I0610919

Jenny excels at depicting small-town life, and this novel showcases her talent. But even in the charm of small-town living, there are those who want more. Jenny excels in showing that, too, in this sweet heart-warmer.

— LINDA W. YEZAK, AWARD-WINNING AUTHOR OF CHRISTIAN FICTION

Jenny Carlisle weaves romance, suspense, and faith into a heartwarming tapestry. From the beginning I was captivated by John K. and Faith's challenges, wondering "how will they find their happily-ever-after?" What a wonderful reminder that God really does work all things together for our good

— DEBBI MIGIT, AWARD-WINNING AUTHOR OF THE JUSTICE, MONTANA SERIES

FAITH MOVES MOUNTAINS

CROSSROADS BOOK TWO

JENNY CARLISLE

Scrivenings PRESS
Quench your thirst for story.
www.ScriveningsPress.com

Published by Scrivenings Press LLC
15 Lucky Lane
Morrilton, Arkansas 72110
https://ScriveningsPress.com

Printed in the United States of America

Paperback ISBN 978-1-64917-266-2

eBook ISBN 978-1-64917-267-9

Editors: Amy R. Anguish and K. Banks

Cover by Linda Fulkerson, www.bookmarketinggraphics.com.

To James, my best friend and forever hero.

ACKNOWLEDGMENTS

Praise God, from whom all blessings flow.

My husband, James has never been in the military, or had the desire to be a firefighter. He is, however, the type who can't sit still. He is not afraid of tackling any project or finding the person who will perform it to his standards. I think John K. Billings would eventually be the guy in the neighborhood that everyone comes to with the smallest or largest problem, just like my wonderful hubby. I thank God every day for sending him my way.

Social media, when used properly, can be the spark that keeps my mind active. Thanks to Facebook friend Kim Zweygardt for sharing a story about a huge piece of farm equipment that got my wheels turning, and ultimately exploding (LOL).

This book would not exist without my God-sent critique partner, Julane Hiebert. Her constant prodding mixed with encouragement helped Faith and John K. come to life and cross the finish line just in time. She is a full-circle friend, since I met her in my childhood hometown of Pittsburg, Kansas.

Thanks to Megan Poole for her rodeo queen expertise, Tonya Ashley for insights into rural firefighter life, and Candace West Posey for help with traveling combine crews.

I never expected the "local celebrity" treatment after my first novel was released. Thanks to Elisha Morrison at the Saline Courier, Shelli Poole and Krystal Goodman at

MySaline.com and Alan Robinette at the Saline County Library for making a little girl's starry-eyed dreams come true.

Always, hugs to my six(counting spouses) kids and eight grandkids for keeping my perspective young. Granny loves those weekly video calls!

1

John K. Billings bumped the back door open with his shoulder. He stomped most of the loose mud from his running shoes, then kicked them off on a doormat. His sweaty T-shirt plopped into the hamper. The men in the family laughed when Mom called this little space the mud room. His youngest brother Cody always said nobody told the mud to stay in its room, especially in the rainy month of May in Arkansas. Didn't stop Mom from trying, though.

After padding through the larger living area he stepped into the tiny bathroom between the two bedrooms, rubbing his stubbly cheek. A shave would feel great. Many of his army buddies skipped this grooming step when they came home, but it was good to be able to recognize himself when he looked in the mirror. Relatively short hair, clean face. Yep. Almost like the old John Kennedy Billings. At least on the outside.

He whistled a little tune as he searched under the sink for the shaving cream and reached with his right hand to open the hot water spigot. Nice to have these little creature comforts, even in a hunting cabin. Wait. Where was the new razor he'd bought on his last trip to town? Outside in the truck, of course. He turned the water off. Should he find a clean pair of shoes for the short trip outside? Wouldn't take too long to get that razor. He sprinted to the front door and down the steps to the driver's side of his old pickup.

With the door open, he reached across the seat for the plastic bag he'd left there. A deafening boom rocked the vehicle. Jumping down from the driver's side, he ran without looking back. No more sounds came from the house, but he kept going, instinctively feeling for his cell phone in the pocket of his shorts.

Sharp rocks jabbed the soles of his stockinged feet, but he scrambled up the hill toward a dilapidated shack that had provided shelter for random hunters for longer than anyone could remember. The last few yards to the top of the hill demanded a slower pace, but he climbed on, never looking back until he reached the crumbling front stoop.

What just happened? He tried to collect his thoughts while looking around for the rest of his army unit. Were they okay? Was anyone hurt in the explosion?

He sat down on the concrete stoop. His heart pounded. Cradling his head in his hands, he willed his mind to clear. Flashing images of smoke and flames bombarded his brain. Screams and confused shouts echoed in his ears. He fought the urge to get up and run again, as a gentle gust of wind through the pines reminded him this was Arkansas, not Afghanistan.

Instead of the blazing inferno he expected, a pile of rubble had replaced most of the rooms of the cabin. The hot water tank-turned-missile rested on the gravel driveway next to an azalea bush Mom had planted when they were kids.

His hands shook as he pushed Send on his cell phone to call the last person he had spoken to.

"What's up?" His brother, O.D., picked up on the first ring.

"You driving?" John K. heard engine noise in the background. No use causing another accident.

"I'll pull over. You okay?" O.D.'s voice responded with his usual calm tone.

A damp breeze brushed the back of his neck, raising goosebumps on his bare chest. More than the weather caused him to tremble. He shook his head to dispel images of that other explosion.

"Yeah. I ran."

"You ran? From what?"

Of course, his brother thought he was talking about today. He was talking about today, right? Not that other time?

"The hot water heater. It exploded. Like through the stinkin' roof!"

"What? You're kidding. Did you call 9-1-1?"

"There's no fire. And who hears those calls way out here anyway?" John K. stood, surprised his legs held his weight. Maybe he could collect himself now.

"Well. You got me. I guess you're calling from the old shack, right?"

The squirt knew him well.

"Yeah."

"Call nine-one-one anyway. Somebody needs to come check it out. Dad and I will be out there as soon as we can." O.D.'s general manager voice sounded more natural these days.

"Okay. Thanks." His brother was younger, but he had tons more common sense. John K. was through trying to argue with O.D.'s instincts to take the lead in the family's continuing crises. "Oh, and Dee. Bring me some clothes. I'm out here in my shorts and no shoes. Might need to look through the stuff I left at the house or borrow something from Dad or Cody. Your shrimpy stuff won't fit me."

"Huh? You've always got to get in those digs. Yeah. I'll bring you some clothes. Try to take care of yourself for a few minutes, soldier boy."

John K. sank back to the stoop. The returning hero image was a little tarnished today. Attacked by an exploding water heater. Things could be worse, and they had been. He pushed himself to his feet and used his cell again to call for help.

"Nine-one-one, what is your emergency?" There was a hint of excitement in the young voice. She probably didn't get a lot of calls.

"This is John K. Billings. We have a cabin on the old logging road. My hot water heater just blew through my roof." No easier way to say it.

"Excuse me?" The girl hesitated. "So, is anyone hurt?"

"No." He had tried to tell O.D. there was no need to call the fire department. "And no fire. At least not that I can see."

"Just a moment. I want to connect you to the chief." She was gone before he could say 'never mind.'

John K. wobbled from one foot to the other. He wanted to go see how much damage the cabin suffered, but there was usually no phone reception down there. His inspection would have to wait a few more minutes.

"Chief MacDonald." A gruff voice came on the line.

"Good morning, sir. This is John K. Billings ..." Might as well repeat the whole story again.

"Yeah, Davis's oldest. So, you've had a little water heater problem today?" John K. was grateful the chief had heard at least the first part of the tale.

"Yes, sir. I don't think there's any danger, but I haven't had a chance to really inspect things, yet." His feet flinched as he paced on the rocks in front of the stoop.

"I'm your nearest neighbor, but I'm in town right now. Someone will be there shortly."

"Yes, sir."

"For now, just cut off the power at the breaker box. Wouldn't want a spark to ignite anything else."

"Thanks." John K. peered down toward the house. No need to worry about the breaker box. The wall it used to be attached to was in splinters on the ground.

He began the rocky trek down the hill, wondering how he had made it up here so quickly a few minutes ago. Pure adrenalin. It's what had kept his baby brother Cody climbing on to the backs of those snorting, heaving bulls he rode. It's also the explanation for the distance he, himself, had covered after the blast on the other side of the world. Adrenalin had pushed him too far before he even turned around to check on anything or anyone. If only he could summon some now to get him through the aftermath.

At the bottom of the hill, he stopped short. There was now only one way to get into the cabin, and one, two, three pine trees that had stood too close to the house lay on the ground. His heart sank as he noticed one huge tree stretched firmly across the cab of his vintage pickup truck, where he'd stood only a few minutes ago. A larger one had crushed the front porch roof, blocking the door. There was not much of the small parking area in front of the house that wasn't covered with debris.

"Sorry, old buddy." Didn't everyone talk to their trucks? Made as much sense as talking to horses or dogs, right?

As he reached what was left of the front steps, he heard the distant wail of a siren. Then, another joined. The whole Big River County emergency crew most likely wanted to see this sight. Unsure of the security of the rest of the structure, he decided to wait before venturing inside.

"Wow, you weren't kidding." Chief MacDonald stepped out of his truck as the siren wore down with a feeble whine.

"Not the kind of thing you make up." John K. shook his hand. "I couldn't locate the breaker box."

"No problem. Just lucky you didn't store anything flammable next to the water heater." The chief walked toward the damaged side of the house, kicking aside tin roofing and splintered two by fours.

"Oh, man. Your truck." The big man removed his baseball cap with proper respect.

"Hopefully, we can fix it up." John K. liked this guy. No one was injured, so he recognized the important damage that had been done.

A fire truck that looked about as old as his GMC skidded to a stop, followed by two more pickups and a black and white from the sheriff's office. Vehicles filled the driveway and stretched out into the nearby gravel road. He was glad for the response, but none of them could really help him. Was O.D. on his way with his boots?

The new arrivals walked around the side of the house, stopping to shake their heads as they passed by the pickup. A gleaming bronze club-cab pickup slid in behind the police cars, the passenger side opening and slamming shut.

"John K.! Are you all right?" Faith Caldwell's long blue-jean-clad legs covered the ground between them quickly.

"Yeah." Had he expected the Caldwell sisters to be here? Well, after years of their families being connected, he probably should have. "I'm good." He wished once more for some decent clothes. At least a shirt. Most of the times he had seen Faith lately, she was completely focused on a barrel race, or looking in a mirror to check her flowing blonde hair. "How did you hear about this so fast?"

"You know, these days when you call O.D., you pretty much get Hope too. I was in the truck with her when she heard from him, so we dashed through Amy Lou's new drive-through and here we are." Faith tucked her hands in her pockets and turned to look at the cabin. "Sheesh. What a mess."

"I've been thinking of doing a little remodeling." John K. attempted a joke. "Gotta love demo day."

"Dee is on his way with some clothes." Hope walked up with her super-sized white paper bag bulging. "I thought you and the first responders might need some breakfast."

"My brother snagged himself an angel." John K. hugged Hope with one arm as she placed a paper wrapped sausage biscuit sandwich in the other.

"How did you get out of this?" Faith walked around toward the front door.

"I wasn't exactly inside. I had run out to the truck for a minute. I wish I'd grabbed a shirt, and maybe put my shoes on." John K. rubbed his bare arms.

"I'm glad you didn't take the time. You can always get more shoes and a shirt." Faith glanced in his direction and quickly looked away, picking up a piece of splintered wood.

He'd heard that God protected fools and children. At twenty-four, he supposed he only qualified for the first category. He closed his eyes for a quick prayer. Credit where credit was due.

"Ma'am." Chief MacDonald walked closer to the three. "Please stay away from the damage. I am sure the insurance inspector will want to see it just as it is."

"Sure." Faith stepped back and reached toward Hope to offer the chief a sausage sandwich. "Would you like one?"

"No thanks. I had breakfast earlier." He stood next to John K. as they both faced the forlorn pickup truck. "Have you called your insurance agent?"

"Haven't given it a thought, yet." John K. searched through

his phone for a number. There was a business card somewhere in his wallet, in the house, which he couldn't enter right now.

"Hey, Mac. What's this boy of mine been up to today?" John K.'s dad slapped the chief on the shoulder as he walked up from O.D.'s truck.

"Luckily, staying alive." Mac shook Dad's hand vigorously.

"Son?" Dad wrapped John K. in a hug. "Did things get too boring out here in the woods?"

"You know me, always looking for excitement." Teasing was their usual M.O. It was good to have his family's support. Lesser folks would have told him to shove off by now. Especially if they knew he wasn't the hero they thought he was.

"Here. These were still in the closet. I've got some jeans and a few more things in the truck." O.D. handed over a pair of tennis shoes, along with a Razorbacks hoodie. Tastes of home. The prodigal couldn't have been happier to get his freshly slaughtered fatted calf.

O.D. pulled Hope into a quick hug. "I should have known you'd beat me here, and with food."

"No problem." Hope squeezed O.D.'s arm.

How long would this newlywed attitude last for these two? He leaned against the fire truck for support to pull on the shoes, then shrugged into the red sweatshirt.

"Yeah, thanks for assisting in the rescue." He smiled at the two sisters. Neither of these girls resembled the tomboyish next-door neighbors they once were. Hope had stepped into the role of organized mother figure, and Faith was playing up the rodeo queen image for all it was worth. He laughed as she used the dilapidated mirror on his crushed truck to search for something that might be stuck in her teeth.

"We were on the way to return those two big chandeliers

O.D. rented for the wedding reception." Faith collected paper wrappers from the fire-fighters and dropped them in a bag.

"Aww. I hoped y'all would leave those in the new barn. They were downright elegant." John K. elbowed O.D.

"Nope. They were just a part of the magic of that fantastic day." O.D. winked at Hope.

"And I would have been the one to have to clean the crazy things." Hope tossed her truck keys from one hand to the other. "They're headed back to Paris, to wait for the next wedding."

"Yeah, and we need to get them up there. It looks like it might rain before we get back home. At least we didn't rent them from the real Paris." Faith walked back to Hope's new truck.

O.D. looked up at the clouds. "I could have gotten someone else to return them." He brushed his finger across Hope's cheek.

"We both kind of wanted to go to Emma's Wedding Shop again. Every now and then, every girl likes to feel like a princess." Faith waved from the running board of the truck. "Hey, John K. I'm glad you're okay."

"Yeah, me too." Hope held O.D.'s hand as they strolled toward her vehicle.

John K. smiled at their retreating backs. If you looked up the word "smitten" on a search engine, you'd see their picture. Their wedding had marked the successful restoration of his grandparent's old house on top of the hill between the Billings and Caldwell ranches. John K. had enjoyed helping with that process. It provided a welcome break from caring for his little brother. No one assumed the road back from a spinal injury would be easy, but Cody's continued struggles were taking a toll on all of them.

"The insurance adjuster should be here this afternoon."

Dad's voice refocused his attention to the scene in front of him. "What do you think happened here, Mac?"

"Usually, when a water tank blows, it had a faulty valve, or one that wasn't repaired the right way." The chief walked toward the offending tank, being careful not to touch anything.

"When John K. called about the leak, I called a new plumber who works up this way. He assured me it was an easy fix." Dad ran his fingers through his hair. "I guess he made it too easy."

"Meanwhile, you don't need to go back inside, son." Mac waved as the emergency crews began to leave.

"I guess you'll be coming home for a bit." Dad wasn't trying to hide the hopeful tone in his voice.

"Thanks, but I'd rather stay out here. My camping stuff is in the back of the truck." John K. glanced to the tarp that covered his gear.

"That won't be comfortable for long." Mac looked up at the sky. "This is the rainy season. Sometimes there are some ugly storms in May."

"Yeah. That's crazy. You can stay at home until the work starts here." Dad sounded out of patience.

"Tell you what. I have an old travel trailer that nobody's using right now. You're welcome to set it up here." Mac walked toward the power pole. "You'd have lights, water, a way to cook."

"Hey, that would be great." John K. was still amazed at the kindness of the folks who lived around here. He hadn't really appreciated them so much until he went away for a while.

"We'll pay you rent," Dad spoke up.

"I'll pay the rent. I've picked up some odd jobs." Would his parents never let him grow up? Even after serving in the army?

"We can work something out." Mac extended his leather glove for a contract-sealing handshake.

"Always. Things just have a way of working out, don't they?" John K. shook the chief's hand. But how long would his luck continue? Would God soon get tired of rescuing him from his constant messes?

2

Faith leaned out the open window of Hope's truck as they approached the Victorian house on the edge of Paris, Arkansas. "I still think you should have done the whole wedding here. Imagine, getting married in Paris. You could have wedding pictures at the Eiffel Tower."

"That's not my style at all. Besides, it's not the real Eiffel Tower, sister." Hope laughed as she stopped in the gravel lot and powered up Faith's window. "Let's just get these things unloaded. I want to be home before the rain pours down."

Faith jumped out of the passenger door. "Yeah, riding in a pickup cab in pouring down rain is not my idea of excitement, especially with your sister."

Inside the front door, she scanned the parlor, soaking up the opulence. Candelabras of every description shared tables with crystal vases of fresh flowers. For a moment, she forgot they were in small-town Arkansas. This store was incredibly out of place, but amazingly perfect at the same time.

"Hi ladies. Good to see you both again." Emma Peterson emerged from a side room with her curly auburn hair pulled back in a bandana. "Did everything turn out well at your wedding?"

"It was amazing. I wish you could have been there." Hope reached out to hug Emma's shoulders.

Faith had never imagined her younger sister getting married first. Somehow, though, she had always known Hope would end up with O.D. The two of them just belonged together. Without Faith's help, the wedding would have been sensible, but plain. Hope needed Faith's prompting to make her dream wedding a little dreamier.

"There's so much going on this time of year. Since your fiancé had picked up the chandeliers, I just sent the guys down in the van with the flowers and candles." Emma looked out the window toward her storage barn. "They'll take care of unloading for you."

"Where do you find all of these things?" Faith reached her fingers toward the crystals hanging from a table lamp.

"We get some from estate sales. Lots of folks appreciate nice things, even out here in the hills. The newer stuff is shipped in from the cities, New York, Chicago. I even get a few things from the other Paris when I can afford the shipping." Emma walked to a side door and waved at some young men outside. "Thanks for letting us use some of your wedding pictures on our website. That's the best way to attract new customers. I hope you'll send your friends for their dresses too."

"For sure." Faith leaned through the door of the display area for the beautiful gowns Emma was famous for. "I would love to just stay and look at them. I guess I haven't grown out of playing dress-up."

"Me either." Emma laughed.

"Sorry, you two." Hope walked toward the door as the two helpers approached the porch. "We need to get these huge light fixtures out of my truck. You can try on dresses another day."

Faith followed them out onto the porch. Even though she was dressed modestly, Emma somehow fit here just as naturally as the brocade wing-back chairs.

Faith's phone buzzed in her pocket and she took it out to check the text message as they stood behind the truck's tailgate.

"Who's that?" Hope handed Faith a box containing two vases.

"Just spam." Faith balanced the box on her hip and finished reading the message before replacing the phone in her pocket.

What's up beautiful?

Not spam exactly. Ty Porter was a local dee-jay she'd met on Black Friday when his station helped to promote the Caldwell Family Rodeo. He'd handled the music for Hope's wedding reception, and they'd been out for a supper date after that.

"I'll take this inside." Faith hefted the box, setting it down just inside the front door.

She pulled up Ty's message and answered it.

In Paris at the moment. What's up with you?

Paris. If only it were France. Ty was a city boy, and he seemed to understand her longing to see other places. On their first date, he'd entertained her with stories of his fast-paced life, especially before coming to the Arkansas River Valley.

Outside the window, clouds joined forces. Yes, this was still Arkansas. That sky was looking mean. They needed to get back to Crossroads before the rain made driving difficult.

Had John K. gone home with his dad and brother? Was he camping in this weather? Did he prefer being alone that much? Why was she worried about him? After all, he'd survived serving in the military, and even being missing in action for a while. He could take care of himself.

A message alert from her pocket startled her.

Paris? Ooh la la.

It was almost as if Ty knew she was thinking of John K. She had gotten over the crush she'd had on her hero neighbor long ago. No harm in hoping he stayed safe, right?

Paris, AR, goof. Returning the rented items from the wedding.

Gotcha. See you when you get back to town?

He wanted to see her? Like tonight? Her heart raced. Well, that might be exciting.

Depends on the weather.

That sounded like an old lady talking. She followed with another text.

It's supposed to rain a lot tonight.

Will you melt?

Another message flashed in immediately.

I'll keep you safe and dry.

Faith's face flushed. They'd just gone out for one dinner.

He'd been on his way to work at the radio station that night. He'd crossed her mind once or twice since then, but ...

"Put the phone away. Your fan club can wait." Hope peeked in from the porch. "The guys are going to use a forklift to unload those huge contraptions. You need to help us watch. I don't want so much as a scratch on that truck bed."

Faith's phone buzzed again. "I'll be right there."

So, see you soon?

Another text from Ty?

Faith grinned.

I'll talk to you when we get back to town.

Her finger shook a little as she sent the reply.

She thought of the smile that would just be visible in his red beard, the twinkle in those blue eyes. Her own smile warmed her cheeks.

She ignored several pings from her cell phone while watching the forklifts unload the two crates from the back of Hope's truck. O.D. had packed them exactly the way Emma wanted them. The guys on the forklifts knew what they were doing. Why was she even needed here?

Hope signed the paperwork Emma had prepared to finalize the rental agreement. Faith slid into the passenger side of the truck as thunder rumbled, and rain began to fall.

"Ready?" Hope started the truck and pulled away from Emma's house into the downtown area. "This is a great little town. Maybe we can come again when the weather's better. There is a little bakery with tables in front like a French café. I'd like to do more than just drive by next time."

"Yeah. Sounds cute." Faith scanned the messages Ty had been sending. He was persistent, for sure.

I've been thinking of you a lot.

Do you like Italian food?

There's a great little place with killer ravioli.

Come on, can't I get a response? Are you up for some great food tonight?

She might as well answer. It would be good to see him again.

Sure. Sounds like fun. I love Italian food.

She typed the response as the sky let loose its heavy burden of rain.

Cool! See you about 7:00.

Did he even know how far she lived from town? She had met him at the restaurant last time. Oh, well. Hopefully, this rain would slack up before then.

Faith was grateful Hope had to concentrate on the road and the weather as they navigated the winding roads.

I hope you get back from Paris in time. Trans-Atlantic flights can be killer.

Ty's text came as Hope turned her windshield wipers up to full speed, battling the waves of water in front of her.

You are insane.

She laughed aloud as she responded.

"Having too much fun over there." Hope leaned forward.

"Just a bunch of silliness." Faith turned the phone upside down on the seat. Ty's texts could wait. She adjusted the defroster, hoping to help keep the windshield clear.

"I'm glad you came with me. No fun driving these mountain roads in the rain." Hope reached over to pat Faith's knee.

"No problem." Faith sighed. She knew Hope thrived on days like this. Her job at the Cedar Ridge Therapy Center didn't allow her to get out of the office often enough. Driving around in the Ozark mountains made Hope happy, even in terrible weather.

"Do you ever get tired of living here?" Faith settled back in the seat as the rain slacked up.

"What brought this on?" Hope laughed. "It doesn't rain every day."

"I know. It's not the rain. It's just, I don't know, we have never really been anywhere else." Faith looked to her right, watching the trees passing by her window. "Don't you ever wonder what it's like to live in a city?"

"Sure." Hope smiled. "I guess it would be fun to take a vacation now and then. But I would always want to come back home. Especially now that O.D. has our house almost finished."

"Yeah. I guess it makes a difference when you get married. I'm just not ready to be so settled." It was useless trying to explain how she felt to good old steady Hope. She had enjoyed the past few months so much, as she and their cousin Kayla Grace traveled around the state to rodeo events. Serving as Miss Crossroads Rodeo with Kayla as Miss Teen Crossroads had added some spice in an otherwise ordinary world.

"Well. Sorry I can't provide any more excitement than driving through a tsunami on a slippery road." Hope laughed.

Faith picked up her phone again. Ty was still texting. He had sent a picture of the real Eiffel Tower, then one of Venice. Then, a menu from the restaurant he wanted to take her to. Yes, much more exciting than riding in her sister's pickup truck. She began to picture the outfits in her closet that might impress this fascinating guy.

3

"Yeah, Dad. I'm sure." John K. checked the wedge blocking the trailer's front tire. "I'd much rather stay out here where I can keep an eye on the cabin. You work on getting the insurance guy out here so I can get back inside as soon as possible."

"My wife keeps the fridge and the pantry stocked up pretty well." Mac stepped out of the door of the compact camper trailer. "She even added an extra dozen eggs and a loaf of bread before I pulled out of the driveway. You should be okay for a few days."

"More than okay." John K. shook Mac's weathered hand. "Thanks again. I'll have to figure out a way to repay the two of you after our place is livable again."

"That's what neighbors do around here. Guess I'd better get back and make sure everything at home is ready. That sky is looking kinda mean." Mac opened the door of his massive pickup truck. "See you, Davis, O.D. Tell Felicia we're still praying for Cody." He closed the driver's door and started the engine in one quick motion. Gravel crunched as he turned around to head toward the highway.

"You'd best head home too, Dad. Mom will be standing on her ear." John K. waved at Mac.

The gray clouds overhead grew darker and began to boil. There hadn't been any tornado warnings issued, but at the very least, it looked like they were in for quite a bit of wind and rain.

"You're right, son." Dad removed his baseball cap and ran his gloved fingers through his sandy hair. "I think I heard the first clap of thunder a minute ago. We could use a little rain, but this may be more than that."

"Grandpa Dee would say we're in for a doozy!" John K. smiled. They all looked up to that old man. None of them were ready for the adjustment that would come when their patriarch moved from the local nursing home to heaven. "O.D., this will be a test of that new roof of yours."

"Right. I hope we don't have any leaks. I don't think buckets in the floor would match Hope's décor very well." O.D. laughed.

"Okay, son. You just keep your head where your feet are during all this. I need to get home before your mom decides to hunker down with Cody at the hospital. She needs to trust those nurses a little more." Dad opened the door of his truck. "Use the storm cellar if you need to."

John K. glanced at the heavy metal door marking the shelter half buried behind the cabin. They'd only had to use the tiny room covered in dirt and rocks once or twice. Dad made sure it was free of dampness and snakes but just thinking about spending more than a minute or two inside made him claustrophobic. Maybe it wouldn't come to that.

"Yeah. You can always use the 'fraidy hole'" O.D. waved at him from his own black behemoth of a truck. "Should be fun!"

"You're a barrel of laughs. Just worry about yourself, Squirt." He waved at his brother, who tapped on his phone. O.D. should remember how poor the signal was up here. But, after all, it had been over an hour since he'd talked to Hope. Poor guy.

With only his undriveable pickup left in the yard, John K. realized how stranded he was out here. He heaved a huge sigh and closed his eyes. *Thanks, God. No. I mean it. I can use some quiet after all of this. Being alone is the whole idea. I know You have got this. Just help me to remember that.* His prayers hardly ever ended with *Amen*. Best to keep the conversation going.

The poor truck. He walked closer hoping to get to the driver's side door under the trunk of the massive pine tree. The windshield was shattered, and the roof of the cab was mostly caved in. Maybe he could throw a tarp over it to keep the rain from ruining that new upholstery he had just paid for. There were a couple of large tarps in the little storage building out behind the cabin. The key to that shed was where? On his key ring, in the ignition of the truck. Okay, then.

Squatting to just the right position to open the door, he pushed aside wet, prickly pine branches. With his right hand, he found the keys and pulled them to him. Would the claims adjuster come out here during this storm? Fixing the cabin could wait, but the truck felt like his only lifeline right now.

He jogged to the shed, jumping over pieces of pine trees along the way. He laughed at the irony of this situation. Even before the storm they had trees down. Who knew a water heater explosion could do so much damage? His life was nothing if not interesting.

As he secured the tarp over the cab of the truck, the wind picked up, and howled through the branches of the remaining trees over his head. This was probably just so much busy work, but it would occupy him for a little bit. Soon, there would be no venturing out of the little camper. He tied a knot around the door handle and pulled the rope taut. Thunder rumbled, and lightning flashed in the north. Grandpa Dee's doozy of a storm was here.

Inside the camper, the walls threatened to close in. Rain pelted the roof and the wind howled. He located the remote control for the television above the refrigerator. Maybe he could find something mindless to watch, at least until the power went out.

Seated on the cushioned bench at the dining table, his hands trembled. What a day. Being by himself was what he said he wanted. But it might not be enjoyable for an extended time. He closed his eyes, remembering that long day on the other side of the world. After the explosion he'd run as far as his feet would carry him. Then the awful quiet set in. That afternoon he'd ended up alone too. Tonight, he planned to keep his eyes open as long as possible, to remind himself that he was in a much better spot.

Channels changed idly, moving quickly past the weather forecasts that seemed to dominate everyone's mind. There was nothing else he could do to prepare right now. No use being reminded how bad things might be.

Past the tiny bathroom with its sit-down shower and a passable commode was a bed covered with a cheery comforter, and even a throw pillow or two. Mac was lucky to have a woman's influence in his life. He'd like to meet Mrs. Mac some time. Funny how just when he was enjoying being by himself, he began to appreciate having someone else around.

The tiny closet in the bedroom was empty, except for the clothes O.D. brought. His jogging shorts and T-shirts were in the cabin. And his army boots. With all the rain coming, these shoes O.D. brought wouldn't be much help. No telling what was left of his good running shoes since they had been in the mud room before the explosion.

Mac had warned him not to go inside the damaged cabin. Probably out of an abundance of caution. After his time in the army, he was definitely a rule-follower, but he didn't buy in to the over-abundance theories. The rain had slacked off a bit. If he climbed in the window of the second bedroom, he could stuff some clothes into his backpack and come back before the real storm started. It was always good to have a mission.

Random branches from the fallen pine trees threatened to trip him as he bounded past his truck, rounded the corner of the damaged porch and approached the back of the house. Water blew off the roof as he stopped to survey the situation. That window was higher than he remembered. Luckily, he knew it wasn't locked, because he had opened it just last night to get some fresh air before he went to sleep. May was one of the few months when humidity levels were not unbearable. Except during these blow-up storms.

He jogged to the shed behind the house and found a homemade wooden bench the previous owners had left. The perfect height for a boost into the window.

A long, slow rumble rattled above him, and the tip-tops of the pines swayed as the wind increased. A damp breeze brushed his cheek. *Thanks, God. No need to make this easy.*

He picked up the wooden bench and took three long strides to the side of the house, clambering up to raise the window. He propped both hands on the sill and hoisted himself in and through, landing on the floor with a thump.

It would be tempting to stay inside during the storm. But what if Mac came back by to check on him? It would be dark and drafty in here. Just outside the bedroom door, most of the roof was gone. Okay, back to the camper.

With rolled up socks, some boxers and T-shirts stuffed into

his backpack, he tied the laces of his army boots together and draped them over his shoulders. On his way back to the window, he picked up his Bible off the nightstand. Should he venture to the bathroom for his shaving cream? A bang from the direction of the porch jolted him. Another pine branch falling? No use worrying about shaving. He'd just find out how fast his beard grew.

He shoved the backpack through the window where it thudded to the muddy ground. As he backed out, his foot found the security of the wooden bench. Rain pelted his head as he picked up his backpack, readjusted his boots and made a beeline for the camper. Time to hunker down.

Inside, the camper rocked with the steadily increasing winds. He located a canister of coffee in an overhead cabinet and grabbed the old-school aluminum coffee pot on the stove burner. Exactly what they used when hunting. He laughed to think of some of his friends who thought coffee was always made one cup at a time by a barista.

Ding. A notification from his phone surprised him. He leaned back against the kitchen sink to read a string of messages that had just arrived.

Hope you're staying dry.

That was Mom.

If you see this, let us know you're okay.

Dad chimed in.

Checked on Grandpa Dee and Cody. They both have generators if the power goes out. Now I'm holed up above the garage.

O.D. knew he would want to know about their favorite old timer and their little brother.

John K. typed a quick text to all three.

> Still have power here. Plugging phone in to save battery.

No matter what time of year, they always prepared for power outages. Being isolated from city living had its pluses and minuses.

Hail pinged on the metal roof of the camper. The howling winds resumed. He dropped into the chair that must be Mac's and reached for the remote control. A certain smiling blonde crossed his mind. Nice to know Faith Caldwell had cared enough to want to know how he was earlier. He hoped she and Hope were safe at home by now.

Closing his eyes, he sighed. He'd always functioned better with a goal of some kind. For now, fixing up the truck and then the house would occupy him. But then, what?

At least O.D. was the one helping Dad with the family's truck dealership. That was too much project management. Better to be the guy building fences on the ranch than the one making sure the workers had enough wire and posts to finish the job.

So, ranch work? Maybe. But he wanted to make a difference for people, not just cattle and horses, or even pickup trucks. That's why he'd come out here. To get ideas to the surface and see where his life would lead. Before the water heater launched itself into space, he had been enjoying this new life. *Okay, God, a pretty extreme way to get my attention. And this wind storm? Maybe a little overdramatic.*

A huge crack was followed by a rushing noise as the top of another tree crashed through other branches on the way to the ground. The mighty thump as the pine hit the ground jolted

John K. to his feet. His forehead broke out in tiny beads of sweat as he peered out the window. Was it safe to stay in this tiny mobile home?

He sat down on the couch, tightening the laces on his army boots. There would be more protection from the storm in the cellar behind the cabin. He grabbed Mac's oversized flashlight from the top of the refrigerator, shrugged into a hoodie and opened the door of the camper. A gust of wind threatened to yank the door out of his hand. What was that Dad said earlier about looking for excitement?

4

"Okay, kiddos. Looks like everything is battened down out here." Dad closed Belle's stall door, opening the top so the horse could look out at them.

"Good night, Girl." Faith patted the big sorrel's nose and took a last glance at the feed bucket just to the right. Lid down tight, ready for feeding tomorrow. Wouldn't want any mice crawling in to keep dry and get their fill before morning.

"I still say we've wasted good hay on those silly goats." Junior peered in at Hope's favorite pair of pets, who jostled around each other noisily in another stall.

"We could just let them bunk with you." Hope poked their brother on the way to the door of the barn.

"Worthless little critters. If they just acted a little more civilized," Junior grumbled.

"All God's creatures deserve a chance to stay dry and healthy, son. Even nincompoops." Dad dimmed the lights in the barn.

"Hey. Are you talking about me or the goats?" Junior whined. After years of bantering back and forth at the rodeo, these two had a natural way of teasing each other that wouldn't quit.

Faith followed the family out of the barn, toward a vapor light in the yard. So far, only light rain was falling. But she knew the heavier rain and wind could be on its way.

"Okay, I'm headed home." Hope jogged toward her truck. "Thanks for watching the kids, Dad. O.D. says their spot in our barn will be ready soon."

"Your turn to pick the movie after supper, Faith." Junior opened the back door, ushering her inside.

"I'm going out." Faith pulled the phone out of her pocket to see if Ty had answered her latest text.

"In this weather?" Junior leaned out to take another look at the darkening sky.

"It may not even do anything. I will keep an eye out and give myself plenty of time to get home." Faith pulled off her cowboy boots. She'd grab her high-heeled half boots to go with the jeans she planned to wear.

"Dad. Faith's going out." Junior always felt it was his responsibility to keep their dad updated on her business. He could be such a pain.

"Your sister can make her own decisions, and she probably knows how to speak for herself too." Dad hung his rain jacket on a hook before walking into the kitchen. "But seriously, be safe, Princess."

"Yes, sir. I will." Faith knew it was tough for him to fill the role of both parents these days. For the most part, he did a good job of letting them live their lives. Still. It would be nice not to have to feel like she had to clear every move through a family council.

The mirror in the half bath gave her a quick glimpse of her makeup. When she reached her closet, she selected a tight-fitting T-shirt, adding a necklace with a fake diamond that dropped to just the right length in front. Turning her head upside down, she shook out her wavy hair and stood back up, arranging things quickly in front of the mirror. A quick spray and a dab of perfume on each wrist and one just under the necklace completed her preparations. She smiled at her reflection. Any guy that wasn't impressed wouldn't be worth her time.

Grabbing her favorite rain jacket on the way to her truck, she made it just in time. Huge raindrops pelted her back as she jumped behind the wheel. The engine of her pickup leapt to life, and she adjusted the wipers to intermittent before checking the latest message from Ty.

Do you know where the radio station is?

Yes.

Faith pictured the spot in her mind. Not the best neighborhood after dark, but okay.

Meet me there, and I'll drive to the restaurant.

Okay. I can be there in 15.

Faith's heart tapped against her chest as she typed.

Make it 10, beautiful. Can't wait.

Wow. It was probably just his way of flirting, but none of the guys she had dated before made a habit of talking like that. She caught a glimpse of the Caldwell house in the rearview mirror as she left the driveway and turned out onto the gravel road. Most of those same lights would be left on until she got home. She wished Dad would just give up and go to bed. She was an adult now. He could shift his worry to their little brother. Like that would happen.

Her windshield wipers fought the sheets of rain. She glanced to both sides each time she crossed over a bridge or culvert. Dinner with Ty would be fun, but she'd need to keep a watch on these low water crossings. They would flood if this rain kept up much longer.

Most of the fast-food places in town were empty and quiet when she passed. It looked like everyone was at the grocery stores, stocking up for the bad weather to come. Any impending storm caused the rush for supplies. Oh, the worries of small-town Arkansas.

She 'brighted' her lights as she reached the other side of town and the parking lots got further apart. Funny, Ty hadn't offered to come out to her house to get her. She would have turned him down, of course. She knew those country roads better than anyone, but still, it might have been nice to have been asked. Another way he was different than the other boys she had dated. They were boys. This was a man. Huge difference.

A billboard advertised the local radio station in front of a small concrete building and lots of imposing looking satellite equipment. There were only two vehicles in the lot. One, an old sedan of some kind, and the other, a shiny red Mustang sitting in the best spot to reflect what little light existed. She turned her motor off as she parked next to it, noticing the rain had slacked up for the moment.

"Okay." She sighed aloud as she turned on the tiny light in her visor to check her lipstick. Her hair was decent, though she wished she had retouched the curls. She flipped the visor back up and stepped out. Primping too long would not make a good impression. What kind of impression was she going for? No use over-thinking it. It was dinner. Tell that to her pounding heart.

"Hey!" Ty jumped out of the driver's side of his car and ran around to open the passenger door. "Finally. You look gorgeous!"

He wrapped her in a tight hug, then took one of her hands, leading her to the car. "Let's get in where it's dry."

Faith perched on the edge of the seat for a moment as Ty ran around to climb in on his side. He filled up the entire seat and seemed to fasten his seatbelt and shift the car into gear in one smooth movement. She fumbled with her own seat belt as the car left the parking lot, and she slid back into the support of the reclined seat.

"Hungry? Or did you get your fill of fancy food in Paris?" Ty sped through the dark streets.

"Oh, no. We didn't eat. There was too much to do at home to make sure the animals were ready for the storm." Faith tried to watch for landmarks. She had grown up here, but even this small town was not as familiar as the dirt roads she lived on. Things seemed to speed by in a blur.

"We have reservations at this great little Italian place I found." Ty slowed to make a sharp curve. "Coming from the city makes you seek out the authentic food. Italian is not easy to find around here, but I just looked for the Catholic churches and went from there. Did I tell you how great you look, by the way?"

"Yes. You did." Faith laughed. On previous dates, it had taken hours to decide where to eat. Not with this guy.

"Mrs. Gino said there wouldn't be a lot of customers. Most everyone has gone home, but she'd save an extra piece of Italian cream cake for us." Ty slowed down again and navigated his car into a space in front of a small diner. A new light bulb in the sign would help, but the words 'Gino's place' were still visible and welcoming.

Faith's stomach growled. Since she'd been trying to watch her weight, she had avoided pasta, but she had a feeling this meal would send healthy choices out the window.

"Come in, Mister Ty Porter. It's wet outside!" A large woman with flowing black hair and rings shining from every finger held the door for them as they entered the building.

"Hi, Mrs. Gino." Ty reached around Faith's waist and guided her toward a table with a lighted candle and two wine glasses placed carefully on the long white tablecloth. "I'd like to introduce you to Miss Faith Caldwell."

"*Benvenuti.*" Mrs. Gino nodded in Faith's direction, then patted Ty on the arm. "There's wine left from the last time you were here. I corked the bottle for you." The lady bustled off toward the kitchen as Faith settled into the chair Ty held for her.

Reservations had been overkill for sure since they were the only customers. She tried to recall the last time she'd driven past this place. When their family was busy with the rodeo, there hadn't been many occasions to eat out, and Italian food was certainly not the preference of her meat-and-potatoes dad. Oh yes. They were near the river. They had passed this place on the way to Junior's favorite catfish restaurant.

"She certainly makes her customers feel at home." Faith tucked her phone and billfold next to the wine glass on the table.

"Well, I'm sort of a regular. Like I said, I crave this stuff at least once a week." Ty reached across the table, rubbing his thumb in the palm of Faith's hand. "I won't even need a menu. Her ravioli is to die for. Okay with you?"

It sounded like a rhetorical question.

"Sure." Faith tried to take a deep breath. Not easy with the persistent touch of his hand on hers.

"So. We'll let Mrs. Gino handle the food. Let's spend some time getting to know each other. I think we were both in a hurry the last time." Ty's blue eyes found hers and locked in.

"You had to go back to work. Do you like working at the radio station?" Faith looked down at her hands.

"Yeah. It's a job. I like being on-air, but with such a small staff, I have to do some of the engineering stuff too. In fact, because of the storm, I'll end up staying there watching lights blink all night tonight. But what about you? What are you doing with yourself now that the Caldwell Rodeo is not happening every two weeks? Well, other than getting ready for the Miss Rodeo Arkansas pageant. Which you are guaranteed to win." Ty moved his chair around to get a little closer to her.

"I think I'm pretty well ready for the pageant. It will be bigger than the Miss Crossroads Rodeo contest, so I'm kind of nervous. Other than that, I am still working as a CNA at the nursing home." Was he really interested in her work? Helping old people with their basic needs didn't seem as glamorous as hosting radio programs.

"You like that nursing stuff? Doesn't match the rodeo queen image." Ty sat back as a teenager brought their salads. He poured himself a second glass of wine and reached over to fill Faith's glass.

"No thanks. I'll stick with just water." She placed her hand over her glass.

"Don't know what you're missing. This stuff takes the edge off." Ty swirled his glass under his nose before taking a sip.

"Yeah. So CNA. That's like the lowest rung in the nursing world." Ty took a bite of his salad. "Surely that's not your ultimate career goal."

Maybe he was interested. "No. I want to be a nurse

practitioner. That's the real reason for entering a pageant. If I could win some scholarship money that would help pay my way through school." Faith ran her finger around the base of her water glass.

"Yeah. I bet it costs a lot. If you're spending all that, why not just go ahead and be a doctor?" He tore off a piece of hard crusted bread and slathered it in butter.

"Well," Faith thought back about narrowing down her career choice. "When my mom had cancer and we had to go so many places for treatment, the doctors were great, but the nurse practitioners were the real lifelines for us."

"Any patient would be lucky to have you for their nurse." He winked at her, and turned his head toward the kitchen. "That ravioli should be on its way. I am starving."

Faith chewed a bite of bread. So much for revealing her heart to Ty. If he heard her mention her mom's cancer, it just rolled off his radar. No need to bore him with any more of that story.

Mrs. Gino arrived in a flourish with the hot bowls of ravioli. Faith savored each bite, realizing she had never tasted anything quite like this. Not overly saucy, the tender packets of meat and cheese warmed her stomach and delighted her tastebuds.

Ty was smiling when she caught his eye again. "The best thing ever? Right?"

"Wow." Faith nodded between bites. "So good."

"Being raised around immigrants, this tastes like home to me." Ty closed his eyes for a moment.

"So, where is your home?" Faith sat back, trying not to devour her food too quickly.

"Baltimore." He caught her eye for a moment, and immediately looked away. "Now, it's wherever I can get a paycheck. Nothing for me there anymore."

Faith used the cloth napkin to wipe her mouth. Strange. He had been the one to suggest they get to know each other. Now, he seemed to be shutting down that conversation.

"This has been great." She reached to pat his hand. "But I'm afraid we don't need to stay long. There are a lot of low spots around here that could flood." Rain pounded on the window next to her to emphasize her point.

"You're probably right. They're expecting me to mind the station tonight and switch over to auxiliary power if the lights go out." Ty waved to their young server. "Hey, could you bring us the check?"

Faith found the ladies room as Ty took care of paying. Another glance in the mirror revealed her flushed cheeks. She closed her eyes and took a deep breath. Something about this evening, this guy, set her heart racing.

"I fixed your cake to go." Mrs. Gino handed a Styrofoam package to Faith as she returned to the table.

"Oh, thank you." Faith smiled at their hostess. Sweets had not been a regular part of her diet for a while, but she knew better than to refuse such a precious gift.

"See you next time." Ty leaned in to peck Mrs. Gino on the cheek, before opening the glass door leading out to the covered porch.

"I guess I left my raincoat in your car." Faith laughed as the cold wind slapped her cheeks. The restaurant's sign clanged noisily against the metal awning above them.

"We'll be fine. It's just rain." Ty clicked a key fob and the little car's engine roared to life.

Faith felt his left arm encircling her, and she juggled the cake container as he turned her to face him. The strength of his embrace pressed her against him. She struggled to get her breath as his mouth claimed hers in a firm and insistent kiss.

As he released his hold, she couldn't find any words. She stared dumbly at the twinkle in his blue eyes.

"Sorry not sorry. I just couldn't resist." He whispered gruffly. With his left arm still around her, the rain pelted her face as they ran together toward the car.

She found a spot in the back seat for the container of cake, retrieving her rain jacket from the floorboard. She turned to the front, drying her face on the lining of the coat. Her hands trembled as she fastened her seatbelt. Where had that kiss come from? Was she happy about it? She had not had much time to react.

Ty turned the music up and concentrated on keeping the windshield clear during the ride back to Crossroads. Would he be okay driving after the wine he'd had with supper? She closed her eyes each time they entered a curve in the road, hoping the little car would come out safely on the other side. Her fingers tied knots in the drawstring of the jacket. She was relieved when Ty actually seemed to slow down as the rain increased.

When they reached the parking lot of the radio station, rain poured buckets from the sky. Faith could picture the laps her dad would be making around the living room, waiting for her to come home.

"So, do you think the road to your house will be flooded?" Ty turned off his ignition as he parked next to her truck. "Listen, they have a foldout couch in our station, and there's even clean sheets for it somewhere." He ran his hand up her arm, pulling her closer to him. "The guy I work with will go home, and I'd be close by, just watching the lights blink. You'd be safer here. And we've got Mrs. Gino's cake to eat." His finger touched her cheek, making its way to her lips.

"No." Faith pulled away. "I mean. Thanks, but I need to get

home." She reached for the door handle and found her door still locked.

"Okay. I just want you to be safe." Ty pressed a button to unlock her door.

"Thanks. I'll be fine." Faith faced him.

"Goodnight, princess." He leaned closer, kissing her much more tenderly than he had on Mrs. Gino's front porch.

She squeezed his hand, then quickly turned to open the car door. Rain bounced off the hood of her jacket as she ran the few steps to the driver's side door of her truck.

Inside her pickup, before starting the engine, she reached for her phone, sending a quick message.

Thanks again for the supper. Sorry the weather sort of freaked me out.

No problem. See you again?

His response came quickly.

She hesitated. That second kiss, though. Much nicer than the first.

Sure.

She found her keys in her handbag and sent another text, this time to her dad.

Headed home. Love you.

Don't drive through standing water.

She laughed out loud. Dad must have been sitting with his phone in his hand.

She started the truck, turned on the windshield wipers, and headed for familiar territory.

5

John K. pushed up on the heavy metal door and stepped out of the storm shelter with his flashlight scanning his pathway back to the camper. When he heard the last big crack of a pine tree breaking, he knew there would be no electricity this morning. Now that the storm had finally stopped, he hoped for a mattress and a blanket so he could catch a few hours of sleep. When the sun came up, today's tasks would be much clearer.

Stars above the remaining pines caught his attention as he neared the tiny trailer house. *Thanks, God. Those pinpoints of light are encouraging. It's so good that Mac's camper is still intact. You could have piled on in a big way, but Your mercy in ending this storm is appreciated. Really.*

His flashlight revealed a cabinet above the dining area. Inside were extra quilts for the full-size bed in the back room. He kicked off his boots and covered the last few steps to the bed in a hurry. This would feel so much better than the metal bench in the storm cellar.

John K. left the stove burner lit while he filled up the little coffee pot. There was just enough dampness in the air to bring a chill after the May windstorm. With no electricity, any bit of warmth helped.

Time would have passed more quickly if he could have slept, but most of the night he was wide-eyed on a hard metal bench in the cellar. He was never frightened. He'd spent quite a bit of time just talking to God. But these couple of hours he crashed under homemade quilts refreshed him.

He opened the compact refrigerator and found eggs and a loaf of bread. If there was a drinking glass in the cabinet, he could attempt an egg in a basket. He remembered mornings spent with Grandpa Dee and Grandma in the little house that looked down on theirs. There were not a lot of memories of Grandma. She was usually just very quiet. But when Grandpa Dee wasn't working out of town, she always seemed to enjoy fixing breakfast for him. He'd even helped her make the "holey" bread a time or two.

Aha. He should have known that Mrs. Mac's cabinets would have clean glassware and a good heavy iron skillet.

He set to work, dropping a slab of butter in the skillet, cutting a hole in the center of two slices of bread, frying them on one side before flipping and cracking eggs into the perfect spots. After one more flip, he watched the eggs until they were perfectly medium. When he was home with Mom and Dad and the brothers, he didn't let his cooking skills show. No use taking away Mom's joy. Grandpa Dee told him he would keep that little secret, and so far, he had.

The window next to the dining table gradually filled with light, and as he enjoyed a second cup of coffee, he could see some of the damage outside. He decided to take a run up the hill where he could get a better look.

Wearing a fresh pair of jogging shorts and his running shoes, he bounced out of the camper and headed up the hill. A damp breeze slapped his cheeks and prompted his legs to move faster. His breath came in short puffs as the grade steepened. Thankfully, there were not a lot of fallen branches along this path.

When the wind took a rest, familiar, peaceful sounds tempted him to forget about the events of the night before. Songbirds trilled, and a mockingbird picked up the tune to make it part of his repertoire. Truck noises from the distant highway carried through the stillness.

He stopped in front of the old shack and pulled his phone out of his sweatshirt pocket. No surprise, the usual messages popped up from Mom and Dad, O.D., and even one from his Aunt Candace. He created a new group text to check in all at once. It was always best to communicate with everyone to prevent any hurt feelings. Except for those long weeks when he'd talked to no one. He shook his head to dispel that memory and drafted a quick message.

> Lots more trees down. Mac's camper is a life saver. Had a good breakfast. Talk to you soon.

Wait. There was one more message. Faith Caldwell? Strange she didn't choose to get updated through Hope and O.D.

> Looks like your county was hit hard. Hope you see this and you are okay.

Those Caldwells were a thoughtful bunch. He remembered how his mom and theirs used to check on each other. Hard habit to break.

Thanks. I'm good. How are things on the Caldwell ranch?

He hit send, wondering how long it took his messages to leave this remote area. Maybe communication between locals was quicker. He searched to find his new friend Mac's number.

John K. here. Thanks for the shelter.

Surprisingly, he noticed the little dots that indicated his message was being read.

Yep. Gas holding up?

10-4. Everything OK with you?

Headed out to check on neighbors.

Through the trees, John K. spied smoke from a nearby chimney. That might be Mac's place.

Need help? Wanna swing by and get me?

Reading what he had typed surprised him. It was a natural reaction. Helping just seemed more fun than bumping against the walls inside the tiny camper.

Great!

Mac's message came instantly.

Now to get down the hill again before Mac arrived.

We are okay. Power went out, using generators in the house and barn.

Huh? Oh. That was Faith. One thing about her hadn't changed while he was in the army. Sitting in one spot generated boredom for both of them.

Take care!

The phone was tucked safely in his pocket for the trek back to the camper. Going downhill was much faster, even a little dangerous on the jagged rocks.

Slowing down a bit, he reached more level ground next to the cabin. Maybe Mac could help him find some more tarps to protect what was left of the structure. There would be extensive repairs needed, but maybe at least some of the flooring could be protected from the elements. Hopefully, Dad was in touch with that insurance adjuster, and this scene would begin to change soon.

Inside the camper, he found a pair of blue jeans and a clean T-shirt. Donning his Razorbacks cap, he stood just outside the camper door, watching for Mac's truck to come up the road. He faced away from the pitiful green truck for now. Restoring power and helping the neighbors came ahead of talking to Dad about repairs to his old buddy.

The roar of an engine pierced the silence just before John K. caught sight of a white four-wheel-drive truck coming around the curve just north of their cabin. With huge wheels, and the cab suspended above them, Mac's ride looked ready for the next monster truck rally.

"Hop in." Mac's gruff voice reached out, as the passenger side door flew open. "You had breakfast?"

"Absolutely." John K. shook Mac's hand as he climbed aboard. "Thanks again for the fully-stocked fridge. I hope you're running a tab so I can pay you back for all this."

"Depending on what we find, you may pay me back with

sweat today. I haven't heard from many people, so I'm a little worried about what's going on." Mac drove carefully, glancing to the right and left as they made their way up the road that led to the main highway.

"So part of your job as fire chief is disaster recovery?" John K. lost count of the downed trees they passed.

"Ha." Mac's chest moved with a silent chuckle. "I've never seen a list of job duties. It's just what we do. Neighbors helping neighbors. My truck is able to get out and go no matter what, I've got a full tank of gas, so ... here we go."

John K. nodded. Nothing had been harder for him than sitting still. His dad would come home from work every day ready to relax, watch television, etc. But John K. hadn't gotten that old yet. He was never comfortable unless he was moving around. Growing up on a ranch had been perfect. Plenty of roaming room.

Mac turned right at the main highway and traveled around a curve before turning down a narrow lane surrounded by pines. At least, there were a few pines still intact. The larger ones all seemed to have the tops removed. Branches littered the ground, and Mac had to stop once to clear debris from the road.

"This place is like yours, tucked into a lot of trees. I'm sure their power is out too, so we need to see what's up." Mac accelerated, and gravel flew around them.

"Sounds like a plan." What would they find at the end of this road? Would Mac's neighbors be injured? Would their roof be intact?

"Uh-oh. That's what I was afraid of." Mac stopped abruptly, as they confronted a huge tree completely blocking the road.

The sound of a chainsaw greeted them from farther down the lane.

"Evidently, Brad is working down closer to the house. We can start here and meet him."

Mac jumped out and went to the back of the truck, handing John K. a pair of leather work gloves as he unloaded a chain saw from a tool box in the bed of the truck.

"This has got to be cleared. Brad's wife, Christy is due to deliver their second baby any day. No way for anyone to get in or out till we get this road clear."

"Lead on, chief." John K. pulled on the gloves and followed Mac to the huge tree. He would throw branches out of the way as Mac cut them. Evidently, the sweat payments for borrowing the camper started right now.

"Hey, over there!" A voice shouted during a quiet moment when both chain saws stopped.

"It's Mac here. How's Christy?" Mac set the saw down at his feet and peered through the branches in front of them.

"She says she's okay. But she's having contractions. These trees blocking the road are not making me feel very confident." John K. could hear the anxiety in the young man's voice.

"Have you called her doctor?" Mac reached for his cell phone.

"Yeah. She talked to them. Lucky our phones were charged last night."

"Oh boy." Mac stood back, removing his cap and running his hand through his graying hair. "I can see you through this brush. We'll get it cleared away. Why don't you go back to the house and check on her and big brother. I've got help out here." He waited as Brad headed away from the downed trees.

"We need to make a path through here so at least someone can get to the house." Mac turned toward John K.

"What can I do?" John K. was throwing any branches he could pull loose to the side of the road.

"If she's about to have that baby, we need my wife. She'll

be a lot more help than you. No offense." Mac tossed a large limb to the side of the road.

"None taken." John K. took a deep breath to calm his racing pulse. A new baby? Today? Right now?

"We live the next house up from you on Old Logging Camp Road."

Mac pulled his phone out of his pocket. "Hon? Christy needs you. She has called the doctor, but the road is blocked and that baby might not wait." He paused. "I'm sending the oldest Billings boy to get you in my truck. He should be there in just a minute."

Mac picked up the chain saw and started it up, drowning out any question from John K.

John K. jogged to Mac's truck and jumped in. The four-wheel drive feature came in handy as the tires navigated the muddy road on the way to the main highway and back to the next gravel road. He couldn't help nodding at his own forlorn-looking truck, still struggling under the weight of the tree in front of their cabin.

"You're next, buddy. Today, we've got a baby to bring into the world." Talking to his truck again. Probably certifiable.

Mac's truck bounced up the road and seemed to know exactly where to turn as they passed the mailbox in front of the two-story log house just behind the Billings place.

A short-legged figure in a hot pink sweatshirt stood at the bottom of the porch steps with a bundle of clean towels in her arms. At her feet was a twenty-four pack of bottled water.

"Hi, I'm Betty." She opened the passenger side of the truck as soon as it stopped. "Can you get those waters for me?"

John K. jumped out and ran to lift the plastic bottles, settling them below the toolbox in the truck's bed.

"Pleased to meet you, ma'am." John K. turned to smile at

her as he shifted the truck into reverse and turned around in the graveled space in front of the house.

"It's good to have another neighbor today." She smiled as she locked her seat belt. "Mac would tend to overdo, and the ambulance crew will have enough to take care of getting Christy to town. Wouldn't want to ask them to tend to Mac at the same time."

"Does he have issues?" John K. knew it wasn't normal to ask about such things. But he did need a clear understanding of what he was dealing with here.

"Hopefully not, as long as he takes his heart medicine. Which he did, at breakfast today. That's my job—medication monitor." She replaced the Razorbacks baseball cap on her head. "Like I said, I'm thankful the Lord sent you to us."

"I'm glad to be able to help. That camper of y'all's was a lifesaver." John K. turned onto the main highway and headed back toward Mac. Funny how he had just met these two people but felt totally at ease. What was it Mom always talked about? Kindred spirits? Maybe so.

John K. stopped in front of the pine barricade in the road. The cleared space was almost big enough to drive through.

"Hey, sweetie!" Mac stopped and mopped his forehead with a bandana as he helped Betty out of the truck.

"Christy's baby picked a great birthday, huh?" Betty grabbed the towels and stomped toward the mobile home at the end of the driveway.

"She'll have a doozy of a story to tell her grandkids, that's for certain." Mac followed after.

"You need the bottles of water?" John K. hoisted the package from the bed of the truck.

"Yes. Bring them along." Betty stopped to face him. "I don't know what their pump situation is."

Brad opened the door of the mobile home and ushered the

little troop inside. "I've got coffee going. Christy didn't want me sitting there with a worried look on my face between contractions."

John K. glanced around the neat-as-a-pin living room and dining area. A small brown-haired boy played with a looped racecar track in front of the fireplace.

"Spencer. We have company!" Brad brought three cups to the dining room table.

The little guy ran one more toy car through its loop and walked toward them.

"Hi, Mr. Mac. Hi Mrs. Mac." He held his tiny hand in their direction.

"Good morning, young man." Mac leaned down to greet the boy. "This is my friend John."

"Are you a fireman like Mr. Mac?" Spencer moved closer to John K.

"Nope. I just came along to help today." He walked over to the toys on the floor and found an old-looking pickup truck. "Does this one go fast?"

"Yeah. Watch!" Spencer knelt next to the track and placed the truck in the right place for its journey through the loop. "But the Batmobile is fastest."

Betty walked toward the bedroom, and Mac sat at the table with his coffee.

"I didn't see any roof damage." Mac surveyed the ceiling of the room.

"No, Thankfully, I think everything is intact." Brad stood, looking toward the bedroom. "It's a good thing, since I guess we'll be gone for a day or two with little bit coming so soon."

"Brad!" Christy's voice interrupted the conversation, and Brad cleared the distance to the bedroom in three long steps.

"I guess I'd better finish clearing the road." John K. walked toward the front door.

"Don't you want some coffee?" Mac picked up a mug from the table.

"No. It felt good to rest, but if I get coffee, I'll want to sit for a while." John K. pulled on his work gloves. "Spencer, you have fun, now."

"Thanks, Mr. John. I hope you will be a fireman when you grow up." Another race car completed a loop and sailed across the wood plank floor.

"Maybe so, Buddy." John K. laughed. He wondered how this little guy would do when it was time to share his toys. From the looks of things, his parents would handle that transition just fine.

"I'll be right out." Mac stood next to his wife, who had just emerged from the bedroom. "Little man is coming to stay with Mrs. Betty when his mom goes to bring his little sister home, so we need to get his suitcase packed."

Toys were forgotten. Spencer took Mac's hand and walked to another bedroom. "I already have some of my toys in my suitcase."

John K. smiled and stepped back out into the damp wind. Out here, life seemed to continue, even with a road blocked with downed pine trees. He felt honored to have a part in this new baby's birthday story.

His phone vibrated–there must be a bit of a cell signal here at Brad and Christy's house.

Mom's response to his text from earlier.

> Praising God that you are okay. We are fine.
> Power is already back on here. Love you.

Okay, then. Back to the task at hand. He hoisted a few more large branches to the side of the road, then stepped back to check the width of the clearing.

The wail of an ambulance siren drifted in from the

highway. He jogged out to guide the first responders toward Christy. Working up a sweat was a great way to spend the day when the results were this easy to see.

"This way." The crew couldn't hear him, but he shouted anyway. *Thanks, God, for Your help.*

6

"I can't believe you're so calm. Two weeks from this Thursday, we will be in Fort Smith for the pageant." Kayla's voice was pitched higher than normal, even on the phone.

"Why be nervous? We've both done all we can to prepare. Got all of our paperwork done, sponsors lined up. Now, we just wait." Faith tossed a stress ball up and down as she talked. She wouldn't admit it to her cousin, but she was pretty excited too.

"We still need to go shopping. I need another hat."

"How many hats do you need?" Faith laughed.

"I have that gray, dressy one. And my everyday one for the riding events. But what about for casual stuff, interviews, luncheons? Won't we be wearing hats for that too?" Kayla sounded more and more desperate.

"Possibly. Yes. I have three. Like you said, one everyday, one super dressy, and an in-between one." Faith walked to her closet and scanned the outfits she had picked for the pageant. "I could probably use another pair of jeans now that you mention it. It's only one o'clock. We can run to town this afternoon."

"Okay. I'll even drive. Mom and Dad are gone in his truck, so her car is here."

"No. You don't need to run your mom out of gas. I'll drive. Be there in five." Faith ended the call and ran past the mirror on her way to the driveway. If Kayla needed a shopping trip to calm her nerves, she could oblige. She half expected a text from Ty asking her to supper. So far, nothing. Her palms got a little sweaty as she remembered that random kiss at Mrs. Gino's. Yes, this guy was certainly different.

"Are we crazy to be entering this thing?" Kayla picked up the conversation as if they had never stopped talking. She climbed into Faith's truck, fastened her seatbelt and slammed the door.

"I don't think we're crazy. We've both been rodeoing since we were born. We can compete right along with the rest." Faith scanned the sky as she pulled onto the highway. There was certainly no sign of a storm today. Crystal-clear skies were only interrupted by an occasional fluffy cloud. Folks near the river were still cleaning up storm damage. Well, at least they had a good day for it.

"Imagine winning all that scholarship money and then traveling all over the state being all royal and stuff," Kayla said.

"'All royal and stuff'?" Faith laughed. "Well, I hate to say it like this, but the money part is the most important thing for me. Being an oncology NP is going to take so much of it."

"That's why I'm doing architecture when I get to college. I can stop with the school stuff anytime and get a job. You just have your sights set so high, Lainie."

Faith smiled at the nickname Kayla used. When her youngest cousin was small, she had become obsessed with middle names. She'd called Hope "Cat," short for Catherine, and Faith became "Lainie" for Elaine. Kayla had even insisted on being called by her own middle name of Grace for most of her second-grade year.

"Okay, Gracie. While you're sitting at a drafting table somewhere, I will be helping people." Faith checked the digital clock on her dashboard. Still time to hear from Ty. She'd just have time to go home to get ready for a date.

"Well. Anyway." Kayla stretched and re-stretched her seatbelt. She usually changed the subject when Faith started talking about career plans. "I'm excited. I guess no one is surprised you won Caldwell Family Rodeo princess, and I am the teen winner, but now we're talking the State pageant."

"Hey, we got this. I have confidence." Faith smiled.

A text alert caught Faith's attention when she stopped at the next stoplight. Not Ty. It was the nursing home. When they arrived at the western store, she answered the message as Kayla bounced through the double glass doors. Someone was missing from the three o-clock shift. She'd take their shift, and an extra paycheck. No problem.

Faith moved the radio dial to find something livelier as she drove toward town. Sometimes, the country music she listened to just seemed too "down home" for her mood. She smiled. Of course it was down home. Exactly how they wanted it to be, right? But home was sometimes pretty boring.

"So. I've been here at the station for a long time now. I hope everybody's power is back on." Ty's voice sounded different, maybe a little huskier on the air than in person.

"At this point, my playlist is wearing thin. I don't want to start repeating, so unless y'all have a request, I'll play something for a certain someone who has been on my mind a lot since last night. Her name's not Virginia, but it should be." His low-pitched laugh rumbled through her speakers as the music started. "Listen to these words, Princess, 'cause 'Only the Good Die Young.'"

Faith's cheeks flushed. The message in the song was all too obvious. She glanced around nervously, even though no one else was close by. No one listening would connect what he said on the radio with her. Had he wanted her to hear this? Maybe he would be as embarrassed as she was if he knew she was listening.

Her heartbeat picked up speed and warmed her chest as she listened to the whole song. The singer was obviously trying to convince the girl to give up on her principles. He didn't want to wait.

She'd fought off the advances of boys during dates. But no one had ever sent their plea out as a song on the radio. Just this guy.

The pickup stopped in its usual parking spot on the north side of the nursing home. Faith took a deep breath as she picked up her purse.

Hey. I'm busting out of here at 9:00 tonight.

Ty's message appeared just before she tucked her phone in her pocket.

Wanna do something?

Her fingers shook as she typed.

I work till eleven.

I can stay busy till then. Would love to see you.

Starting a date at eleven? No. Of course not.

No thanks. I will need to go home to sleep.

Sleep is overrated.

Sorry. Thanks for asking.

Wow. He was persistent. She turned her phone off and tucked it away. Her answer had to be *no*, didn't it? She couldn't help smiling, and her breath caught as she stepped out of the truck to go inside.

7

John K. watched as Brad waved to his wife in the back of the ambulance before turning toward the carport attached to their mobile home.

"You're not going with them?" John K. saw the stress on the young man's face.

"No. I might need my truck while we are at the hospital. I'll follow." He jogged to the four-door pickup and jumped into the driver's seat. Just before closing the door, he leaned out. "Hey, thanks for your help today. We weren't looking forward to being trapped here when little Annie Elizabeth shows up."

"That wouldn't be ideal." John K. wiped his forehead with a bandana. His phone buzzed in his pocket. At least Brad and Christy had good phone reception out here.

> Thought O.D. and Me might bring you a truck this evening.

Dad's texts sounded just like talking to him.

> Okay.

Lord knows we have plenty of trucks around here, and yours is out of commission. Just makes sense.

Paramedics tended to Christy in the back of the ambulance as the driver warmed the vehicle and prepared to drive away. Brad drummed on his steering wheel impatiently.

"Hey!" John K. jogged to the passenger side of the truck and opened the door. "Can I catch a ride to town?"

"Sure. I owe you that much." Brad reached to shake John K.'s hand. "But I don't know when I'll be coming back. Spencer is settled at Mr. and Mrs. Mac's, and they are feeding my animals for a few days."

"No problem. I'll have a way back." John K. settled into the seat of the pickup and formulated a text to Dad.

Hey. I have a ride in. I wanted to see Cody and Grandpa Dee anyway. Want to meet me at the hospital?

Good idea.

John K. fastened his seat belt just before Brad accelerated to follow the ambulance past the piles of pine branches. He looked down at his dirty blue jeans and T-shirt. It would have been nice to clean up before visiting anyone. Was this rough appearance part of his new lifestyle? At least for today, it was.

Riding to town with Brad.

He sent a quick message to Mac while his signal was strong. Out here, you were wise to jump on opportunities when they came around.

"So, how long have you and Christy lived out here?" John K.

thought it might be a good idea to keep Brad talking on the way to town.

"Since we married six years ago. She was raised on that land. Her mom and dad moved into town last year, so we're tending their animals along with ours."

"It's beautiful out here." John K. adjusted his sunglasses. The mid-day sun spotlighted some undamaged trees. "Does the power go out a lot?"

"Not really. We are all pretty well prepared for it when it does happen." Brad slowed up going around a curve.

"Yeah. And I guess it is good to have neighbors close by." John K. craned his neck to look toward his family's cabin as they passed the narrow dirt road.

"Mac and Betty are the best. Everyone in the fire department looks out for each other, but since their kids don't live around close, I think they have sort of adopted us. Spencer loves them like his own grandparents." Brad sped up to glide into a spot behind the ambulance.

"Any chance the baby will be born in the ambulance?" John K. instantly regretted saying this. No reason to stress this new Daddy out.

"I hope not. Betty and the paramedics think we still have a few hours left. I just hope Christy has an easy time like with Spencer. That's what we've been praying for, anyway." Brad gripped the steering wheel, and kept his eyes focused on the back of the emergency vehicle in front of them.

Lord, take care of this family. And help the ambulance driver stay safe. John K. figured his prayers couldn't hurt anything. He shifted his body with each curve they rounded and resisted the urge to grab the passenger door handle. No need to make Brad self-conscious about his driving. John K. was always more comfortable doing the driving himself. His brother O.D. said it was a control thing. That kid was right more often than not.

A few more downed trees appeared as they neared Crossroads, but it seemed the brunt of the windstorm was in the more isolated areas. They met several power trucks headed out to assist.

"Boy, this weather sure caught everybody by surprise," Brad said, slowing down as the road turned to four lanes.

"Yeah. I don't think it was a tornado this time. Maybe just straight-line winds. But it was pretty fierce. I was glad to have the 'fraidy hole out at the deer camp." John K. craned his neck as they passed the Billings Boys dealership. No sign of either his dad or O.D. out on the lot. "Thanks again for the ride. My dad said he would have a truck for me to use to get back to the cabin."

"Oh, yeah. You're *that* Billings." Brad laughed.

"Ha! No, just his son." His cheeks reddened as he remembered how disappointed Dad had been that he hadn't wanted to take over the family business. O.D. was much better suited for delegating jobs and keeping balls in the air. Just give John K. a job that allowed him to get his hands dirty. He couldn't imagine making a difference by sitting behind any kind of desk. But he could anticipate the question in all of their minds. Just what WAS he going to do with his life now? At least his driver had a clear direction today.

"Well. Not much longer till you see that new little girl of yours." John K. pointed out an empty parking space. "I think this lot over by the ER is close to where you want to be."

"Thanks. I appreciate you riding with me. I shouldn't be so nervous since this is the second baby. But Annie sure decided to make a memorable entrance. I just hope Christy is okay."

He navigated the truck into a wide spot and turned off the ignition.

"Here." John K. pulled out his billfold and found a twenty-dollar bill.

"Oh. No. Like I said, I enjoyed the company." Brad shoved the bill back toward him.

"It's not a payment for the ride. It's a gift for the new baby. You can use it to get something special for her." John K. slid out of the passenger side before Brad could catch his arm.

"Thanks. It may buy gas for the truck." Brad laughed as he pulled off his coat and threw it in the truck seat. "I forgot all about checking the gas gauge."

John K. jogged along behind the excited young man as they entered the hospital.

"The Women's Center is down this way." Brad waved as he ran into the corridor to their left.

"Good luck, man." John K. pushed the elevator button and stepped in as soon as it opened. Cody had moved from the fourth floor to the fifth for physical therapy. Five months out from his accident, they might be looking at a new facility for him. He knew that Cody's preference was to go home, but they had tried that. When an infection set in, the hospital proved to be the only choice. Time to put on a cheerful face.

Are you in town?

There was no need for Dad's text. John K. opened the door to Cody's room instead of answering.

"Hey." O.D. greeted him with a handshake. "Looks like you've put in a full day of work already."

"Well, you know. We can't all have a cushy desk job. How's it goin', Squirt?" He nodded at his dad while shaking hands with his brother.

"No power at the dealership, and nobody is thinking about buying a truck today anyway. We sent everybody home." O.D. sank into a chair near Cody's bed.

"Hey, Marshall." John K. was the only family member that

used Cody's first name on a regular basis. "Ready for another bull ride?"

"Yeah, bro. Bring it on." Cody laughed. "What could go wrong?"

"Was there a lot of wind damage out towards camp?" Dad walked over to shake John K.'s hand.

"It looks to me like everything over about thirty feet came down. We will have a ton of cleanup to do. But at least nothing hit what was left of the house, and Mac's camper survived." John K. was glad to see Cody smiling, but noticed his eyes seemed heavy. They wouldn't need to hang around here long. He could obviously use some rest.

"I brought you a demo to drive, but you know your mom would prefer you just head to our house until yours is livable." Dad handed him a key ring.

"Sure. Mama hen loves having her chickens all close by." John K. leaned against the shelving unit next to Cody's IV pole.

"I told her you wanted to stay busy out there getting the cabin shipshape again."

"For real. It's gonna be a while. But today, it's been all about giving our neighbors a hand." John K. caught a glimpse of himself in the mirror across from Cody's bed. He did look the part of a mountain man today. He'd definitely clean up when he got back to the camper. But maybe the whiskers could stay. Not a bad look.

"So Mac recruited you for his rural fire department, huh?" Dad laughed.

"Well, not officially. But the walls of that little camper were closing in on me this morning, so I rode along. No fires, today. Just a lot of clearing unnecessary timber out of the way." As the words left his mouth, he wondered what would happen if there was a real emergency out in the woods. Would he be able to help, or would he run, like he did when the water heater exploded? It was probably better for Mac not to depend on him too much.

"Wish I could come help." Cody's low voice rumbled from the bed.

"Hey, me too, buddy."

It must be hard for this kid. John K. had problems staying still as a youngster, but this youngest one didn't even fight the battle. He just stayed constantly moving. When he wasn't riding a horse or a bull, he was cleaning stalls, fixing equipment. Anything to stay busy. Confinement must be killing the kid.

"But, hey. Check the calendar. It's not summer vacation. Aren't you supposed to be in school?" This was a familiar jab that their Grandpa Dee used when they were younger.

"It's Saturday, goof. Junior Caldwell has been keeping me up on my assignments. I can do a lot of them on my computer from this bed." Cody reached for his laptop proudly. "I even got to be in on a discussion in Social Studies class Friday."

"Awesome!" John K. gestured to O.D. to join him in the hallway. He needed to learn what the plan was for Cody's future recovery. "I'll be back in minute. I need to get O.D. straightened out on a few things."

O.D's shoulders rose and fell with a silent chuckle. Not too long ago, a comment like that would have caused them to come to blows. Now, he clapped his younger brother playfully on the shoulder as they walked out the door.

"So, what's the plan for Cody?" John K. knew O.D. didn't expect any beating around the bush. "I get the impression the hospital is not the right place for him anymore. Is he coming home?"

"Not without a lot of adaptations." O.D. removed his baseball cap and ran his fingers through his hair. "And he still needs a lot of therapy. Several times a day sometimes."

"So ..." John K.'s mind charged ahead. What kind of facility did he need? How far would they have to travel back and forth to visit him?

"Believe it or not, the home Grandpa Dee is in has some of the best rehab around." O.D. looked down and spoke softly.

"They're thinking of putting him in Pleasant Oaks?" John K. struggled to keep his voice down. Oh no. Cody would not want to go to an old folk's home. Was that the best alternative?

"It just makes sense. Like I said, keeping him at home wouldn't be realistic right now. A therapist would either have to live with us or come all the way out there once or twice a day." O.D. stood a little taller and faced him. "There are facilities in other places, but Pleasant Oaks is the best one nearby."

"Is money a problem? I could get a steady job and help to pay for another place, maybe even in another city. But a nursing home?"

"Hey." Dad emerged from the hospital room. "Are you about ready to head home, O.D? I've got some work with the cattle before Mom gets supper ready."

"Yeah." O.D. took a step down the hall. "We can talk at supper, John K."

"Okay." He wasn't sure any amount of talking would convince him that his baby brother was ready for a nursing home. "Tell Mom I'm on the way. I want to spend a minute or two with the Marshall."

"Okay, son. Here's your keys. It's the burgundy four-by-four out near the flagpole. See you soon." Dad patted him on the shoulder as he handed him the Billings Boys fob.

"So, I could have used your help today." John K. immediately switched over to cheerful big brother mode as he reentered Cody's room.

"Sorry, I ..." Cody winced as he tried to sit straighter in bed.

"I don't need to hear your excuses. You would have liked this. It involved a chain saw." He removed his hoodie and threw it in a chair. "This whole road was blocked by a massive pine tree that decided to fall right in the way."

"Wow. No wonder you're such a mess. You could have at least taken a shower before coming into town." Cody's smile was a welcome sight.

"Well, the ambulance had just left, and the baby's daddy was ready to follow it, so ..."

"What? What ambulance? What baby?" Cody laughed. "Maybe you'd better start this story over, hot shot. Are you sure this is not one of your tall tales?"

John K.'s cheeks warmed as he grinned. He was thrilled Cody was alert enough to enjoy listening to his stories today. There had been days when he'd just talked to hear his own voice echo off the walls. But the nurses had assured him that his visits to his brother had done a lot to contribute to the healing process. If he ran out of true stories to tell, he would make up some new ones. Anything to see that smile again.

New car smell filled John K.'s nostrils as he opened the door of the pickup and slid into the comfy seat. These new models his dad sold were great, but somehow it just made him miss his old truck more.

He stopped to send a quick text to Mom.

> Headed to see Grandpa Dee while I'm in town. Save me a plate?

> Already did. That's why God made microwaves. See you soon.

He laughed. That was their crazy mom. Most people would have responded with one letter. Maybe two if they decided to add an *O* before the *K*.

Pleasant Oaks was near the hospital. It would certainly make visiting easier if Cody joined Grandpa there. But a nursing home? That would be an adjustment for all of them.

8

"Hi, sweetheart."

Faith smiled at John K.'s grandpa's greeting as she entered his room. "Good evening, Mr. Tolliver." She had learned that addressing him so formally helped him remember who she was. Other patients had pet names for her and she was okay with that, but she must remind him of someone he had known before. It was sort of creepy, even though she knew he meant well.

"Got some pills for me, I bet." He used his remote control to adjust the volume on the television.

"Yes, sir." She handed him the little paper cup with his pills and helped him with the straw in his drinking water.

"Must be time for supper, soon. I hope it's not leftover meatloaf."

Faith laughed. "You know they don't serve leftovers. I think it's something warm like potato soup."

"I never was one for leftovers. But Trixie liked my leftover cookies after lunch."

"Trixie?" Faith straightened the pillow on his bed. He

usually made it up himself. All the CNAs enjoyed helping in this room. Mr. Tolliver was very easy to care for.

"Don't be jealous. Her hair is darker than yours, but she's quite a bit shorter. And her bark is worse than her bite." His eyes twinkled as he enjoyed his own joke.

"Oh, the therapy dog visited today. That's right. I don't usually see you on Saturday evening." The director of the nursing home had balked at first when Faith suggested allowing pets to visit. But the residents looked forward to seeing the furry visitors.

"Knock, knock." John K. spoke from the doorway before he removed his baseball cap, and reached to shake his grandpa's hand.

"How are you, Grandpa Dee?" He winked in Faith's direction. "Looks like you have some very pretty company."

"Sure! All the girls like me." Mr. Tolliver stood slowly before John K. released his handshake.

"Hi, John K. I wasn't sure you would come in today." Faith smiled. She wouldn't mention the dirt on his clothes or the little shadow of whiskers on his chin. It was certainly a different look for this ordinarily clean-cut military man.

"You need a shave, private." Mr. Tolliver didn't hold back the obvious remark.

"Ha. Yes, sir. I do." John K. rubbed his chin. "I had to catch a ride in this morning, and the driver didn't want to wait on me to clean up."

"See that you take care of that." John K.'s grandpa walked toward the window on the other side of the room, and she got the sudden impression that he didn't recognize his oldest grandson.

"I just came to deliver some medicine. Will you be joining us for supper?" Faith spoke quickly, dodging the embarrassment her friend must feel.

"No. I won't stay long. Just came from checking on Cody. Thought I'd drop in here before I go out to the house. Mom has supper ready." John K. looked toward the back of his grandpa's head, some moisture pooling in his blue-gray eyes.

"Okay. Take care." She walked into the hallway, picking up a clipboard that would assist her in helping the next patient. Family visits did so much good for the residents. John K. and his family shouldn't become discouraged as their patriarch's memory slowly dwindled. The well-being of people who had visitors was better than the ones who had been forgotten.

"Faith." Her supervisor brushed past her in the hallway. "Let's get Mr. Murphy ready for supper next."

"Yes, ma'am. On my way." Faith stopped at the door to Mr. Tolliver's neighbor.

This was a perfect example of the difference in someone who had few visitors. It was a chore to get any kind of communication out of Mr. Murphy. He didn't argue when they came into his room. She almost wished he would sometimes. Such a sad life, just existing.

The other nurses told her this was a lesson in staying detached. It was much easier to do their job if they didn't worry too much about each person they served. Easy to say, but not as easy to do. She included the residents of Pleasant Oaks in her prayers each night. Maybe that is why she wanted to be a nurse instead of a doctor. She didn't want to pretend to be unconcerned about her patients. Nurses were allowed to be a little more empathetic.

It took a few minutes to get Mr. Murphy cleaned up, dressed and sitting in his wheelchair. Finally, she pushed out backwards through the door into the hallway, with her patient in front of her.

"Okay, Mr. Murphy. Here we go. Hang on tight. I haven't been driving this thing for long."

She smiled at her joke since the man had no reaction of his own. After turning the chair around, she headed toward the right side of the hallway, and followed John K. who walked slowly with his grandpa toward the dining hall.

"I don't think anyone is in a big hurry." John K. turned to smile her way.

"Well, they should be. The chef's potato soup and yeast rolls are fantastic." Faith laughed.

"So. I've heard. I'll just get him settled and move along." John K. nodded sadly.

"You sitting with me, doll?" Mr. Tolliver reached for Faith's arm.

"Sorry. Mr. Murphy is my date this time." Faith winked at John K.

"I'll bet they all compete to get the rodeo princess for a dinner companion." John K. smiled.

"I don't know about that. I don't feel glamorous in this outfit." Faith turned the corner and steered Mr. Murphy toward his assigned spot.

"Okay, Grandpa Dee. Let's see who is at your table." John K. guided the shuffling man toward a table nearby.

"Say hello to the rest of your family when you see them." Faith tucked a napkin in the top of Mr. Murphy's shirt.

"I will. I understand you may have my baby brother to deal with soon." John K. pulled out a chair for his grandpa. "The hospital says he can get some good physical therapy here."

"Their PT is top notch here. Maybe I can spend some time visiting with him when I'm not busy on my hall." Faith knew this must be a tough pill for the Billings boys to swallow. Physical Therapy and rehabilitation was great for all ages, but the majority of their patients didn't expect to "graduate" once they got here. "Hopefully, they can help him prepare to go home in a few weeks."

"Yeah. That's the plan. Anyway, I guess you'd better pay attention to your date." He nodded in Mr. Murphy's direction. "I'll see you soon."

Her date. Yes, Mr. Murphy would need her attention. She was glad she wouldn't have to answer a bunch of messages from Ty tonight. Working here required her to focus on what she was doing. These people needed her.

"Take care!" She waved at John K. as she settled into a chair near Mr. Murphy's right side. Yes, being needed was a good thing. There was more to life than being glamorous.

She decided to check her messages quickly while they brought food to the table. Kayla had sent a selfie in her new hat.

> Thanks for your help. I think this looks great with my interview outfit.

Dinner with a man who couldn't feed himself and a teenaged cousin primping in her best duds. What a contrast. She took a deep breath and turned off the phone.

Faith sat in the nurse's break room and scrolled through her phone again. Where was that post about the requirements for becoming a nurse practitioner? She knew her first priority was to complete her undergraduate nursing degree and become an RN. But then what?

It seemed like the best post-grad programs were all in the Northeast or on the West Coast. Except for one in Houston. That was fine. She'd spent enough time around Crossroads. She loved this place and her family and friends, but there was a big world out there. Big city life might be part of the big-time degree she was looking for.

There was a respected medical school in Chicago. The requirements were tough. But—Chicago! How exciting. She drew a timeline on a napkin in the break room. About a year left on her undergrad degree. Could she finish that while serving as Miss Rodeo Arkansas? Maybe not. But that scholarship money would help so much. She could probably continue to work here even if she won. If she socked away everything she could and took all the tests at the right time, it might be doable.

She looked again at the website for Miss Rodeo USA. If she won the state pageant, and won in Las Vegas, she would have to take a year off from her studies. She shook her head to try to dispel these big dreams. Her parents taught her to believe in herself. Could she do this?

A cross-stitched sampler hanging above the microwave caught her eye.

"I can do all things, through Christ who Gives me Strength."

Yes, it would take God's help, for sure. She closed her eyes for a quick prayer.

Lord, guide my steps. I know Your plans are perfect. Amen.

9

John K. stretched his arms over his head as he sat on the side of the king-sized bed in O.D.'s old room above the workshop. When Dad asked him to stay over last night, he hadn't put up much argument. It was Sunday morning, but only O.D. was still in the habit of weekly church attendance.

Stretching a fence was a job better started at dawn. He didn't want the crew to wait for him to roll up from Mac's trailer before they got their work underway. He couldn't tell his dad that he preferred finding a paying job to do today. Dad would easily pony up some cash to help him buy groceries. Working on the Billings ranch felt more like a family obligation than a part-time job. He didn't mind helping out. That helped his dad concentrate on the work he loved to do out in the sunshine. Let O.D. take care of the desk job at the new- and used-truck business.

He took two quick steps toward the window to survey the familiar landscape. His dad would have to hire more permanent help if he wanted to make a go of the cattle ranch. There was lots of land out there, perfect for grazing, with enough room to handle a few pleasure horses. It was tempting to just stick around here, where meals were provided, and the work was second nature.

The problem was things were too familiar. At his point in life, he should only be coming back home for a visit now and then. Not to work, and certainly not to live here. There were perks, though. Mom would have breakfast on the table on her way to check on Cody.

A clean T-shirt was tucked in before he fastened his belt in a new notch. Those morning runs up and down the mountain were keeping his waistline under control. He pulled his socks up before stepping into his old cowboy boots. As Grandpa Dee would say "better wear your working clothes and pull your hat down tight." Plenty of good old-fashioned work to be done today.

Ping. A text arrived from a Highway Department connection. A temporary job was available tomorrow. Another chance for hot, sweaty work. Goody. But at least this one had a paycheck attached. He pressed the button to accept and headed out the door and down the stairs for Mom's famous biscuits and gravy. *Thanks, God. It's all good.*

The clouds that had signaled springtime turbulence were completely gone as John K.'s borrowed truck bounced out to the edge of the pasture. The sun tinted the sky above the hillside with a soft pink hue. He stopped his truck and jumped out to locate the come-along that would enable them to stretch the spools of wire across the gap. Dad had wanted this new divider in the largest grazing area for a long time. It might be an all-day job for him and Billy, but it was definitely doable.

"Hey, how's married life?" He greeted the young man stepping out of an old brown Jeep.

"Good. It's all good." Billy met his handshake. "So, I guess you know where this fence goes?" Billy tilted his cowboy hat back.

"Yep. Dad and I brought the posts and laid them out after supper last night." John K. pointed down the fence line.

"I'll bet he's glad to have you home." Billy lifted the first spool of wire.

"Yeah, but I hope he doesn't get used to it. I've got lots of work to fix up the cabin at the deer camp." John K. pulled his leather gloves from his back pocket.

"Hey, one job at a time." Billy laughed.

"For real."

They settled into a routine as the sun rose higher, and both shed their shirts, lifting the wire carefully to avoid the sharp barbs. Billy pounded the first post in place and fastened the top strand before John K. placed the second one, stretching the metal wire tight. He twisted the wire firmly onto the metal fence post and prepared to stretch the next strand.

"Hey!" A familiar voice called from the hillside above them. "Don't you two know about taking the Lord's day off?" Faith waved from her horse, and Hope galloped up behind her.

"Gotta stretch fence while the sun shines." John K. glanced up to meet her smile as rode closer.

"So, you think you need to add an extra fence to keep the Caldwell neighbors out?" Faith stopped near him.

"Nope. Trying to keep our cows out of Hope's front yard." John K. reached into his back pocket for a bandana and removed his hat to wipe the sweat off his forehead.

"They'd have a lot of hill to climb before they reached our yard." Hope brought Champ to a halt just a few feet away.

"Dad just got tired of following them up into the rocks." John K. waved at his partner. "Take a minute, Billy." He gestured toward the gravel road leading up to O.D. and Hope's house. "Trespassers can still use the road."

"Glad to see your dad is getting some work out of you." Faith paced Belle back and forth. "You can't hide out in the woods all your life."

"That's not fair," Hope said. "He's got plenty of work out there too."

"Just a mild to moderate remodel," John K. laughed, reaching for the come-along.

"Hey, O.D.'s friend Tara called this morning asking about your storm damage. She said her station is thinking of sending a crew out this afternoon for an interview on the cleanup efforts." Hope stood next to her horse, allowing him to graze for a moment.

"Yeah. She's welcome to come out. But most of my damage was caused by the flying water heater." John K. said.

"Her viewers won't know the difference." Faith laughed.

"Hey!" Dad rolled up in his two-seat pickup. Cool air poured out of the driver's side window as he stopped next to them. "Need some more lemonade?" Dad cut the engine and stepped out of the truck with a plastic jug in each hand.

"Hang on!" John. K. nodded at Billy. "Hold what you got, man."

"We're headed back to Hope's house." Faith turned Belle to head back up the rocky path. "Don't work too hard."

"Come back when you can stay longer," John K. called after her.

Faith and Champ dodged boulders as if they were in a barrel race on their way back up the hill. That girl. He wasn't sorry for the interruption, though. He was always up for a smile from that one.

"Are you staying over tonight too?" Dad handed the jug of lemonade to John K.

"No. We'll finish today if Billy is up for it. I need to get back to the cabin. Didn't you say the insurance man cleared us to get started on reframing?" His to-do list was growing. Staying busy was one thing, but this was on its way to overwhelming.

"Fine with me. The sooner we finish, the sooner I get paid." Billy took a swig from his jug.

"Okay. And, yeah. The insurance adjuster took a look at the house and the truck. We can get busy fixing both any time." Dad pulled his own pair of leather gloves out of the cab of the pickup. "I'll just pitch in, and we can get this fence knocked out in no time."

What were all of these vehicles doing at the cabin? John K. rolled to a stop near Mac's camper and stepped out. He'd like to get inside to the miserable excuse for a shower, but he'd better see what all this commotion was about first.

"Hi, John K." The blonde reporter from KRVA TV stepped out of one of the vehicles, a black SUV with some sort of satellite contraption on top.

"Hey, Tara. Hope said you might come up this afternoon. Can I talk to this other guy for a minute before you get started?" He walked toward the rollback wrecker that backed toward his old green GMC.

"Hi!" Wouldn't it be best to clear the rest of the timber off the thing before they tried to move it?

"Oh. I guess you are the owner." The driver stopped his engine and stepped down from the driver's side of the wrecker. "Mr. Billings asked us to come get your pickup as soon as the insurance guy had seen it. The agent said he came by just before dark last night, so we're here to take it in to the body shop."

"Do you mind waiting just a minute?" Tara ran up to stand

between the two men. "Tom, come over and get a shot of this truck in front of the cabin before they move it."

The cameraman ran over and turned on his lights, filming Tara looking toward the smashed vehicle and the damaged house.

"Thanks. We'll get out of your way now." She stepped aside, and John K. reached for a large limb that lay across the bed of the truck.

"I thought you might want me to move this stuff. And I've got some camping gear I need to get out of here." John K. pulled the canvas bag to the back, opening the bent tailgate to make removing the cargo a little easier.

"Man, I hope they can get this looking good again. She's a beauty." The tow truck driver helped pull branches away.

"Yeah." Funny he'd never thought of his truck as a female. He guessed folks thought of trucks like boats, calling them 'she.' But this vehicle seemed more like a male, an old friend of the family. He stood back and looked for a moment at the scratched green paint, the bent bed, the crushed cab. He had missed it almost as much as his family when he was in the Army. It might never be the same again, but it was worth the effort to restore it.

With the tree moved away, the rollback moved into position to load the pickup for hauling. Tara rocked from one foot to the other, and John K. realized she probably did not want to wait until the tow truck left to start her interview.

"Okay. If you can handle a little motor noise, I'll answer your questions now." Where was O.D., the family spokesperson, when needed? At least after a day of stretching fence, he looked the part of a bedraggled storm victim.

"Thanks, John K." Tara moved into position and the cameraman pointed in her direction as he started filming.

"We're just across the county line from Crossroads to

report on the cleanup efforts after the storm that struck earlier this week. We found one of our locals, John K. Billings, whose family owns a deer camp. Can you tell us what happened here?"

After a deep breath, he couldn't help turning his head as the tow truck began to pull away with his old buddy. *Sure. Just a typical day in the neighborhood, Tara.*

10

Faith walked away from the group that always surrounded her dad after the cowboy church service. Hope and O.D. followed another young couple, and Junior waved to his friends as they rejoined their families. She still felt a little bit at a loss right after services were over. Mom had always had a plan of action for all of them. These more relaxed Sundays would take some getting used to.

A buzzed notification reminded her that her phone remained on mute.

What's up, princess?

She smiled as she read the text. Ty was the only person other than her dad who called her that.

Not much.

She texted back her standard reply.

Meet me for pizza?

Sure.

Easy decision. Why not?

"See you at home." Junior jogged away from Faith and her dad. He ran the last few steps to the driver's side of his dad's truck.

"Dad, I won't be coming straight home." Faith stepped up to her truck and opened the door. "I've been invited for pizza."

"Okay. Sounds more exciting than our ham sandwiches I guess." Dad patted her knee before she could close the door. "Be careful."

"So, 'fess up." Hope caught her just before she turned the ignition key. "Who's the mystery man?"

"No one special. At least not yet." Faith smiled into her rearview mirror. Her lipstick could use a touch-up.

"Okay, then. Be that way. But like Dad said, be careful."

Faith hated it when her younger sister's gaze bored into her eyes like that. Now that she was married, the mothering instincts were stronger than ever. She blinked to break the eye contact.

"Just give me a break. I can handle things." Faith waved off her meddling sibling and managed to get the truck out of the church parking lot.

Cranking up the radio, she ignored the texts that kept coming in from Ty. Couldn't he give her a minute to get there?

The quiet downtown area displayed lots of CLOSED signs. Only a few restaurants took advantage of hungry church-goers. She glided into a parking space at the pizza place. Ty's Mustang was already there.

Booth for two in the back.

That was the last text he had sent. Okay, then.

Just past the brightly lit pool table in the darker corners of the room, a couple with small children tucked safely into the inside of the booth shared their messy supper.

Ty's waving hand led her to the high-backed booth he had chosen. A pitcher of beer occupied the center of the table, and a waitress followed her with a notepad.

"Are y'all ready to order?" The young girl stood next to Ty as Faith slid into the booth.

"I like all the meats on mine with thick crust." Ty winked at Faith.

"I'd like veggies if it's okay." All of that grease would make her afternoon unbearable.

"Okay. A large, half Meat-Overload and half veggie. And we're hungry, so make it snappy." Ty moved to her side of the table and scooted in next to her.

"And I'd like a glass of sweet tea." Faith leaned out around him to speak to the waitress as she walked away.

"Sweet tea?" Ty laughed. "You're gonna make me drink this whole pitcher?"

"I don't imagine I can make you do anything." Faith's heart pounded as Ty's hip pushed her firmly against the inside wall. "Can I have a little space here?"

"Woo-hoo! I'm happy to see you too!" He moved an inch or two, then pulled her chin toward him. "Rough day at church?"

"No." She took a deep breath as his smiling blue eyes caught her attention.

"Well, I'm glad you're here. Our jobs make it hard for us to have much time together, and I'd love to make this happen more often." Ty's hand dropped from her face to her arm, and then rested on her left leg. "Having you next to me makes me think I can handle the week ahead."

She moved away enough to remove his hand. Nice to hear he thought about her, though.

"So, what did you do today?" A sip of cold tea soothed her throat.

"A lot of nothing. That's what Sundays are good for in my opinion. A little grocery shopping, bare minimum laundry. But you don't want to hear about that stuff. You've got a big pageant coming up. Have you got a press crew following you and Kayla to Miss Rodeo Arkansas?" He poured himself a second glass of beer from the pitcher.

"A press crew? Ha. I don't think the community is that concerned about the Caldwell girls going to Fort Smith." Faith mouthed 'thank-you' to the server as she brought their pizza.

"Well, they should be. If the high school football team was going to the state finals, they would be all over that, right? So, you two deserve some attention too." Ty picked up a glass jar of parmesan cheese and motioned to the waitress. "We could use some more of this."

"Tara Williams is having us drop by the station Wednesday afternoon for an interview before we leave Thursday." Faith moved Ty's hand, which had inched its way back to her leg. This was a little beyond distracting.

"Well, I'll talk to my manager at the radio station. He's always saying we should be more involved in the community. Maybe I can do some live reports from the State pageant." He moved his hand to the table and grabbed a piece of his half of the pizza.

Faith chewed a bite of a veggie slice. How would that work? Live reports on the radio? Would he follow her around asking questions? She was glad he was interested, but how would he fit in with a hotel full of ladies? Hmm. He'd probably say he'd fit in just fine.

"So, you said you were from Baltimore. What's that like?"

Maybe she could change the topic and get some more insight into this guy's brain.

"The greatest." Ty sat back in the booth. "You can go from the ultra-modern and flashy area around the inner harbor to seedy little restaurants on the side streets by just walking a few blocks. My brother and I used to hang out in the Italian neighborhood, just inhaling the smells." He laughed.

"You have a brother? Older or younger?" Faith sat up straighter. An actual detail about his life. What a surprise.

"Younger." Ty fidgeted with his napkin. "But I haven't talked to him in a while."

Ty ate another piece of pizza. Faith didn't want to stop with just one question.

"Hey, Faith!" Tara Williams walked past their table. "Good to see you!" She nodded in Ty's direction. "Mr. Porter, how's it going?"

"Just great, Ms. Williams." Ty took another drink of his beer.

"See you later this week, Faith." Tara waved as she passed by them.

Faith sipped her tea. Tara was always friendly, but there had been something different about the way she looked back at Faith before she left the pizza restaurant. Maybe she could ask her about that backward glance later. Now, she'd like to see if Ty would share more about his background.

"And you moved here from Baltimore?" Could she get this conversation going again?

"With a couple stops between. The job before this one was in New Orleans. Talk about culture shock." Ty sprinkled his pizza liberally with crushed red pepper.

"I'll bet." Faith laughed. "So why Crossroads?"

"My station down there switched to a national format. No local deejays. The country station here still has live personalities, and they had an opening." He scooted closer to her again. "I interviewed with the TV station too. That's where I met your Miss Tara."

"Being on television might be fun." Faith couldn't read the shadow that crossed his face.

"Maybe. I just didn't fit their 'image.' But enough talking." He turned to face her, reaching around her shoulders with his right hand, and using his left to trace her cheek. "I'd rather just be quiet and look a little closer at my beautiful date."

Faith flinched as he pulled her close and his lips found hers. Her cheeks flamed, and she stiffened.

"What's wrong?" He whispered, without moving away.

"You just surprised me." She looked down at the table.

"Well, it shouldn't be surprising that I can't resist you. You look beautiful, even in this dim light." He reached into his back pocket for his billfold. "But, yeah. I get it. Maybe some of your church-going friends might see you here. Let's find somewhere a little more private." He stood without another word and walked toward the cash register.

Faith followed, standing a few steps behind as he paid for their food. Had he even bothered to tip the waitress? His repeated compliments to her contrasted with the way he seemed to treat other people. At this point, she didn't want to go anywhere else with him, especially somewhere more private.

Ty reached for her hand as they walked out toward the parking lot.

"You want to follow me, or just leave your truck here?" They had reached his car, and he turned toward her before opening the driver's side door.

"Where are we going?" Wouldn't this have been a good piece of information to share with her?

"My apartment isn't the greatest, but it is clean at the

moment. Maybe we could find something to ignore on the television." He pinned her against the side of his car and kissed the side of her neck.

"Sorry. I think I had better just go home." Faith moved her hands up in front of her and pushed against his chest.

"Really? I know you're a princess, but don't you ever have any fun?" His hands moved down her back.

"Yes. Really." She pushed a little harder. "I'm not interested in being alone with you. Since I'm not sure that pitcher of beer was the first you've had to drink, I don't even want to ride with you." Her heart pounded, but she tried to keep her voice firm.

"Wow. Okay, then. I'm sorry I don't meet your standards, your highness." He stepped back and gave her an exaggerated bow. "I will see you at the rodeo queen contest, though. I still think you and your beautiful friends deserve some publicity. I'll try to behave myself a little better in the future."

Faith backed away as the red car sped out of the parking lot. She knew turning him away was the right thing to do, but why did she suddenly feel hollow inside?

Her phone dinged with a text notification as she started her pickup. She hadn't received a text from Tara Williams in a long time.

> Just thought you might want to research that guy. His real name is Paul Tyler.

Tears stung Faith's eyes as she drove home. She would definitely check to see what Tara was talking about. But maybe when she had a little more time to think things through.

11

John K. adjusted the neon yellow-green vest over his plain white T-shirt and flashed his "STOP" sign at the oncoming SUV. The morning sunshine blazed into his sunglasses and reminded him why he usually worked shirtless. The female road-crew foreman had informed him that option was off the table.

"You'd be an attractive nuisance." She smiled.

"That doesn't sound like a totally bad thing." He laughed. "But okay. I'll cooperate. I need this job."

She handed him a walkie-talkie, which already squawked.

"Five—no, six coming your way."

He pressed the button. "Ten-four." He raised his eyebrows, and the foreman answered with a nod. She walked to her pickup to retrieve a clipboard.

John K. counted vehicles as they passed him. He flipped the metal sign to "Slow" as the last car passed and pressed the talk button again.

"Only four headed up this time."

"Got it."

"Today is a little boring compared to tomorrow. I need to go down and post a couple more signs to warn everyone." The foreman stepped into her truck and started it.

"It's that serious?" John K. returned a friendly wave from a small boy in a sedan's back seat.

"Yeah. The road will be completely closed for thirty minutes when we blast the biggest boulder out of the way. They're drilling holes in it right now so the dynamite can go in." She drove down the shoulder of the road and was soon out of sight around the next curve.

Blasting. Dynamite. Sweat broke out on John K.'s forehead. He knew the explosion would be controlled, and everyone would be safe. Could he stand here with only a hard hat and a metal sign for protection while something like that happened just up the road?

After switching his sign to STOP again, the drill pounded its way into the granite somewhere out of sight. Though it didn't happen often, boulders did occasionally slide down hillsides, especially after a heavy rain. If the road was blocked even slightly, it would create a dangerous situation. There was just barely enough room for two lanes on most of these mountain roads. What would be his task tomorrow? Would he still be standing here with a sign, or did they expect him to be stationed closer to the explosion?

A teenaged boy ran up to take his sign and walkie-talkie. John K. jogged to his borrowed truck, eager for a good long swallow of lemonade from the jug Betty had loaned him. He unwrapped the ham sandwich he'd brought and opened a bag of chips. This wasn't a bad way to make a few bucks. The temporary employees got the easy jobs. If he hung around, the pay would increase, but the work involved would probably be tougher too.

He scrolled through the updates on his phone, stopping to

look at the latest Billings Boys ad. O.D. was doing a good job of letting the dealership marketing team shine. That sort of thing was certainly not John K.'s cup of tea.

A crash from atop the hill startled him. Probably just a dump truck delivering some filler material for the road's shoulder. He imagined how much louder dynamite would be.

Hey, give me a call when you get a minute.

The message from his dad popped onto his screen.

"Dad, what's up?" John K. took another drink of lemonade as the phone was answered on the other end.

"The contractor wants to know when he can come talk to you about the cabin." Rushing wind distorted the conversation. Dad must be driving somewhere on the ranch.

"I can be there tomorrow morning." He made the decision quickly. No dynamite work for him tomorrow.

"Don't they need you on the road crew?"

"I'm sure they can find someone else to hold a sign." John K. removed his cap and ran his fingers across his short hair.

"Well. That would be good. This guy needs to get you on his schedule. Okay, I'll tell him."

"Thanks, Dad. Cell phone service is spotty out there. I appreciate you making those calls for me." He breathed a huge sigh. Dad had no idea how great his timing was.

"See ya. Be careful out there today." Dad disconnected.

Yep, being careful was about all he had accomplished lately. John K. stepped out of the cab of his truck and looked up the hill. Tomorrow, he would meet with the people who would do the real work. Was this the way the rest of his life would be? Would he always be avoiding danger, instead of facing it? This was not the way he had pictured his life.

Back at his post on the side of the road, he was stationary, safe. When the foreman's pickup returned, he'd let her know he was weaseling out of work tomorrow.

Truthfully, there was a lot of work to be done rebuilding the cabin. He could save the family some money by doing some of it himself. Sweat equity was respectable. Talking through his decision in his head, it didn't sound so bad. But, that kind of work wouldn't pay his expenses for long. A regular paycheck would need to be in the picture, soon. Maybe the next gig would not involve dynamite.

12

"Aren't you on your way to work?" Hope sat near Faith on a barstool next to the kitchen island.

Faith opened her laptop on the granite countertop. O.D. and Hope had done such a good job remodeling this old place.

"Yeah. But I need to talk to you. I am tired of keeping secrets." She pulled up the news report she'd found a few minutes before. "You remember the guy from the radio station, the cute red-headed one?"

"Oh yeah. Ty Porter. The one who gave the rodeo truck giveaway so much publicity on Black Friday." Hope took a drink of the hot tea she'd served both of them.

"Well, I've been seeing him. We've had dinner a few times." Faith deliberately avoided her sister's eyes. "But not anymore. Tara Williams saw us together yesterday and told me his real name and said I should research him."

"His real name? How did Tara know that?"

"Evidently, they interviewed him for a job at the TV station. I need to show you what I found."

Faith turned the screen of her computer toward Hope.

"Local man found innocent in death of local beauty queen ... Oh, Faith!" Hope pulled the screen closer. "This happened in Baltimore?"

"Yeah. They found him innocent, like it says. But that is scary." Faith shredded a paper napkin on the kitchen island with her fingers.

"No wonder he changed his name and moved away. I would imagine a lot of people still think he did this." Hope was still reading. "It says Ty, or Paul, told the police she got out of his car on a secluded road, and he never saw her again. Wow."

"I know. I can understand why she got out of the car." Faith stood up and closed the laptop. "He's very pushy. I made it clear I don't want to see him anymore, but I'm tired of keeping secrets."

"Of course." Hope stood to hug her close. "You were right to break it off, and I'm glad Tara warned you. I love you, sister."

"I love you too. I just feel so stupid." Faith pulled away, walking toward the living room area of the open concept space. "I thought Ty would be different since he was older than anybody else I've dated. It was exciting to spend time with someone who has lived in big cities. The guys around here haven't been anywhere more exotic than Panama City Beach."

"Hey, you can't go wrong with the Redneck Riviera." Hope laughed. "But I know you want an adventure. That's why you want to go to nursing school somewhere else, right?"

"Yeah. I've been looking at a school in Chicago." Faith took a deep breath. It was good to talk about something other than Ty. "If I'm lucky enough to win some scholarship money at the Miss Rodeo Arkansas pageant, it might actually be possible. There's even a program at M.D. Anderson in Houston that accepts a few applicants every year at no cost."

"But, if you win, you will be traveling to all kinds of rodeo events for the next year, right?" Hope removed glasses from her dishwasher and placed them on the open shelf units above her cabinets.

"Yeah. It would be totally worth it, though. Surely, I can stand to promote rodeo events for another year before I start my medical studies. We've been talking that talk and walking that walk all our lives, right? One more year won't kill me." Faith closed her laptop at the kitchen bar and zipped it into the black carrying case. "Hope, please don't say anything about Ty to anyone else. Especially Dad."

"Are you sure you aren't going to see him from now on?" Hope reached for Faith's hands and stared directly into her eyes.

"Cross my heart." Faith used the familiar hand signal they had made promises with since they were small.

"Okay, then. Of course, I don't keep anything from O.D. Not anymore." Hope closed the dishwasher.

"Sure. I get it. But maybe you just won't have to work it into your conversation. 'By the way, Dee, Faith was dating this guy that probably isn't a murderer.'" She sat at the bar again, with her head in her hands.

"You're right. There may not be any reason to bring it up." Hope massaged her shoulders. "No more secrets, Lainie."

Faith smiled. Her childhood nickname sounded good coming from Hope. It also reminded her to call Kayla. She was super glad she and her cousin had the upcoming pageant to think about.

"No more secrets." She rinsed her tea mug and placed it in the dishwasher. "See you soon, little sis."

"Shouldn't you be at home with that new baby?" John K. shook Brad's hand as he stepped down from his truck in front of what was left of the cabin. Funny, he'd never thought to ask what Brad did for a living. They'd had something more important to worry about last time they'd met. Dad said he'd found a local guy with great recommendations to repair the house. Pretty cool that it was Spencer and Annie's dad.

"Christy's mom is still with us, taking care of Spencer. The new baby sleeps most of the time, and I just get in the way. They'll need me more after the grandparent visits are over with." Brad stepped back, surveying the damaged part of the house.

"Hey, it's great to have so much support." John K. meant that. He also sympathized with Brad for wanting to get out of the house to work now and then. "So, the ramp could come down this side of the porch?" John K. stretched a tape measure across the rubble that remained in front of the cabin.

"Yes. That's doable." The contractor backed up to take a wider view of project. "Remember, the cost of a ramp is not included in the insurance settlement."

"Yeah, I get it. They are just paying to restore the place to the way it was before. But I won't rebuild anything my brother can't use. We'll find a way to cover the difference." Cody had looked down when he last saw him at the Pleasant Oaks home. Therapy should be a good thing, but he couldn't wait until his little brother could have some sort of a normal life again. Hanging out here at the cabin was definitely part of getting back to normal.

"Other than the ramp, is there anything else I need to know about?" Brad took notes on his phone.

"I have this sketch of the old layout." John K. held the paper out. "Porch, mudroom, roof over the main room. I'd like to make adjustments to the bathroom for Cody too, but that may be another project."

"Hey, this is good. Ever thought about going into the construction business yourself?" Brad took a closer look at the drawing.

"No. Not for me. But, hey, could we save some money if I put in some sweat equity while you and your crew are here?" He picked up an odd piece of lumber near his feet and tossed it to the scrap pile.

"Sure. That may be how we work out the cost of the ramp." Brad shook his hand. "I will get in touch with my guys, and we'll get started tomorrow morning."

"Thanks, Brad. I'm not a builder, but I am pretty good at following directions." John K. picked up a piece of roofing. "I'll have the rest of this junk picked up and in a pile by the time you come back."

"Great. We'll look through it. You never know what might be usable. The rest will make a good bonfire. See you in the morning." Brad jumped into his pickup and backed out to the road.

John K. pulled out his phone to text his dad.

The contractor will start on fixing the cabin tomorrow. He doesn't see any major problems.

Great.

Dad's quick response surprised him. Reception must be extra good for some reason today. Might as well take advantage of it to check on Old Greenie.

How's my truck coming along?

It hadn't been easy to stay away from the body shop as they worked on his old friend.

It may be a while. The guys are having some problems finding parts

Thanks. The loaner will work for now. Talk to you soon.

See ya!

John K. walked toward the camper that would be his home for a few more weeks. Might as well change into his hiking boots and his old jeans to work in. Gravel flew as someone pulled in behind him.

"Hey, neighbor," Mac shouted from the driver's side of his pickup. "What's up?"

"A lot of work. That's what's up," John K. laughed. "Brad starts fixing my house tomorrow."

"Sounds great. So, you won't be working for the highway department anymore?" Mac asked.

"My sign-waving career is over."

"Good. I came by to see if I can put you on the volunteer fire department's call list. We always need people who don't commute to their jobs. Pickings are slim during the daytime." Mac pulled out his phone.

"Yeah, sure." What was he agreeing to? He'd never thought about being a firefighter. Mac's vote of confidence made him a little nervous. Maybe that's what volunteering was all about. Say yes first and ask questions later.

"Yes, Kayla. I think we are ready. I'm glad your mom is going with us." Faith was eager to finish this phone conversation so she could go inside the nursing facility to start her shift. "Don't forget about our interview with Tara on Wednesday."

"That's exciting." Kayla's voice was an octave higher than normal.

"Okay, sweetie. See you soon." Faith disconnected as a text came up in a group message that included Hope, O.D., and Tara Williams.

Tara started the conversation.

> Hey, can we get the old team together? I have a great idea to honor a couple heroes you know and love.

O.D. answered quickly.

> Sure.

> Amy Lou's diner?

Hope was already in too.

The last time Tara became involved in Caldwell family business, Hope and Faith had talked O.D. into a scheme that didn't save the Family Rodeo. But it did bring Hope and O.D. together. Tara had been a big encourager that time. The girls probably owed her a favor.

Tara answered.

> Yeah. How about right after Faith's interview on Wednesday?

Hope responded.

> See you then.

What in the world was Tara up to? Did Faith and O.D. already know? What did it have to do with local heroes? She couldn't help but be curious.

> Okay. Sounds like I'm coming in on the tail end of this, but I will be there.

Faith hit send and jogged across the parking lot to greet her own heroes.

13

John K. stepped back from the wheelbarrow he was mixing concrete in to answer his phone.

"Hey, Dad. What's up." He mopped his forehead with a bandana from his back pocket.

"You busy?"

"I can take a minute. But not long. I'm helping with the concrete footings for the new front deck." He was grateful for the break. The other, younger guys on this job were leaving him breathless.

"I have a favor to ask. It's Billings Boys business, but maybe you won't mind. It has to do with your old truck." Dad talked over the background noise of pneumatic impact wrenches.

John K. smiled. He knew they wouldn't be able to keep Dad away from the service bay for long. "Fill me in. But no promises. I am committed out here too."

"Okay, I'll be quick. We have had a devil of a time finding a replacement for the roof of your cab. We could get a new one fabricated, but I think you want it to look vintage, right?" Dad shouted.

"Sure, as close as possible." He just wanted the old truck back like it was before the storm.

"We found a salvaged one from the same model as yours, and we've arranged for it to be shipped to our dealership in Fort Smith. The extra cost for the trip to Crossroads is crazy."

"Yeah, yeah. Let's do it." John K. visualized his bank account. He hated for Dad to bear more of this burden than necessary.

"Okay, it will fit in the bed of one of our newer pickups. So, if you can drive over there to get it, I wouldn't have to send one of my services techs."

"Yeah. Sounds good. When?"

"It comes in Friday."

"Yeah. I'll do it. Let's talk later, okay? I need to get back to this concrete pour."

"Okay, son. Love you."

"Love you, Dad."

John K. used an old shovel handle he'd found in the shed to finish mixing the water into the batch of concrete. Did everyone have a dad who was this concerned about the things that were important to his son? Even after that guy was supposedly grown and on his own? He sent up a quick prayer of thanksgiving. He was blessed, for sure.

Faith waved to direct Tara to their favorite booth at Amy Lou's. Her stomach had just stopped quivering after the interview at the television station. Why was speaking on camera so hard? She could ride in front of an arena full of people and even use a microphone when necessary. But that box with the cameraman behind it was a whole different story.

"Faith, you and Kayla were wonderful on my show today!"

Tara slid into the booth with a tall glass of sweet tea she had grabbed on her way in.

"Thanks." Faith nodded at her. "We appreciate the publicity. I'm afraid pageants are sort of going out of style, along with rodeos. We need people to support them as much as possible."

"Hey, not in our family." Hope stirred more sugar into her own tea. "We think Arkansas needs a Miss Rodeo and a Miss Teen Rodeo who both have the last name Caldwell."

"Kayla has a better chance than I do." Faith smiled as O.D. walked through the front door, setting the entry bells to jangling. The dark-haired cowboy grabbed the attention of all the diners. It was strange to think of him as her brother-in-law, even though he'd seemed like one of the family for quite a while now.

"So, what's up, guys?" He slid in next to Hope.

"I won't keep y'all long. I just have a crazy idea and need some Billings/Caldwell buy-in." Tara pulled up some pictures on her phone. "Bear with me, these two things I'm about to mention will tie in."

Hope and Faith smiled at each other. Tara was a big talker. Easy to see why she and O.D. had been friends since high school.

"So, y'all know that Crossroads has a big Founder's Day parade coming up on June 6, right?" Tara took a sip of her tea.

"Yep. Happens every year." O.D. smiled.

"And since that is also D-Day, there is always a big emphasis on our veterans?"

"Yes." Faith fidgeted against the hard wooden bench. Why were they here exactly?

"Stay with me," Tara continued. "O.D., your dealership is repairing John K.'s old truck, right?"

John K.'s truck? What? Faith caught the strange, puzzled look on Hope's face.

"Yes." O.D. looked at Tara's phone.

"What if we made his truck look something like this? And had it ready for him to drive in the Founder's Day parade?"

O.D. took the phone from Tara and scrolled through the images, showing them first to Hope and then to Faith.

The customized paint jobs on the vehicles were amazing. Most of the time, these colorful designs were used for advertising, not on a personal vehicle. Faith smiled, but a strange shiver ran up her spine as Hope and O.D. responded to Tara with enthusiasm.

"I don't know." Faith finally mustered up the courage to speak. "You know how John K. hates attention." She was surprised O.D. hadn't said the same thing, after the struggle those two had gone through last winter. Didn't he remember how his older brother pulled away from the family for a time, just to escape the pressure of hero worship?

"Well." O.D. took another look. "He does deserve this. But he is also very protective of his truck."

"And he still considers it Grandpa Dee's truck too." Hope handed the phone back to Tara.

"Your Grandpa is a veteran too, right, O.D?" Tara scanned through her pictures, showing them a more patriotic example.

Faith could almost hear Tara's wheels turning.

"How about we honor both in some way? We could have their names painted on the truck." Tara spoke quickly, smiling at all of them.

"Yeah. Maybe painted under the windows, like a NASCAR driver." O.D. sat up a little straighter. "Just do most of the patriotic stuff on the tailgate or something."

"The rest of the truck still needs to be green." Hope added. "Its name is Old Greenie."

"Sure!" Tara started making notes on her phone. "Now, O.D. can your body shop have the truck ready in time for my friends over at Kenny's Customs to do their magic?"

"Hey, everybody can do with a little magic." O.D. laughed. "Yeah. In fact, John K. is picking up a salvaged part in Fort Smith this weekend that will help our body shop get it finished in a hurry.

"Great! Now, y'all need to promise to keep this a secret until the big reveal. Our station wants to witness his reaction." Tara made more notes.

Faith picked up a napkin, shredding it to tiny bits. Hope and O.D. knew John K. as well or better than she did. Why was this whole idea of Tara's giving her such bad vibes?

14

"Now, I want you to meet a very important member of the Miss Rodeo Arkansas team." The tall auburn-haired lady addressed the group of contestants and families from the stage.

Faith squeezed Kayla's trembling hand. Her young cousin's face was pale.

"This is Ms. Patricia May." A petite, older lady with long blonde hair waved from the stage. "I know some of you teen contestants brought your moms. But this lady will be an extra mom for all of you. As a past queen, she knows the ins and outs. I know it may be hard to believe, but she has a *grand*daughter competing in our pageant this year. Because of that, Ms. Pat will be serving as a judge for some of the teen events, but not the Miss Rodeo Arkansas events. She's a real pro, ladies. We are fortunate to have her."

The room exploded in applause. Faith saw heads nodding and even some who had obviously been past contestants smiling and waving at their friend.

"Call me Pat." The jewels in the lady's oversized earrings flashed as they caught the spotlights. "I'm here to answer questions, especially for moms and grandmas helping your young ladies succeed. Just stop me in the hallway anytime. I'm hoping all of you have the most awesome Miss Rodeo Arkansas experience ever."

The girls applauded and cheered. Aunt Tina hugged Kayla's shoulders.

"Okay, you're free to head to your rooms for the night. See you bright and early with your best smiles in place for breakfast at 7:00." The director replaced her mic on the stand. Happy chatter erupted as everyone stood to leave the conference room.

"See, Mom. I told you we'd be fine." Kayla locked arms with Aunt Tina as they walked into the lobby of the hotel. "You didn't even need to come."

"Miss Pat makes me feel better, for sure." She turned to wink at Faith. "But she won't be in your room with you to be sure your hair and makeup are right before each event."

"I could have roomed with Faith." Kayla pouted.

"I don't know." Faith piped up. "Our schedules don't always coordinate. I'm glad you're here, Aunt Tina."

She swallowed a lump in her throat as the elevator took them to their floor. Mom would have loved being here with them, experiencing the rewards of years of work. The first Crossroads Rodeo Queen contest turned out to be the last, as their family business was sold after Mom died. So many nights of carrying the flag for the opening ceremony of their bi-weekly rodeo. So many pasted-on smiles when she was bone tired after long days at school. Mom had been her chief encourager, but there had been times when she'd felt more like one of their cattle being prodded than a beautiful princess.

Aunt Tina and Kayla stepped out of the elevator. "I wouldn't miss it for the world, Lainie. Call us after you get settled in. We'd like to meet your roommate."

"Sure. Talk to you soon." Faith followed the signs to the room where she'd dropped her luggage earlier.

She scanned her card at the door. A soft voice spoke from somewhere inside.

"Hi, it's me, Faith Caldwell." She began talking as she entered the room.

The tall raven-haired girl waved from a chair near the sliding door leading to the balcony.

"Yeah, Mom. I'll call you in the morning. Good night." The girl rose from her chair and crossed the room. "I'm Alex."

"Hey, it's great to meet you. I'm Faith. I guess I already said that. Where are you from?"

"South of El Dorado. Almost to Louisiana. I've been to Fort Smith before, but this part of the state is different." Alex walked to the window, holding back the curtains to reveal the view.

"Yeah. It's growing so fast." Faith plugged her phone in on the nightstand. "But it's still just Arkansas."

"Is this your first time in the pageant?" Alex picked up a hairbrush and ran it through her long hair.

"Yes. I won the regional contest back home. My cousin Kayla is the teen winner too. We're both here representing the rodeo in Crossroads." Faith strolled to the bathroom, peeking in to see if there was room to get ready in the morning.

"Crossroads? Your family ran the Caldwell Family Rodeo, right? I've actually been there. My boyfriend is a bull rider, and I came up to watch him compete once. I remember you. That opening ceremony is amazing." Alex finished brushing her hair and stopped in front of the mirror.

"Well, that is part of the past now. My dad and uncle sold out. The arena belongs to a hippotherapy place now." Faith sat on the side of the bed. It was still not easy to say that out loud. The bi-weekly rodeo had been part of her life for as long as she could remember. She was sad about it, but a little relieved at the same time.

"Hippos?" Alex giggled.

"Horse therapy." Faith laughed too. "Riding helps people recover from all types of injuries. Physical and Emotional."

"I'll need to check that out. Fits right into my platform of promoting rodeo for everyone. It's such a great sport. I truly believe that." She sat on the bed across from Faith. "Some of these ladies have been in this pageant two or three times. I probably don't have a chance."

"Well, they haven't won yet. You have just as much chance as they do." Faith's phone notified her she had a text message.

We found a coffee shop with hot chocolate in millions of flavors. Bring your roommate.

She smiled. Kayla did love hot chocolate.

I'll see if she wants to come down.

"Want to go downstairs for a bit?" Faith checked her hair in the mirror.

"Sounds good. My grandma is down in the lobby too." Alex tucked her phone in her back pocket.

"That's great that your grandma came to support you." Faith smiled.

"She was in pageants before my mom was born," Alex said. "In fact, you've already met her. Patricia May. Former Miss Rodeo Arkansas." Alex laughed as they stepped into the hall.

"And you've never been in a pageant?" Faith took a closer look at Alex. She had queen written from the crown of her hat to the toe of her boots.

"Just not in Arkansas. We moved up from Louisiana last year, I'm eligible here for the first time." She led the way to the elevator and pushed the button.

"Well, what do you know?" A familiar voice came behind Faith made her stiffen. Ty jogged a few steps to catch up with them. "The lady at the desk told me some of the contestants had rooms in this hall, so I took a chance."

"Hello, Ty." Faith tried not to meet his eyes.

"Looking beautiful, princess." His hand reached out to caress the hair on her right shoulder.

She stepped away from him and closer to Alex.

"Alex, this is Ty Porter, a radio personality from my hometown."

Alex flashed her best smile at Ty. "Happy to meet you."

Ty whistled softly through his teeth. "I can't believe all the pretty girls around this place. Cowboy heaven, for sure."

The elevator arrived and Alex stepped on.

"We'll grab the next one, doll." Ty caught Faith's arm and pulled her to the side. Alex's questioning look disappeared as the door closed.

"Ty ..." Faith pulled her arm from his grasp.

"I just need a minute." Ty stepped back, looking into Faith's eyes. "I owe you an apology. I acted like a real jerk the other day. I don't normally drink that much. I should have known you don't like it."

"It's not really that." He backed her up until a raised sign posted next to the elevator pressed against her back. "I was ready to go home." She kept her voice strong. No need to waver.

"I know. I have a lot of trouble controlling my impulses when I am around such beauty. You really send me, Princess Faith." Ty leaned forward and placed a soft kiss just to the right of her lips.

Faith stiffened. How could she get this message across without slapping him?

"See, there I go again." Ty stepped back, grabbing her fingers. "I promise, if you'll give me another chance, I will try harder to be good."

"I am going to be busy here for the next few days."

He held her hand loosely.

"Yeah. I get that. Maybe we can get together for coffee or something. And of course, I will interview you and your cousin for our radio station. I'll see you around." His thumb moved up onto her wrist, and he grasped her arm with his other hand.

The elevator opened. Faith pulled away and stepped inside, grateful other people rode too. The dad of the family moved his rolling suitcase over, but the stroller and grocery bags near the mom's feet left no room for another passenger.

"One, please." Faith reached over to push the button. She didn't even look up as the door closed. Rude? Maybe. But this guy. The quivering in her stomach returned. Was it excitement, or a warning?

The elevator stopped on the first floor and she hurried to the coffee shop. Kayla waved from a table near the back, and she hugged the side of the room on the way, hoping Ty would not see her if he passed the door of the shop. Ms. Pat stood at the cash register next to Alex as the barista took their orders.

"You okay?" Kayla pulled out a chair next to her.

"Yeah, yeah." Maybe repeating herself didn't say calm and collected. "Just in a hurry. Alex, over here." She waved and pulled two more chairs to the table.

"Alex, Ms. Pat, this is my Aunt Tina and my cousin Kayla

Grace Caldwell, Miss Crossroads Rodeo Teen." Faith took a deep breath. Normal. Work on acting normal.

"Happy to know you." Pat shook Aunt Tina's hand and nodded at Kayla.

"Such a pleasure." Aunt Tina scooted closer to Kayla. "I can't believe we didn't have these two girls in the pageant system earlier. My husband and Faith's dad and mom were just so busy keeping the rodeo going."

"That takes a lot of work, for sure. But this is a great pageant. I think you can catch on quickly." Alex returned to the table with more sweetener for her grandma's coffee.

"Alex just moved here from Louisiana." Faith looked out to the hallway. No sign of Ty. Yet.

"We've been through on our way to the Gulf. What we saw of Louisiana was pretty."

Kayla blew on her hot chocolate, disrupting the foam.

Faith's phone chimed, and she looked down to see a notification from Hope.

> O.D. and I will be there Friday afternoon. Will you have any free time?

Faith pulled up a schedule of activities.

> Lunch on our own from 11:30 to 1:30.

> See you then.

Faith took a deep breath. It would be good to spend some time with Hope. Maybe she could help get her mind back on the pageant, and off Ty.

"Woo-wee!" As if he could read her thoughts, Ty walked up behind her. "Would you look at all the royalty at this table."

Kayla giggled, and Alex leaned forward, smiling broadly.

"Ladies, since I have you all together, could I ask a few

questions? Our listeners would love to know what it's like to be in a rodeo queen pageant. I can record it and use it in a few minutes." He pulled out his phone, reaching around Faith to hold it in the center of the group.

Faith scrunched down into her chair. Could she ever shake this guy?

15

John K. pulled off his work boots and scanned the canned goods in the cabinet above the little sink. Mom would cringe at the "bachelor" food he kept on hand. Right now, nothing sounded better than a quick supper of Beanie-weenies or canned beef stew after a hard day of house-building. Hmm. He did have a can of corned-beef hash. That would require heating something up in a saucepan, but with the addition of some maple syrup, this breakfast-for-supper idea could be just the ticket.

Squee, squee, squee. The siren alarm he had set up on his phone notified him of a text from Chief Mac.

Garbage fire getting out of hand.

Rats. The next text followed quickly.

Meet at the fire station.

John K. pulled his boots back on and grabbed his truck keys from the hook by the door. The siren on Mac's pickup screamed past. John K. was in his truck following the chief in less than a minute.

Three more pickups glided into the gravel lot of the metal building just a half mile from John K.'s cabin. Mac stood in the driveway, passing along information as each driver ran inside to grab their gear.

"Pull your truck over here," Mac yelled as John K. drove in. "You'll take Dumbo."

"Dumbo?' John K. stopped his truck where his friend directed, and Mac hooked a trailer up to the hitch below his tailgate. It wasn't hard to see where the water tank riding on the trailer had gotten its name. Long and round, with a makeshift nozzle that resembled an elephant's trunk, it was filled and ready to go.

The old fire engine led the way, with two men hanging on in the back. Mac went next, followed by two more pickups, and John K. brought up the procession's rear. He followed for over half a mile when he realized he had not entered the fire station to don protective clothing. Maybe his only function would be to get Dumbo out to where he was needed.

As the crew pulled up in a gravel driveway, Mac motioned to John K. to stop.

"You take Dumbo to the edge of the mowed area. Soak this area real heavy to make sure the fire can't get out into the woods." He turned toward the other men and the teen who furiously shoveled dirt on the part of the fire nearest the home. The old fire truck pulled up closer to the house. Mac motioned the young man away and the fire crew took over, concentrating on the area between the brush fire and the structures on the property.

"I'm so sorry." The teen came to stand next to John K. as he continued to wet the perimeter of the yard.

"Hey, it can happen to anybody, bud." John K. knew the feeling. He and his brothers had managed to control their little outbreaks, but there had been some close calls. "Good thing you called for help in time."

"Grandpa's gonna kill me. And then Dad will kill me again." Hands in back pockets, he watched the firefighters work.

"I seriously doubt it. The fire is almost under control now." John K. completed his row of moist grass and started another, closer to the flames. "Give yourself a break."

The kid walked back to his shovel, and the crew finished their work. Black grass marked the massive front yard, and one old rose bush had taken a hit, but no structures were affected. To John K.'s amateur eyes, this looked like a win.

Mac approached the teen from his post near the fire truck.

"Okay, young man, think you can watch for hot spots now? Next time, easy on the accelerant. Good thing the wind wasn't a lot stronger today." Mac shook a still quivering hand. "Let's go, Billings."

John K. replaced the nozzle in its spot near Dumbo's "head" and climbed into the cab of his borrowed truck. This was nothing like his vision of a firefighter's job. If overly aggressive trash fires were the extent of things, he could probably handle helping the crew out more regularly.

Back at the station, he unhooked Dumbo's hitch and refilled the tank from the water hose on the side of the metal building. Mac walked out, his fire helmet and suit replaced by cowboy hat and blue jeans.

"Thanks for coming along." Mac shook his hand.

"Looks like I had the easiest job today." John K. turned off the outdoor faucet.

"We had plenty of help today. Sometimes, it might just be me and you. Could you stay awhile so I can show you the other tools and fill you in on how we use them?" Mac waved at the rest of the crew as they drove away from the station.

"Sure. I may not be close by every day, though. Tomorrow, Dad's sending me to Fort Smith to get a new cab for my old truck. Then, I need to help O.D. bring the herd up from the south pasture to the new area he fenced off near the house. We've got a creek that just might strand them if we get any more rain." John K. led the way into the station.

"Busy man. Are you not working for the highway department too?" Mac stepped inside, turning on the overhead lights.

"Not right now. I need to be supervising the re-construction at the cabin when I can." He flinched as a distant boom echoed off the hills.

"Was that thunder?" Mac looked up into the sky.

"No, I think the highway department was doing some blasting today. When I was there, they said there was a boulder blocking the main road up the mountain. There may have been even more blasting needed." The real reason for his temporary resignation from the highway crew.

"So, you're staying busy, but these volunteer gigs don't pay very well." Mac stopped to look him in the eye.

"You're right." John K. hoped Mac didn't resent the loan of his travel trailer. He should be paying rent.

"Well, if you like the volunteer fire department, our board is thinking of hiring an actual paid employee to hang around here full time. You'd have to go to the fire academy, but that would help you with future jobs too." Mac walked to a large cabinet and opened the door to show him the gear inside.

"Hmm. Something to think about." Could he train to be a

real firefighter? What would happen the first time an aerosol can exploded in a trash can? Would he run first and ask questions later? What would the other trainees think of Mister All-American War Hero if that happened?

16

Faith stood near the elevator, unsure of her next move. She realized before entering Miss Rodeo Arkansas that interviewing would not be her strong point. But the words that echoed in her ears when the pageant judges asked about her platform, her reasons for promoting rodeo as a sport, sounded so hollow.

"Rodeo has been my life since I was very small." That was a true statement, but she sensed the interviewer wanted more. She had no trouble outlining her objective, to attend medical school with the goal of becoming a nurse practitioner. But, how did her personal aspirations translate to a platform that Miss Rodeo Arkansas could bring to audiences across the state? If she wasn't clear on the connection, how could anyone else understand it?

The elevator doors opened but she stepped back. Maybe a walk outside the hotel would clear her head. She would excel this afternoon in the horsemanship events. Nothing put her in her comfort zone like guiding a horse around a ring, or through a barrel course.

"Hey!" Kayla approached from the breakfast room. "Are you already finished with your interview? How did it go?"

"Okay, I think." The judges had smiled, even laughed in all the right places. Maybe it had been more successful than she thought.

"I'm going to mine in fifteen minutes. Could I bounce something off you really quick?" Kayla's green eyes sparkled.

"Sure." Faith was happy to see her cousin so excited. Of the three Caldwell girls, Kayla had been the least passionate about riding and competing. There was no lack of confidence apparent today. Her hair and makeup looked perfect, and the clothes she had selected were just the right combination of elegant and understated.

"When they ask about my platform, I hope they understand how access for disabled people works in. You know, like what they do at Cedar Ridge, where Hope works." Kayla glanced at a note card she held.

"Right. You can just say that rodeo is a sport that can make everyone feel better by watching or participating. Your goal is to help make that happen regardless of physical limitations." Faith smiled as Kayla began writing.

"Ooh. That's good. I wish I had recorded you saying that, so I could just play it back." Kayla moved to a quiet corner of the lobby.

"You'll do great, Gracie." Faith waved at her, then stepped out into the sunshine in front of the hotel. She held her hat in place as the wind tried to catch it. Maybe she'd just go check out the arena where the horsemanship events would happen. Then, it would be time to get ready for lunch with Hope and O.D.

"Hey, Faith!" Alex met her at the door of the arena. "This is a great facility."

"Do you think they got the dirt floor right? It's strange to ride in a place that was a hockey rink or a basketball court yesterday." Faith held the door open for her dark-haired roommate.

"Right?" Alex smiled. "But, yeah. It looks to be pretty good. I'm a little nervous about riding someone else's horse for the judging."

"I guess they need to see how comfortable we are with horses in general, not just ours." Faith was actually grateful that Belle was safe at home. Hauling her own mount would have added another layer of stress.

"Well, I am on my way to my interview. This part spooks me. I am great at mentoring younger kids. That's what my platform is all about. But, making nice for older, stuffy people is not so easy." Alex tucked her shirt in above her belt in the back.

"Knock 'em dead." Faith reached around her for an awkward hug. "You will be fabulous."

"Thanks. See you at horsemanship!" Alex jogged to the double glass doors of the hotel.

Faith stepped into the entryway of the arena. She blinked as her eyes adjusted to the interior lighting.

"Yeah. This should work." Tara's familiar voice drifted in from the arena floor.

"Let me check this spotlight one more time." The station's cameraman spoke up just as Faith peered in their direction. "Should be fine." He turned off the light and packed it away in the bag that hung over his right shoulder.

"We'll try to find the Caldwell girls after their horsemanship events." Tara waved at Faith. "Well, speak of the devil."

"Hey, Tara." Faith walked toward them. "Pretty cool facility."

"Yes, it is. I've been here several times, but it's my first Miss

Rodeo Arkansas pageant. I'm hoping to get a quick minute with you and Kayla this afternoon. Will you be here at the same time for horsemanship?" She pulled out her phone, typing as she talked.

"I'm not sure. I know my judging is first thing after lunch, but the Teens may be a little later." Faith felt her phone vibrating in her pocket. Probably Hope arranging their lunch.

"Yeah, it might take two trips. Folks back home are so proud of y'all!" Tara hugged her shoulders.

"Yes we are!" Ty ran up behind Tara, waving at Faith. "Hey, Tara, my boss said I could grab a little airtime this evening too. Mind if I crash the Caldwell interviews?"

"Our news director told me you might be around." Tara's voice dropped as she turned to face Ty. "If you've got a minute, let's talk about how this will play out."

Faith pulled her phone out to see Hope's message.

We got a table, and we're waiting to order.

Rescued. Thank the Lord.

"Well, I'll see y'all later!" She turned to head out the way she had just come in. Hopefully, Tara would keep Ty busy long enough for her to get to her pickup.

"Over here!" Hope waved at her as she walked into the busy steakhouse a few minutes later. O.D. stood as she approached, allowing Faith to slide in next to her sister, and seating himself across from them.

"Dee picked the place, and I know you want to eat light before you ride but they have a whole list of salads along with their steaks." Hope showed her the menu as O.D. answered his phone.

"Yeah. What's up, bro?" O.D. spoke softly into the phone, while he nodded at the waitress who unloaded their drinks.

"Give us just another minute," Hope whispered to the T-shirt clad server.

"Oh man. That stinks. But you don't want to go home and have to come back tomorrow." O.D. spoke into the phone, then mouthed 'John K.' to the girls. "No. We have a pull-out couch in our motel room. Just hang out here with us. They're having a rodeo tonight and introducing the participants in the pageant. You can help us cheer for Faith and Kayla." He paused. "Hey, and why not just come over to Big Star Steakhouse right now? I'll buy your lunch." He laughed. "Seriously ... Yeah, it's on the main drag in town. Just put it in your GPS, man ... See you soon."

"What's up?" Hope waved at the server. "We need to order. Faith has to get back to the pageant."

"That's okay. Sounds like John K. has a problem?" Faith was glad Hope had at least ordered her sweet tea.

"The part he was picking up for his truck didn't arrive in Fort Smith today," O.D. said. "He will have to stay over until tomorrow."

"Can you handle two Billings boys at lunch, sister?" Hope poked Faith in the ribs.

"Hey, we've handled all three of them since we were kids." Faith laughed. "No problem."

Their table kept the servers hopping, as John K. arrived and ordered just as the food arrived for the other three. Faith was impressed by the brothers' apologies to the staff, even though she was sure they were more than happy to accommodate. She knew from past experience that the charm these two handed out was real and natural.

"So, sorry your trip to Fort Smith will last longer than you expected." Faith nodded in John K.'s direction after finishing most of her salad.

"Hey, no problem. It will be worth it to get a new cab for

Old Greenie." John K. put a straw in his second glass of Coke. "But, enough about me. Let's hear about the Miss Rodeo Arkansas experience. Are you wowing all the other contestants along with the judges?"

"Wowing?" Faith laughed. "I don't know. Apparently, pageants are a way of life for some of these ladies. I feel like a newbie."

"A newbie? What?" John K. leaned across the table toward her. "You've got this thing wrapped up. I've seen your showmanship during the flag ceremony. And your barrel riding, well, you've got buckles to prove how good you are at that."

Faith blushed. The Billings guys had been at the rodeo their whole lives too. But had John K. noticed her in particular? She flashed back for a moment to the days when John K. was a bronc rider. He'd excelled at that sport, just like everything else he took on. His skill, along with his muscular body had fueled a long-standing crush until other girls caught his eye. She'd resigned herself to being thought of only as a neighbor.

"Thanks. I hope you're right." Faith sipped her sweet tea.

"And then when you win, you'll spend all next year traveling around just getting more and more famous." Hope smiled.

"Not trying for famous. Just want that scholarship money. No fun ending up with a pile of student loan debt."

"I know one thing. Caldwell girls have got what it takes." O.D. spoke up between bites of steak. "These other princesses don't stand a chance."

"Thanks, y'all. I think the lunch was just the boost I needed." Faith waved at the waitress to get her ticket.

"So, you've got a rodeo tonight?" John K. asked.

"Yes. All of us will get to participate in their opening ceremony. Should be fun." Faith said.

"We'll all be there." Hope picked up the menu. "Don't you have time for some cheesecake?"

"No. That defeats the purpose of eating a salad for lunch, little sister." Faith placed cash on top of her ticket.

"Okay, then. Go knock out this horsemanship competition. Dad and Junior are planning on coming to the final night tomorrow night." Hope hugged Faith.

"That will be great. Love all of you." Faith stood up, looking over shoulder, hoping she wouldn't see a familiar radio personality with curly red hair. She would not let Ty cast a shadow over her competition.

17

The arena floor was packed with ladies on horseback. John K. leaned forward to try to spot the Caldwell girls. There was Kayla, near the front of the line, with the American flag. She was followed by more teens, alternately carrying the Stars and Stripes and the Arkansas flag. The riders at the end of the line looked older. Those must be the Miss Rodeo Arkansas contestants.

The very last cowgirl to emerge from the entryway stood out from the rest. Maybe he was prejudiced since he had known Faith since she was barely able to mount a pony. Her blonde hair waved gracefully behind her. Her smile was extra confident. The outfit had obviously been chosen to emphasize her patriotic mission. His next-door neighbor was totally in her element tonight.

"That's Faith's roommate, Alex." Hope pointed at the raven-haired rider of a matching black horse next to Faith.

"Pretty, but no competition." John K. smiled at O.D. "Well, am I wrong, bro?"

"Spot on, sir." O.D. reached for Hope's hand. "But I've always been partial to Caldwell cowgirls."

They stood as the entry music stopped and the formalities of an opening ceremony began. John K. blinked back a tear as "The Star-Spangled Banner" echoed through the building. The meaning of that song had changed so much for him. Now, wherever he heard it, he just took a deep breath, grateful to be in the moment. Safe, happy, free.

The riders held their horses at perfect attention, Arkansas flags dipped in deference. Indoor arenas lacked the breeze necessary to unfurl the flags, but this was still impressive. All around him, every head was uncovered, right hands over hearts. At this event, they all understood.

"Now, ladies and gents, we ask one more favor before we get our competition underway." The announcer's voice held the same familiar tone and cadence that Smiley Caldwell had made famous back in Crossroads. "We ask that you take your seats, with the exception of those who have served in any branch of the military."

The crowd complied and John K. looked around at the men and women who remained standing. Yes, these folks understood. Did he deserve to be counted in their number after the way his service ended? His knees bent and he started to sit.

"Hey." O.D. poked him. "Not on your life, man. Get up there."

"Let's give these heroes our total respect. Without them, we would not continue to enjoy the blessings of living in a free country. Ladies and gentlemen of the armed forces, we salute you!"

The crowd applauded as the familiar strains of Lee Greenwood's "God Bless the USA" filled the arena. The riders carrying the Arkansas flags backed out of position and circled up in the center of the floor before leaving.

Right on cue, the rest of the crowd stood as the lyrics prompted them, and the American flags took center stage. Spotlights searched and then focused on the flags. Was he dreaming, or did Faith catch his eye and smile? He was a total sucker for the magic of this song. Surely that's all it was.

The riders and horses stood at attention for the remainder of the ceremony. The whole rodeo experience was familiar and comforting. He could understand that Faith might want to escape the routine. He knew she wanted more from life, and he couldn't blame her. She just didn't realize how hard it would be to shake free from such a firm foundation. He'd tried, with his military service. The rodeo was a big part of both of them.

The sly smile she sent his way as the horses left the arena was real. He was not imagining things. The other contestants in this pageant were facing a real pro in the oldest Caldwell girl.

"Ready for the bronc riding?" O.D. handed John K. a tub of popcorn.

The first contestant bolted out of the gate on a wildly upset black stallion.

"How did I ever do that?" John K. leaned forward, flinching with each jolt the rider was experiencing. "They make it look easy, but it's like a non-stop beat-down. And that's if it's a successful ride. Getting bucked off starts a whole different level of pain."

"You were younger." O.D. laughed. "You didn't get all that beat up. As far as any of us knew, you were in total control all the time."

"Ha! Had you fooled." John K. laughed. "Do you miss tie-down?"

"You know, I kind of do." O.D. finished his hot dog and helped himself to a handful of John K.'s popcorn. "I'm thinking of dropping in now and then. Not going pro, mind you. But, Buck misses it, I think."

"Yeah. It's all about making the horse happy." John K. sipped his soda. "I might have known now that you have a full-time job with Dad at the dealership, you are looking for a diversion."

"What are y'all talking about?" Hope leaned past O.D. with her funnel cake.

"Just our normal. Nothing much." O.D.'s eyes widened in a cautionary sideward glance at his brother.

"Whatever. Just letting you know, I'm looking forward to the barrel racing, but I may have to leave during bull-riding." Hope wrapped her arm through O.D.'s.

"Yeah. I get it." O.D. squeezed her hand. "But if Cody was here, he'd say we should enjoy it for him. Life goes on."

John K. was quiet through the rest of the events that night. Memories of his little brother's hospital stay were hard to chase from his head. It had to be harder for Hope and O.D. who had been there during the colossal wreck that paralyzed Cody from the waist down.

The three managed to stay put, and they cheered along with the rest of the crowd as the evening came to its climactic end.

"Thanks to all of you for coming," the announcer spoke up as fans started for the exits. "Special thanks to our favorite cowgirls, the contestants in Miss Rodeo Arkansas and Miss Rodeo Arkansas Teen. Tomorrow is the big finale of their pageant, and we wish them all the very best. Good night, God bless, and please drive to arrive alive! See you next time."

"Looks like Faith and Kayla are getting interviewed for the KRVA news. Who's that guy with Tara?" John K. pointed to the spot next to the chutes where the TV cameras focused on the reporters. The one with the bushy red beard seemed a little too focused on Faith. *Stick to your job, dude.*

"That's Ty Porter from the radio station." Hope started down the bleachers. "He can be such a pain."

"Huh? I thought we liked him." O.D. shrugged his shoulders as he glanced towards John K. "He gave the Caldwell rodeo and the Billings Boys some good shout-outs last Black Friday."

"Old news." Hope's boots echoed on the metal bleachers. "Let's just say he's not such a nice guy in real life."

"Huh. I'm behind." O.D. backed up to let a family go ahead of him. "I can't keep up with who the good guys are anymore. They all need to go back to wearing white hats."

John K. shook his head. "Come on, O.D., get with the program." Faith's body language right now seemed to verify what Hope said. She stood close to Tara, with Kayla between her and Porter. The radio interviewer leaned in with his mic and Faith shrank back. There was more to this than just an interview, that's for sure. He'd keep an eye out for his guy. Anyone who made Faith feel so uncomfortable had better keep his distance.

"Are y'all going back home first thing in the morning?" John K. asked O.D. as they reached the bottom of the stands.

"No, Hope and I are making a little mini-vacation out of this. We're both spending too much time working these days." O.D. placed his hand comfortably in the small of Hope's back. We plan to explore Fort Smith a little bit tomorrow, then go home after cowboy church on Sunday. You're welcome to stay in our room tomorrow night too."

"No, no." John K. shook his head. Something about that invitation for tomorrow didn't sound sincere. "I've got to find that guy with the cab for Old Greenie, then I'll head home. Tell Kayla and Faith I wish them all the best at the finale. Didn't

Dad say something about moving the cattle to higher ground tomorrow?"

"Yeah. Hopefully, that can wait." O.D. took Hope's hand as they walked toward their pickup.

"Well, thanks for inviting me to come along tonight." John K. spotted a Waffle House nearby. "Hey, I think I'll just go get a piece of pie and some coffee. See y'all in a little bit."

"Yeah. It's room 322. See you soon." O.D. opened the passenger door for his wife. It was still hard to think of them as married, but they were certainly well matched. At least some people seemed to be living their happily ever after. His was yet to be determined.

18

"You looked fantastic tonight at the rodeo." Faith held the elevator for Alex as they arrived at their floor. "That royal blue outfit is perfect."

"Thanks. You're sweet. Your outfit is awesome too." Alex removed her hat as they reached their room. "I love the embroidery."

"There's a lady in Paris, Arkansas, who runs a bridal shop. She has a connection who does custom embroidery. I told her I wanted roses, and she did a wonderful job." Just inside the door, Faith removed her heavy jacket and hung it in the closet. "They don't realize how many clothes we have. We need a closet for each one of us."

"I know, right? I can take some things to my grandma's room if you want." Alex changed into shorts and a T-shirt.

"I'm fine, but you do whatever works for you." Faith took off her boots and packed them in their box.

"I think I'll take the things I've worn and won't repeat. That will help me keep track, anyway." Alex moved some items into a garment bag.

Faith stepped into the bathroom to check her makeup. It was a little strange to have to stay in performance mode all day long. She had been used to getting made up for the rodeo once every two weeks, and a dressy date or event now and then. But imagine having to look like this every day for a whole year as Miss Rodeo Arkansas. Goodness.

"Okay. I won't be wearing my horsemanship clothes or boots tomorrow. And the outfit for tonight can go." Alex carried the garment bag and a boot box toward the door.

"So you're going to your grandma's room?" Faith watched from the bed, after changing to a casual dress and slip-on shoes.

"Yeah. Then, I thought I might go down to check out the game room I saw just off the lobby. I think they have board games and a TV down there." Alex waited by the door. "Want to come?"

"Sure. Is your grandma still up?" Faith grabbed her clutch purse and her room key.

"Of course. She's like me. She takes a while to wind down after a big event like the rodeo. She'll be in her room watching a movie or something." Alex tucked her wallet in her pocket.

Faith stepped into the hallway with one of Alex's boot boxes. She didn't have as much trouble 'winding down' but she didn't want to stay in the room by herself. Maybe Kayla would join them.

The girls walked past lots of closed doors after reaching Ms. Pat's floor. Alex stopped in front of a room. The door across the hall popped open.

"Hey!" Ty stepped out in a pair of baggy shorts and no shirt, holding an ice bucket. "You're just in time. I'm on my way to the ice machine, then y'all can join me for a nightcap."

Alex's grandma peered out from her room.

"I think they were coming to see me." Ms. Pat stepped into the hallway.

"Alex, I need just a minute." Faith handed Ms. Pat the boot box she carried.

"You sure?" Alex's gray eyes sent her a questioning look.

"Yes." Faith's cheeks warmed, and she opened and closed her fists. How could she make this guy understand she wanted nothing to do with him?

Alex stepped inside the room. Ms. Pat's lips were closed tightly when she nodded at Faith before closing the door.

"I'm glad they're gone. I was trying to be polite, but I only wanted to invite you." Ty breathed into her ear, wrapping his free hand around her waist.

"Ty." Faith stepped away. "Look. I'm trying to be polite too. I am not interested in spending any time with you."

"Yeah. I know you're busy here at the pageant." He held the ice bucket behind his back, leaning toward her. "You need to relax every now and then. Let me go get come ice. I've got something in my room that will help you take the edge off. Then, you'll be rested and ready for tomorrow."

"You don't get it." Faith struggled to keep from shouting. "I am not interested. Not tonight, not ever. We're just not meant to be."

"Not meant to be. Oh. You thought I wanted some kind of long-term commitment. Sorry. I just wanted to have fun. I can be a pretty okay guy." He looked down at the floor. "But, yeah. I get it." He stepped backward into his room. His eyes seethed with anger as he closed the door.

Faith shook her head and took a deep breath. She had turned down boys before. This gave her a strange feeling. Was he hurt by her rejection, or just angry? That was his problem, after all. She knocked on Ms. Pat's door. Maybe she'd let Alex go down to the game room by herself. Right now, she just wanted to be alone, and put a bit more space between herself and this infuriating man.

19

"Okay, buddy. Tell your dad it's great doing business with him. This will make my old truck look almost new again." John K. shook the young man's hand before taking a final check of the crate in the bed of his truck. It might have been overkill to build this makeshift box out of old pallets. He just couldn't risk the vintage red roof structure shifting and getting damaged on the way back to Crossroads.

"No problem. Hey, send me a picture when they finish it. Should be cool."

"Will do." John K. sat behind the wheel of the big four door loaner. He would be happy to have his bench seat, stick shift and hand crank windows.

In this big fancy truck, the drive back to Crossroads did not seem long enough. Maybe that's why he missed Old Greenie. No one expected him to move quickly when driving a vintage truck. This one promoted an image of setting the cruise control a few miles over the limit. Instead of buying into that, he'd just enjoy the drive as he always did.

Fluffy white clouds danced a slow two-step across the sky

in front of him. He passed a few slower tractor trailers and families headed for weekend adventures. Every curve in the road presented another fantastic view. He'd enjoyed seeing new places while in the army, but his home state was unbeatable.

After exiting the freeway, the view narrowed. Tall pines shielded each side of the road. Yellow signs warning of sharp curves became more and more frequent. Their designs changed from simple curves to the left or right to "s" shapes, and even hairpins. Though the automatic transmission in this truck made the curves much easier to navigate, John K. missed the rhythm of using his clutch foot and his shifting hand in sync. He checked the rear-view mirror to be sure the crate holding Old Greenie's new top didn't move.

One last shady mountain presented itself before he descended part way back down. Left turn on a blacktop road with no yellow dashes in the middle, past two gravel roads, he turned left on the third one. He dialed his dad's number while sitting in a known sweet spot for cell reception just before reaching the travel trailer.

"Hey," he returned their traditional greeting. "I'm home. The top looks great. Too bad it's not already green."

"Painting is no problem. How about the headlights?" Dad replied.

"What headlights? First I've heard of that." John K. removed his hat so he could scratch his head. What was Dad talking about?

"Oh man. Didn't I tell you? That guy had headlights from the same truck. Yours popped when the tree came down." Dad spoke much more softly now. "I thought they would be right there with the top."

"Oh, for the love of ...." John K. bit his lip. No need giving his dad grief over this oversight. "I guess he forgot to tell his son too. The guy you talked to was nowhere around."

Neither of them spoke for a few seconds. John K. hated miscommunication worse than almost anything. He shouldn't be angry with his dad, but this was a tough one.

"I'm sorry, son. I guess we can just have him ship the headlights to us." Dad finally broke the silence.

"How about this? I will bring the top of the truck to the dealership tomorrow, then head back to Fort Smith. You're paying for the gas in this monster I'm driving, right?" Might as well make the best of this situation. He'd been looking forward to a visit with his mom and didn't want to change that.

"Sure. I just hope the rain holds off. I will be moving those cattle up to higher ground but I should be able to find enough help. The sooner we get those headlamps, the better."

"Okay then." John K. started the truck and began to move closer to his bed for the night. The clouds overhead had changed from fluffy to dark and menacing. "See you tomorrow, Dad."

Back and forth, back and forth. This demo of his dad's would get a workout tomorrow. He stopped in front of the trailer and walked over to see what had been done on the cabin. Brad and his crew had accomplished quite a bit today. With a few more days like this, he might be sleeping under a new roof soon.

All right, God. Thanks for getting me here safely. I will appreciate the same favor as I make the trip tomorrow.

He walked up the narrow steps into the trailer. Might as well get some running clothes on and stretch his legs before settling in for the night.

Crickets and tree frogs greeted him as he headed to the top of the hill above the cabin. Full dark would descend before he came back down, but this trail was familiar. His running shoes would find the way.

At the top, he paused as the cool evening breeze brushed the back of his neck. The sky peeking through the trees was tinted with orange. He took a deep cleansing breath or two and started back down. What was happening at the pageant in Fort Smith? Hope and O.D. were probably on pins and needles about now, waiting on the judges' decision. How would Faith react if she won this pageant?

He had the strange impression when they talked that she wasn't fully committed to the responsibility that would come along with the Miss Rodeo Arkansas tiara. What a crazy thought. Why would she have entered if that were the case? He certainly couldn't get inside that pretty blonde head. It might be fun to try, though.

Bumping around the last few boulders as thunder rolled again, he headed for the porch light burning in front of the trailer. Better get some sleep before the trip to Crossroads and back to the big city tomorrow.

Faith shredded a tissue she held in her hands as she sat with the Miss Rodeo Arkansas contestants during the finale of the Miss Teen Rodeo contest. The butterflies in her stomach were probably nothing compared to the ones battling each other inside her cousin's belly.

From where she sat, she had the perfect angle to take it all in. The smiles on the faces of the top five Arkansas Rodeo Teen princesses barely concealed their emotions. Kayla pressed her left hand to her stomach while waving bravely at the crowd with her right.

The five stopped waving, and held hands as they

announced the Fourth, Third and Second runners up. Hugs were exchanged as each of these girls stepped forward to acknowledge the audience's applause.

"So, that leaves us with two." The rodeo announcer stood onstage with the girls. "Miss Heber Springs, Tori Ann Waters, and Miss Crossroads Rodeo, Kayla Grace Caldwell."

Alex reached for Faith's hand. Faith scanned the crowd to locate Kayla's mom and dad, seated with her own dad, Hope, O.D., and Junior. The next second lasted at least a minute and a half.

"The First runner-up has a very important role. She will fill the role of Miss Arkansas Rodeo Teen if the winner is unable to fulfill her obligations." The announcer took a deep breath. Kayla and Tori stood arm-in-arm.

"The first runner-up is Tori Ann Waters, Miss Heber Springs."

Kayla's mouth formed an *O* as she released Tori.

Faith covered her own mouth with her hand. It was the height of bad etiquette to react loudly when the runner-up's name was announced. She had never tried so hard to hold back a scream.

"Arkansas, your new Miss Teen Rodeo is Kayla Grace Caldwell from Crossroads!"

Faith dropped her hand and released the pent-up scream. The Caldwell cheering section was on their feet, hugging each other, and cheering loudly.

Last year's queen pressed the tiara into Kayla's hat and draped a banner around her neck. Someone handed her a huge bouquet of roses, and she stepped forward, waving with her free hand as tears streamed down her face.

Faith's Uncle Dub and Aunt Tina left their seats and made their way to the arena floor.

"Let's have one more round of applause for your new Miss

Teen Rodeo." The announcer moved to the front of the stage. "And then, we will take a five-minute intermission to get the stage reset for our big event of the night, the crowning of Miss Rodeo Arkansas."

Alex hugged Faith.

"I can't believe it!" Faith said. "I knew she had a chance to place in the top five, but she WON!"

"Yes, indeed." Alex laughed. "I'm afraid you don't have time to congratulate her yet, though. We've got to get down there for our own big announcement. Good luck, my friend."

Faith swallowed hard and looked into Alex's eyes. "And to you. I'm so happy we roomed together."

"Me too. Let's keep in touch." Alex started toward the stairs leading down from their reviewing stand.

"Definitely." Faith struggled to calm her pounding heart. Kayla had won! What would happen when they announced the next winner?

"Hey fella." Faith patted the handsome palomino's neck before mounting him to ride into the arena. The organizers said this was a rather unique grand finale, but she liked their idea. The horse would calm her a little. She could concentrate on keeping him headed in the right direction through traffic, instead of worrying about the judges' scoring. No need in that. Everything was tabulated and decided by now.

After a couple of big circles around the arena, the contestants performed the figure eight pattern they had practiced this afternoon. They all shared a love for performing on horseback. The competition in the horsemanship event had been crazy. Faith felt fortunate that she had received the highest score.

The audience applauded as the horses stopped in a circle facing outward, and the contestants dismounted. The lively music faded out and silence pervaded the arena.

Faith stood firmly on the dirt floor but remembered to bend one knee slightly. No use locking up and fainting in front of all these people. A squadron of cowboys dressed in black appeared and led their horses to the opposite end of the arena.

"Okay, ladies and gents. We'll try not to keep the suspense building any longer than necessary." The announcer stood on a metal stage along with the director of the pageant and several past queens, including Alex's grandma Ms. Pat. Next to the beautiful blonde, Kayla grinned. She held her hands together in a heart shape and mouthed 'I love you' in Faith's direction.

"I have here in my hand the list of the top five finalists for Miss Rodeo Arkansas. But first, a word from our director, Mrs. Georgina Small."

Faith tried to keep her smile firmly glued in place. The last few days had felt more like a week. Her stomach turned flips as she glanced beside her and caught Alex's eye. A confident wink from her new friend settled her nerves ever so slightly.

"This pageant has been such a joy for me and all of the Miss Rodeo Arkansas family. These contestants, and our teens have shown us the future is bright in the Natural State. These young ladies are strong and resilient. They demonstrate that the time and effort their parents, teachers, and community support system have invested have been well placed. To those who don't make it up here on stage tonight, please know we love each and every one of you. We couldn't be prouder of our statewide rodeo princesses. Thank you."

She stepped back, and the announcer took the mic.

"Our first award is very special because it was voted on by all of tonight's contestants. She will receive a prize package assembled by our sponsors, including gift cards for merchandise, hotel stays, and restaurants. Mrs. Small tells me that this year, the People's Princess award was unanimous."

The contestants began to applaud and cheer before the announcer could read the name.

"Miss Brittany Farris, please join us on stage."

A petite young lady with bright red hair stepped up, followed by the sign language interpreter who had accompanied her for the past few days.

Faith waved at her, and then turned to Alex to share in the happiness. This girl had inspired everyone with her "can-do" attitude, despite being totally deaf.

"Thank you." The interpreter said as Brittany signed her acceptance. "But you are not correct. The vote was not unanimous. I didn't vote for me."

Everyone laughed, and Mrs. Small hugged her as Ms. Pat presented her with an overflowing gift bag.

"Okay, now. At long last, the top five. These young women are the best of the best, and all deserve to wear the Miss Rodeo Arkansas tiara. But, only one gets that honor."

Five of the black-clad cowboys returned to escort the contestants to the stage as their names were called.

"Miss Vilonia, Cassie Hunt."

"Miss White County, Terry Lynn Hastings."

"Miss Southern Arkansas University, Alexandra Landry."

Alex squeezed Faith's hand before taking the handsome cowboy's arm to walk toward the stage.

"Miss Central Arkansas, Dominique Williams."

Faith closed her eyes. Maybe not being called to the stage was for the best.

"Miss Crossroads, Faith Elaine Caldwell."

She swallowed hard. Well, then. *Okay, God. Stay with me here.*

"All right! Go Faith!" She smiled. That was Junior's voice coming from the stands. It was good to have her family here.

Her escort left her on the stage next to the other girls. Faith closed her eyes again and took a deep breath. The only event she had been completely confident about was horsemanship. She knew they had been judged on so many things that weren't measurable. A winning smile, a positive attitude, willingness to promote products they may not have heard of before the pageant.

Had she been involved for the wrong reasons? There were other ways to finance her education. Did she want to move all of that back for a whole year while she fulfilled her obligations as Miss Rodeo Arkansas?

Spotlights twirled around the arena as the director of the pageant thanked the sponsors for the event. Faith looked to the right of the stage. Tara Williams talked to a technician, and Ty Porter whispered to another reporter nearby. Hopefully, he understood how she felt about him now. Maybe there was a girl out there for him, but she was not the one.

She pasted her smile back on. Better be prepared to step forward for one of the runner-up prizes. She was grateful for this opportunity. She had a feeling Alex would be a lifelong friend.

"Fourth runner-up ... Dominique Williams."

Faith turned to hug the girl on her right. "Congratulations, Nikki."

"Thanks. Good luck!" Dominique stepped forward to the applause of the arena.

Please, Lord. Let me hear my name next.

"Third runner-up is Miss Vilonia, Cassie Hunt."

Faith's stomach turned flips. *God, are you listening?*

"Second runner-up .... Miss White County, Terry Lynn Hastings."

What? It was down to her and Alex? She turned to her roommate, and they moved closer together, arms wrapped firmly around each other. This time, Faith wasn't thinking of the events of the last few days. Instead, her mind whirled with what she would be expected to do for the coming year.

"The two young ladies you have before you both have tremendous responsibilities ahead of them. Miss Rodeo Arkansas will have a full schedule of events and appearances for the coming year. She will also travel to Las Vegas as our state's representative in the Miss Rodeo USA pageant."

The crowd cheered wildly.

"But the first runner-up must also be prepared to step in if Miss Rodeo Arkansas cannot fulfill her role for any reason. And the name of that backup, our first runner-up ..."

Stay with me. Thy will be done. Faith trembled as she prayed.

"Miss Rodeo Crossroads, Faith Elaine Caldwell!"

Thank You, Lord. Faith hugged Alex tightly, then stepped away to receive a bouquet of flowers and an envelope holding her prizes. Polite applause came from the grandstands.

"And the winner of Miss Rodeo Arkansas is Alexandra Landry! Ladies, and Gentlemen, Your queen!"

20

John K. pulled up to the dealership gate and waved at the security guard. An hour after sunrise, dark clouds threatened. The river valley had been inundated again while they slept last night. The drive back to Fort Smith to finish this crazy parts delivery mission might not be easy

"Howdy, Mr. Billings." The guard entered numbers into a keypad to open the door of the body shop behind the service bays.

"Thanks for opening for me." John K. pulled the behemoth he was driving inside and killed the engine. Old Greenie looked much better than the last time he'd seen him. He'd never pictured his truck as a convertible, but at least it was cleaned up and ready for the next step in the repair process.

"Let's get this unloaded. Do we need a forklift?" The guard turned from side to side, looking for available equipment to help them.

"Nah. I think you and I can pull it off. I'll bounce up in the bed and push it toward the tailgate." John K. dropped the massive tailgate and crawled up beside the crate. Pushing this thing back was more of a challenge than he anticipated. He needed to find a way to work on his upper body instead of just running every day.

"Okay. Can we move it from here?" The guard grabbed the crate.

"Sure. On three." John K. found a good place to hold onto the slats. "One, two," Brace and lift, "Three."

They both added a good "oomph" and settled the crate on the concrete floor near Old Greenie.

"Hey, that was above and beyond for sure. Thanks." John K. shook the guy's hand.

"Yeah, can't wait to see how she looks when she's all decked out and ready."

"I hope they can get the color close to the original." John K. ran his hand over the undamaged portion of the truck bed.

"Should be better than new when it's done. I've seen the guys here after hours some days. I think your dad has put a big priority on this baby." The guard made his way closer to the shop doors.

"Yeah. Thanks. I won't keep you any longer." John K. stepped into his loaner truck.

The guard waved as John K. backed out into the lot and turned around.

'All decked out and ready.' That was a strange way to describe this effort to fix the old truck. Repairing and repainting seemed a little simpler than 'all decked out.' Everybody had their own way of looking at things.

Thunder rumbled as John K. drove toward the Billings ranch. Oh boy. Too bad he couldn't just head toward Fort Smith for those headlamps. Too late now. It had been his idea to work in a visit home between the trips. Maybe someday he'd be able to keep his mind from moving to the next task. Easier said than done.

Faith shoved the last garment bag into her back seat, slamming the door to the accompaniment of a long low roll of thunder. She was grateful the worship service was planned for early this morning. Dark clouds boiled overhead.

Hope rushed out of the hotel, her arms overloaded, pulling a large suitcase behind her. O.D. followed with a similar load.

"Morning." Faith walked over to hold a small bag for her sister as she wedged the larger bag behind the passenger seat. "You had the same idea. Pack before church so we get ahead of the rain."

"Yeah. Well. Change of plans." Hope hugged her as she retrieved the roll bag. "We're leaving now."

"I knew Dad and Junior hit the road before breakfast. He never wants to let anyone else preach in his place. But I thought you might stay and worship here." Faith had looked forward to spending time with her sister this morning.

"I'm sure it will be uplifting. Everyone is still on a high after the pageant last night. But ..." Hope stepped up on the passenger side running board.

O.D. leaned over from the driver's side. "It's my fault. My dad called a few minutes ago. He's extra worried about getting our herd up from the lower pasture. They got more rain last night than we did here. The creek has been rising all night."

"By the time we get there, he'll have our horses ready, and he's even trying to talk O.D.'s mom into manning the four-wheeler." Hope fake-whispered behind her hand. "I sort of can't wait to see that."

"I'm packed up too. Do you need me?" Faith asked.

"No, no. You can tell Uncle Dub and Aunt Tina what's going on. Since our side of the hill is higher anyway, I think the Caldwell cattle will be fine."

"Hey—don't forget, you live on the Billings side now." O.D. teased.

"Yeah, yeah. Whatever." Hope laughed.

"Well, y'all be careful going home. I'll be along soon." Faith closed Hope's door and headed toward the arena.

Once again, she was glad not to be pulling a horse trailer this weekend. She hadn't heard anything about strong winds with this storm, but heavy rain would be tricky enough. Oh well, there was still time to worship. She opened the glass doors and followed the sound of guitar music into the arena.

"Good morning, dear." Ms. Pat hugged her as she reached the grandstand. "Did you sleep well?"

"You know, I did. I am so happy for Alex. She has a big job ahead of her." What a strange feeling to be relieved about NOT winning the pageant.

"Yes, but she's up to it. In fact, I think this is what she has been working for all her life." Ms. Pat held Faith's hand and waved to Alex with the other one. "Let's go praise God together."

Kayla had saved her a spot near the stage set up at the end of the arena. Uncle Dub and Aunt Tina sat next to Ms. Pat, and Alex came to sit next to Faith.

Thank You, Lord, for these ladies who will help our family navigate Kayla's adventure over the coming year. Faith quickly lost herself in worship and enjoyed the preacher's lesson about David and Goliath. There would be plenty of giants to face in her life, and she loved the reminder that she didn't have to fight any battles alone.

"Now, brothers and sisters, please join me in a very special prayer." The preacher moved to the edge of the stage. "I would like to ask our new Miss Rodeo Arkansas and Miss Arkansas Teen to come forward. Alex, Kayla, would you join me, please?"

Aunt Tina reached for Faith's hand as Kayla walked to the stage.

"Lord, these young ladies have been recognized for years of hard work this weekend. They are excited right now, but soon, the reality of the task they have ahead may sink in. Please go with them for every appearance, every encounter with others across our great state this year. Help them to represent You, to bring Jesus to each person they touch. Only You can provide them with the strength and inspiration to complete the work ahead. Bless their families, as well, as they support these young women. We ask for Your grace and protection on all of them. In Jesus' name, Amen."

"Amen." Faith squeezed her aunt's hand. They couldn't have asked for a better send-off for this important journey.

"Are you sure you will be okay driving back to Crossroads by yourself?" Uncle Dub stood next to Faith's truck in the parking lot between the hotel and the arena.

"Of course." Faith smiled. She knew her dad would be grateful that his brother was concerned about her. "It's less than two hours to our front door."

"Ms. Pat has invited us to eat lunch with her and Alex. We need to get some idea about the next step in this process for Kayla Grace." Aunt Tina joined him.

"That's a great idea." Faith tossed her truck keys up and caught them. "But I'm going to hit the road. I've got leftover snacks from this weekend in the truck."

"It looks like we're in for a rainstorm, so be careful," Kayla added her warning.

"I've got this!" Faith laughed. "See y'all back at home. Tell Alex I will text her later, and we'll be in touch." Evidently the only way to stop this never-ending goodbye session was to get in the pickup and start it. She did just that, waving as she left the parking lot.

The faster pace of the freeway felt good as she accelerated up the ramp and headed east. Dark clouds followed through with their threat, and a steady drizzle increased to a full-blown rainstorm. She was thankful for bright headlights and strong windshield wipers. The wind buffeted the truck from first one side and then the other. She slowed down to stay behind a tractor-trailer several times instead of attempting to pass. It would be hard for drivers to see her coming around. She didn't want to risk being in a blind spot.

A new bumping noise started from the rear of the truck. Faith turned off the radio, slowing down to figure out the source of the sound. She fought with the steering wheel, trying to keep the pickup straight on the freeway.

Boom! She held the wheel tightly and eased over to the right shoulder, slowing to a stop. A flat tire? Today, in the pouring rain? Well, then. *Stay close, Lord. I'm going to need some help.*

21

Davis Billings stood next to the massive new gate separating the lower pasture from the recently fenced-off area nearer the house. "O.D., you flank around on the right, and Hope can get the left. Mom will have the four-wheeler down here if one of them heads the wrong way."

John K. sat tall on Dad's horse, General. The cool western breeze slapped his cheeks with moisture. If the cattle weren't in danger of being stranded, he would have loved to just ride, enjoying the cool air until the rain started.

"Dad." John K. couldn't picture his role in this operation. "I think y'all have this covered. I need to get back to Fort Smith to get those headlamps. Do you want me to take the General back to the barn?"

"No. Leave him here. I'll ride him." Dad took the reins as John K. dismounted. "Yeah, looks like I have a pretty good crew today. Sorry about your extra trip."

"Might as well go get it done. They were making a lot of progress when I checked at the body shop this morning. I'd love to give you back the giant I'm using. Greenie and I understand each other."

John K. leaned across the handlebars of the four-wheeler to hug his mom. "Thanks for dinner."

"Ha. Cold sandwiches. Not much of a meal." Mom hugged him tightly. "Come back, and I'll actually cook something."

"Sure thing. Love you." They all missed Cody whizzing around on that four-wheeler. He could see the strain in Mom's face. She much preferred all of them being here.

The cattle lined up to move toward the higher pasture, lodging their complaints with low moos.

"This is only temporary, guys. They only want to keep you safe." Was he trying to carry on a conversation with the livestock now? Better just get in the truck and hit the road.

He checked the gas gauge. First stop would be for fuel. He had to admit that driving back and forth was more comfortable in this truck than it would have been in Old Greenie. At least he had good windshield wipers.

With the tank full, he unwrapped a beef jerky stick. He placed an energy drink in the cup holder on his right. Now, to test the connection O.D. had made between the truck's fancy radio and his cell phone playlist.

"Well, check this out." He sang along with each country song that emerged through the speakers and filled the cab with vibrations. Maybe this fancy vehicle had its advantages after all.

The truck nearly drove itself back toward the garage he'd visited the day before. Was this what his life would look like? Running errands for his dad's dealership, occasionally attending church with his family, and sharing a meal? He certainly had nothing to complain about right now. Then why did he feel so lost?

"Got time for a cup of coffee?" The garage owner's son placed the box with the headlamps in the cab of the truck.

"No. I think I'd better try to beat this weather." Thunder rumbled overhead, and a fat raindrop hit John K.'s forehead.

"It's taking it's time rolling in, but the weatherman said it may be another toad strangler." The young man removed his baseball cap and examined the sky above him.

"Yep. It hasn't been a good May for toads around here." John K. started the truck and waved as he shifted into reverse.

His phone pinged with a message at the edge of the busy road.

Flat tire. Called Triple A. Estimated time one hour.

A Text from Faith Caldwell?

Apparently, he and O.D. had been included in a group text when he met them for lunch the other day.

Hope answered quickly.

Where are you?

Between Alma and Ozark on the side of I-40.

He didn't want to read while driving so he waited before pulling out onto the highway. Maybe he could help.

I'll tell Dad. We can be on the way soon.

Hope again.

No need. I'm closer.

He typed his message and hit Send. Why bother Mr. Caldwell?

Faith answered quickly.

I know how to change it.

It's pouring down rain.

He wasn't challenging her abilities. But everybody could use some help now and then, right?

Thanks, John K.

O.D. chimed in.

I'll tell Dad anyway. He'll want to check on you.

Hope posted.

John K. put his phone down and started driving. It wouldn't be hard to find a baby blue pickup truck on the eastbound shoulder. Hopefully, the truck was safely off the road. Those tractor-trailers passing at over seventy miles an hour could be brutal. *Lord, sit with Faith and keep her safe for a few minutes until I can get there to help. Thanks.*

Faith stared through the windshield as rain pounded down. She turned off the engine and the windshield wipers. Only the illuminated button on her dashboard and the flashing emergency lights outside the truck broke the dreary gray curtains waving on every side.

She found a video on her cell phone demonstrating changing a tire on the same model truck. Her dad had insisted on practicing the process when her truck was brand new. He would never send one of his kids out without the ability to change a tire and at least diagnose more serious issues. Watching the video again would be useless, except for the possibility that the rain might ease up a little bit.

A red Mustang whizzed by and she immediately saw a text on her phone.

Was that you in the blue truck?

The message came from Ty's number.

Yes

Thank goodness for AAA, right?

There was no chance he would turn around to help her.

Her cheeks flamed. *"You thought I wanted some sort of long-term relationship? I only wanted to have some fun."* If that was not the last thing Ty said to her, it was very close. Maybe not a long-term relationship, but at least some simple kindness and respect.

"Get mad at it, and get it done." One of Mom's favorite phrases rang in her head. No use putting it off any longer. She reached into a pocket on the back of the passenger seat to find a full-length rain suit. One-size-fits-all might be a little large, but it would keep most of the rain off her. She stretched out across the front seat, and squirmed into the pants, and then the hooded jacket. If anyone was coming to help, maybe they would give her a minute.

Rain pelted her boots as she crawled feet first out of the passenger side of the truck. She stepped down and opened the rear passenger door, lifting both seats to find the equipment she needed.

When everything was removed and sitting beside the

truck, she looked up for a moment. Too bad the weather was not like the crisp autumn day when she and Dad had rehearsed. Standing here wouldn't stop the rain. Might as well get to work. She would just keep visualizing a hot shower and curling up on the couch with a bowl of popcorn.

"First things first, Lainie." She tried to sound confident as she spoke aloud to herself. "Let's get this done."

John K. stopped several yards behind Faith's truck on the shoulder. He had seen police cars angle their vehicles with the tail end out closer to traffic, so he tried his best to replicate the position. Maybe it wouldn't do any good if a car plowed into the borrowed truck, but no harm in trying to protect them while they changed this tire.

He left his flashers going and jogged up to where Faith squatted behind the truck, using a long handle device to lower the spare.

He waited until the tire reached the ground before he spoke. No use breaking her concentration.

"Good job there."

"Hey." Faith stood up, pushing the hood back from her forehead. Her customary smile was not present today. "Thanks for coming to my tire-changing party."

"Nothing better to do today." John K. reached past her to lift the tire, pushing the bracket that held the spare in place through the center of the wheel. He pulled the tire out behind the truck and rested it in front of her feet. "You're making good progress. I think I can probably jack up a truck and adjust lug nuts in my sleep. So, if you want, I'll be glad to do that."

"Be my guest. They're already loosened a little." Faith stepped back.

"Front tire scotched?" John K. looked toward the front of the truck.

"Yes, sir." Faith gave him a mock salute.

"Should have known." John K. hoisted the tire and brought it to the shoulder of the road. Faith handed him the handle for the jack. He squirmed under the back frame to find the right spot, cranking the jack up until the flat tire was off the ground.

"Keep up with these for me?" He handed the lug nuts to Faith as they were removed.

"No problem."

He pulled the old tire up and off, walking to the back of the bed to toss it over the tailgate. Was there a rain suit like the one Faith wore in this fancy truck he was driving? Not likely. He hadn't even taken time to locate the jack and the spare tire in his truck.

Rain splattered around them, bounced off the side of the truck, dripped off the brim of his hat and ran in rivulets down his cheeks. A tire change was a tire change, no matter the weather. At least there was no lightning. *Keep us safe, Father.*

"Thanks for your help." Faith tossed the jack into the truck bed. "I could have done that, but not nearly as quickly."

"I wouldn't qualify for a pit crew, but I changed a lot of tires in the army." He wiped his grimy hands on the front of his blue jeans. He would have to remember to store some rain gear in his truck.

"Let me at least buy you something to eat. You know that famous burger place in Russellville?" She opened the passenger door of her truck, wriggling her arms out of the sleeves of her rain jacket.

"Sure." He could handle a burger right now.

"See you in a few." She climbed into the passenger seat and closed the door before he had a chance to answer.

He laughed as he jogged back to his truck. Evidently, there was no arguing with the oldest Caldwell girl.

Faith removed her rain gear, stowing it behind the seat before scooting over to drive.

She picked up her phone and noticed a text from her dad.

Need help princess?

She had hoped Hope and O.D. would not even call him. As the pulpit minister of the cowboy church, Sunday was his busiest day. If he managed to get any rest between services, she didn't want to interrupt.

All done. John K. helped.

Headed home now?

Her dad was not done checking on her.

Stopping in Russellville for a burger. See you soon.

She started the truck and checked the traffic behind her. John K. was waiting on her to pull out. He knew where they were going. Why didn't he just leave? She knew the answer to that one. Not the way the Billings Boys operated.

Thank You, Lord. God did send angels sometimes. This particular angel was handy to have around, for sure.

The rain slowed down and clear skies emerged ahead of her truck. No use complaining about God's timing. She accelerated and watched the mile markers. Not too much further before the restaurant. Maybe their coffee wouldn't be too stale.

She exited the freeway and found a parking space in front of the familiar restaurant. John K. pulled up next to her. His chambray work shirt clung to him as came near. She should have at least held an umbrella over his head while he changed her tire.

"So now it stops raining." He laughed as he held the restaurant door open for her.

"Arkansas weather, right?" Faith stepped in and stood behind several other customers. The line would move quickly because there weren't a lot of decisions to make here. One patty or two, with or without cheese, what to drink. The owners had tried to add menu items from time to time, but most customers stuck with their burgers.

"I think I'm ordering coffee instead of a coke." Faith commented. "Trying to chase the chill."

"Good idea." He agreed. "I'll pick up the napkins and other stuff. Ketchup for your fries?"

"Of course!" Faith laughed. "That counts as a vegetable, right? This is the only place we go that I don't order a salad."

"That would probably violate a local ordinance."

That grin of his. It didn't show up often, but it lit his face. Just before she ordered, she watched him wait as a family with several kids gathered straws, napkins and ketchup packets. So many other guys she knew would have pushed ahead, or at least acted impatient. This one was the model of manners.

"So, how did you do at the pageant?" John K. stood up as she settled in to a table near the window.

"First runner-up. I was relieved I didn't win." Faith stacked the packets of ketchup he placed in front of her.

"What?" John K. laughed.

"Alex is the perfect Miss Rodeo Arkansas. She came in with

her platform fully formed, ready to go out and mentor younger kids all over the state." She handed the waitress the number from their table as their burgers arrived.

"You could have done that too." John K. salted his French fries. "You speak rodeo better than anyone I know."

"I haven't confessed this to anyone." Faith used both hands to hold the messy burger. "I was ready to move on when Dad and Uncle Dub sold the rodeo. It's time to get my education finished and get my career started."

"I get that." John K. paused after finishing his first bite. "So, now you won't have a commitment for the next year or so."

"Right. All those personal appearances and social media posts. It would have been fun. But, a full-time job." Faith nodded. "I may end up going along with Kayla and Aunt Tina sometimes. But at least I won't be obligated."

"Oh, yeah. That's right. She's Miss Teen Queen. Cool. I live next to royalty."

"Miss Rodeo Arkansas Teen." Faith laughed. "Yes. Another good choice. Kayla grew up at the rodeo just like Hope and I did, but she is the one that could sell ice cubes to an Eskimo. She will be so excited to represent the sponsors and wear their newest products. She'll be fantastic."

"But back to you." John K. stirred more sugar into his coffee. "So, you need more education to be a nurse? Can't you just work up through the ranks?"

"I want to be a nurse practitioner. So, besides being an RN, I will have post-graduate work." Was he interested? Ty had always changed the subject when the conversation got to this point.

"Oh, so you have to go to school in Little Rock, right? Or do they have that program in Fayetteville?" He leaned his chair back, balancing on the back two legs.

"I want to concentrate on oncology. The nurse

practitioners were lifesavers for us when Mom had cancer." She finished her coffee. "I wouldn't just pick where to go, I'd have to be accepted into a program. The best ones are far away, in big cities."

"Wow. Living in one of those places would be a major adjustment." He wiped his mouth with a napkin, leaning back in his chair.

"Another true confession." Faith paused. "That's what appeals to me most about this idea. I have lived right here in this same area all my life. Big cities are more exciting."

"I get that too." John K. placed the front feet of his chair back on the floor. "But take it from the guy who enlisted in the Army to see the world. There's a lot of advantages to living in a small town or out in the country."

"Everyone appreciates your service so much. You have been a hero for our community since you were in high school." She took another bite of her burger.

"Nope. The real heroes didn't come home." He stared into his coffee cup.

"I know." He had managed to pull so much truth out of her today. Now, he was giving her a glimpse of the problem he had with being called a hero. Not only was he good at changing truck tires, but he seemed interested in what she had to say. She hadn't had to worry about him getting too close or making inappropriate comments. Of course not. He was a Billings after all. Solid, secure, dependable. Boring?

"Okay. You bought my meal today. But I get to plan the next time." John K. replaced the lid on his empty coffee cup.

"Next time?" She wasn't upset he assumed there would be a next time.

"Yeah. Let me know when you have a full day off from the old-folks home. If Old Greenie is ready, I want to take you on a drive. I can prove to you that you can get big city advantages without going too far from home." He stood up, gathering her trash along with his.

"Okay. I'll check my schedule and get back to you." What would he think when he saw what they were doing to Old Greenie? Probably no chance that reaction would be boring.

22

John K. limped the last few steps past the travel trailer. His ankle twinged when he stepped on a rock. Maybe running was not the best thing right now.

"Hey, boss man." Brad pulled a two-by-four away from the saw blade in the cabin's front yard. "Come see how we're doing with the framing. Your living room is almost done."

John K. reached the porch but stopped short of climbing the newly built stairway.

"Looks great, man!" He waved his cap in Brad's direction. "I need to go inside for a minute, but I'll come look later." Maybe he should just sit with an ice pack for a few minutes. More than six months after his surgery, it should be completely healed. Had he re-injured it?

Pops and bangs echoed from the cabin, as work resumed. He found a package of frozen vegetables in Mac's freezer and placed it on his ankle as he propped his foot up on a pile of pillows on the couch. Maybe he'd find another bag for his head.

Squee, squee, squee. He jumped up, sending the package of

peas sliding to the floor. He should probably change that notification on his phone. "What's up, Mac?"

"No fire. It's a truck down in the ditch up on the main highway. The sheriff just wants us to be there to help direct traffic. I'll swing by to get you."

"Okay. I'll get my boots on and watch for you." John K. disconnected and worked his sore left foot into his hiking boot. His body had aged ten years during the three he was in the army.

Can you give me a call?

A message from Faith popped up on his phone, this time without the group text including Hope and O.D.

Got a Fire Dept. run right now. Can it wait?

Did she have another flat tire?

Sure. Not urgent.

Well, she had his curiosity up now. At least she wasn't angry that he wanted a second date so quickly. He had enjoyed talking to her while they dried out on Sunday.

He stepped out of the trailer and waved at Brad again.

"Got a fire department run to make. I'll come look at the house when I get back." Brad gave him a thumbs up as he and his helper carried boards inside the cabin.

"Thanks for coming along." Mac opened the passenger door of his truck. "I didn't even try anyone else. The driver got out of his car safely. I think they just want an extra pair of emergency lights sitting on the side of the road while the wrecker pulls him up out of the ditch."

"No problem." John K. leaned back to rest his head.

"You okay?" Mac asked.

"Just a little headache." John K. straightened in his seat.

"That reminds me. None of my business, but I was wondering if you have checked in with the local VA office since you moved up here." Mac turned his siren on as they reached the main highway.

"No. My surgery was done while I was still overseas. Since I came home, I haven't needed anything." John K. stared out the passenger side window. A conversation with the local VA would not be fun. His commanding officers had filled out the initial reports after he was injured. Now that he was home, he didn't deserve to spend any more of the taxpayer's money on his medical treatment.

Faith reined Belle to a stop just outside their barn. The air felt so clean and clear this morning. Now that the sun was fully awake, the day could turn hot very quickly.

"Thanks for coming with me on short notice. It's harder and harder to find time to ride these days." She dismounted, patting Kayla's horse on the neck as they came near.

"No problem. You know I love an early morning ride." Kayla grabbed a brush to help Faith groom Belle. "Are you sure it's okay for Alex to ride Champ in the parade?"

"I don't know why not." Faith hung the bridle up on a hook outside Belle's stall. "You've got Sissy, and I'll be on Belle. Hope said she has no reason to ride with us, so Champ is available."

"Alex said she could bring her horse up from their ranch, but she wants to go to Little Rock after the parade, and she'd have to board him somewhere. Won't it be great to have three rodeo queens in the parade this year?" Kayla patted her horse's nose. "Well, technically they call us Ladies in Waiting, I guess."

"I don't fit in with the group." Faith said. "Newly crowned Miss Rodeo Arkansas, Miss Rodeo Arkansas Teen, and the runner-up."

"You're still the Crossroads queen. We need you, Lainie. Besides, if you don't ride, Mom might. That would be embarrassing." She tucked her braid back into her baseball cap.

"Talk about embarrassing. I called John K. Billings today to try to prepare him for the big truck reveal." Faith scuffed the toe of her boot in the dust outside the barn.

"You think he'll be mad?"

"I don't know. He just seems extra sensitive when he talks about his active-duty time."

"All heroes deny doing anything brave," Kayla said. "He'll appreciate the attention."

"I hope so." Faith walked toward her house as John K.'s number appeared on her cell phone. "Speak of the devil."

"Okay, I'll see ya!" Kayla mounted Sissy and headed up the driveway toward her own house.

"Hi!" How should she start this conversation without spoiling the truck reveal?

"Are you sitting on the side of the road again?" He made that question sound playful instead of insulting.

"No. Just for the record, I could have changed that tire." She stopped to sit in Mom's favorite Adirondack chair, under a huge oak tree.

"I have no doubt." John K. laughed.

"I did appreciate the assist. Hey, you wanted to know about my days off. I'll be working the overnight shift this Saturday so I can ride with Kayla and Alex in the parade." Okay, good lead-in. Make it about the Rodeo Queens.

"Yeah. The Founder's Day parade. I think Dad and O.D. want all the Billings Boys to drive a truck with an ad for the dealership on the side." John K.'s voice dropped. "Well, all except Cody."

"That will be cool. And I heard they are making a big deal out of the local veterans too. So, there is that." *Awkward, just a bit?*

"Yeah. Too bad Grandpa Dee is not up to riding with us."

"I heard some talk at the home. They might take some of the residents outside during the parade since it comes right in front of the building." He was okay with his grandpa being honored. That was a start. "I'll ask the nurse on duty to see if Cody wants to go out with them too."

"Great. So, when is your next day off? I've got a cool idea for a little Arkansas sightseeing."

"Next Wednesday. I'm off all day that day."

"Okay. I'll come get you in Old Greenie if he's ready. We'll have to leave early. How's seven-thirty?"

"In the morning?" Faith wrinkled her nose. Not many dates started that early.

"Yeah. If you're up for it," John K. said. "Plan on being gone all day. We'll be back around sundown."

"You've got me wondering now." What was he up to? It didn't matter. Just riding with him would be fun. He was so easy to talk to.

"I hope the old truck is ready. It will be a good road test for him."

"All-righty then. Well, I guess I will see you at the parade this Saturday." She leaned back in the Adirondack.

"You got it. Keep checking the air in those tires." He disconnected.

Fluffy clouds ambled overhead. Would they be lucky enough to have a beautiful day like today for the parade and

John K.'s planned adventure next Wednesday? Somehow, the weather was secondary. Both days promised to be full of excitement.

Here's the plan.

Tara's text on the chat with Hope and O.D. was perfectly timed.

The custom paint man says John K.'s truck will be ready Friday night. What do y'all think of him picking it up just in time to drive it in the parade on Saturday?

Hope responded instantly.

Sounds good. Where will this happen?

Can you have the guy bring it back to the dealership?

O.D. chimed in.

We'll tell John K. we are meeting there so that each of us can get a fresh, shiny truck with signs on it to drive that morning.

Hope responded.

Perfect. What do you think Faith?

Sounds like a plan.

Maybe not a great plan, but a plan. What if John K. totally hated what they did to Old Greenie? She wished she had told him more in their phone conversation. After he came to her rescue on the side of the road, didn't she owe that to him? It was too late now. What was done was done.

A mockingbird practiced its repertoire at the top of a maple near the back door.

"I wish I was as confident about this as you sound." She mumbled in the general direction of the bird. Her new friendship with the oldest Billings brother might be over before it started when he found out she had been in on this surprise.

"Hey, what's for breakfast?" Her brother's standard question greeted her as she walked through the mudroom. No time to worry about John K. As the Bible said, this Saturday would have enough worries of its own. Or something like that.

23

"Are you sure you don't need me to drive one of your newer models?" John K. stayed a half step ahead of Dad as they neared the Billings Boys body shop.

"No. There are three floats that need pulling in the parade. Me, O.D., and Hope will handle that. Aren't you excited about driving Old Greenie?" Dad punched a code on a pad to raise the shiny shop door.

"You know I am." John K. stared as the door lifted to reveal a small crowd of people forming a line across the width of the bay. Tara Williams rushed forward with a cameraman, and an insanely bright light flashed into his eyes.

"Hi, John K. I hope you don't mind if we film as you see what your truck looks like." She smiled at him while holding a microphone to her side.

"Huh?" Why would she want this on television? His gut tightened, and he clenched and unclenched his fists, battling the urge to run out of the shop. What was happening? Had they done more than a regular paint job on his old truck? He searched the shop for a sign of the familiar vintage green.

"It's okay, son." Dad stepped closer, looking directly in his eyes.

He swallowed and tried not to sneer. These people cared about him. They didn't know that he was the total opposite of a hero. His feet were rooted to their spot. He nodded to Tara. Might as well get whatever this was over with.

Tara waved the cameraman closer, and the bright light shifted to the side. Hope and O.D. stood in the center of the group in front of him. His dad walked over to join his mom and the body shop crew.

"We're here today with John Kennedy Billings, one of the local heroes we honor today at our Founder's Day parade." Tara stood beside him. "John K., when we found out that your favorite truck was being repaired here in the Billings Boys shop, we asked our friend Kenny at Kenny's Customs to get involved. KRVA TV and the whole community of Crossroads appreciates you so much. This is our way of showing you how proud we are. Thank you for your service!"

He tried to peer past Tara and the camera. What had they done to Old Greenie?

The body shop crew applauded as the man Tara had called Kenny handed him his truck keys. Hope moved to her right, and O.D. to his left so that he could get a better look. He had to force himself not to close his eyes.

At least it was still green. In fact, this was more of an army green instead of the original faded Kelly green it used to wear. He was okay with that reminder. Grandpa Dee had been in the army.

He walked toward the driver's side door.

"O.D. told us not to get too carried away." Kenny stood next to him. "We hope you like it."

Under the driver's window, his full name was written in a

fancy cursive font. On the driver's side of the bed, more words. "All gave some, some gave all."

He blinked back tears. *And I gave up.*

"What do you think?" Tara followed him to the back tailgate.

"Just a lot to take in." John K. tried to keep his voice upbeat. Whose idea was this? It was so unnecessary. His major concern was whether the cab he brought from Fort Smith would fit the rest of the truck.

He took a deep breath, both hands in his pockets as he stood behind his truck. A painting of the American Flag fluttering in the breeze completely covered the tailgate. Beneath the flag was written "Total respect for our American Heroes."

Hero. There was that word again. He couldn't act like he didn't appreciate their efforts. But he didn't deserve this at all. If only they knew.

"You okay?" O.D. stood at his elbow. "I was afraid this would be too much."

"Hey. I'm blown away. I just thought the dents would come out and Greenie would get a new paint job. This is overwhelming." He forced a smile and shook his brother's hand.

Tara followed with the cameraman as John K. completed the circuit around the pickup. On the passenger's side, they had written a famous quote from his namesake, President Kennedy.

"Ask not what your country can do for you, ask what you can do for your country." Tara read it aloud, and the assembled crowd cheered.

Dewayne Tolliver. He nodded as he silently read his grandpa's name written under the passenger's window. He had to admit, this was all tastefully done. Maybe he could at least give Grandpa Dee a ride in his favorite old truck. John K. didn't deserve kudos, but his grandpa did.

"Well?" Tara rocked back and forth and placed the microphone close to him.

"I want to thank whoever was involved in this makeover." John K. wished he had the eloquence of his calf-roping brother O.D. or the swagger of Cody the bull-rider. "I didn't expect all this, but I appreciate it."

"You are more than welcome. Thank you for your service." Tara shook his hand and signaled the cameraman to turn his light off. "Now, we've got a parade to launch!"

She hurried away, and John K. ran his hand across Grandpa Dee's name again. A parade. So many guys would be proud to be honored by their hometown. He wished he could get past the bitter lump in his throat and enjoy this, even a little bit.

Faith pulled into the gravel lot at the end of Main Street. Aunt Tina's truck and trailer were nearby as well. Maybe it wouldn't take long to get unloaded. After parking, she walked back to the door of her trailer.

"Easy, Belle." The horse took several quick steps down the ramp. "Want to stand here a minute before we get that fancy saddle on?" The wraps Dad always insisted their horses wear on their legs when they traveled came off easily. They were both used to this routine. "Good girl."

"Hey, Faith." Kayla and her horse walked across the gravel lot near the railroad tracks. "Thanks for bringing Champ for Alex."

"No problem. I'll get him out in just a minute." She patted Belle's flank as she noticed Kayla's outfit. "You look beautiful, girlie."

"Thanks. I thought I'd wear the baby blue shirt today. I like the way it looks with my gray hat." Kayla turned to look up the street. "Oh, there she is." She waved at Alex, who talked to Aunt Tina.

"Are you sure you've got that saddle cinched up tight?" Aunt Tina stood next to Sissy, running her hand over the shiny new leather.

"Mom. I've been riding since right after I learned to walk." Kayla turned back toward Faith.

"Hi, Alex." Faith gripped her new friend's hand. "This is Belle, my barrel horse. I've got Champ over here in the trailer. Do you want to help me unload him so he can get used to you?"

"Sure." Alex's royal blue shirt would complement Kayla's outfit so well. Once again Faith felt like a fifth wheel, even though she had always gotten compliments when she wore gold.

"Are you the Queen?" a small girl carrying a colorful poster board ran up to meet them.

"As a matter of fact, I am." Alex bent down to get on the girl's level. "I'm Alex, next year's Miss Rodeo Arkansas. What is your name?"

"I'm Gabby. I made this sign, and I will be walking in front of you when you ride in the parade."

"Perfect!" Alex held the sign, reading aloud, "'Alexandra Landry, New Miss Rodeo Arkansas.' What a great idea. Champ and I will be sure to stay back so we don't crowd you." Alex stood up. "Who's this?"

Two other girls cowered behind Gabby, each holding a sign announcing Kayla as Miss Teen Rodeo and Faith as Miss Rodeo Crossroads.

"That's Sam and Chloe. We are in gymnastics together."

"This is Faith, and that's Kayla over there. We're happy y'all are here today."

Faith smiled. Alex was such a natural. She would be a great Miss Rodeo Arkansas when her reign officially kicked off in January.

Trucks and trailers formed a line behind them on Crossroads' main street. O.D. Billings stood next to John K's newly painted truck, talking to him quietly. John K. paced from the front of the truck to the back as Alex unloaded Champ and removed his leg wraps. O.D. spread his hands apart and stomped towards Faith.

"That brother of mine," O.D. grumbled.

"What's the problem?" Faith checked Champ's cinch.

"He says he's not driving Old Greenie in the parade. Something about not being a hero." O.D. tipped his black hat back. "I don't have time for this. I've got to go pull the cheerleader's float. There's a Boy Scout who is supposed to ride in the bed of the truck with a sign introducing John K. This is such a disaster."

"You go take care of the cheerleaders." Out of the corner of her eye, she saw Aunt Tina rubbing Belle's neck and talking to her soothingly as Kayla and Alex chatted nearby. "I have an idea."

O.D. shrugged and headed back toward Main Street.

"Here you go, Alex. Champ is ready." She spoke softly to Aunt Tina. "You'd like to ride along with these girls today, right?"

"Of course." Tina nodded.

"How about you trail along behind on Belle. I'll find another ride." She waved at Chloe. "Come on, my friend."

"Hey!" Faith jogged nearer to John K. as he stood by the driver's side of his truck with his hands in his back pockets.

"I need a big favor." Would he go for this crazy idea? "We

came up one horse short. Would you mind if I ride with you in Old Greenie? Chloe here is supposed to hold a sign to tell folks who I am. Maybe she could sit in the bed of the truck if she promises to be safe?"

Chloe adopted her best sad puppy dog look as if they had rehearsed this.

Faith's stomach trembled. If he refused, what was Plan B?

"Sure, why not?" John K. threw his hands in the air. "Too hard to get out of this traffic anyway. I might as well go down Main Street."

"Hi. I'm Carson. I'm supposed to ..." A Boy Scout with a very patriotic looking sign stood next to Chloe.

"Hi, Carson. Why don't you climb up here with Chloe? You'll hold your sign on the driver's side, and Chloe will be next to me on the other side." Faith directed the kids into position, then walked around to open the passenger side door.

"Your truck looks great." She ran her hand over the new leather upholstery.

"Way different than I expected." John K. looked straight ahead, moving into place as the parade got underway.

"I appreciate this. Aunt Tina wanted to ride with Kayla, so I had to come up with something fast. I can't wait to see what your grandpa and Cody think when we drive by Pleasant Oaks."

"They'll be surprised. Greenie looks pretty classy."

Did he mean that? Maybe the makeover wasn't such a bad idea.

"What's this, now? Can't we just get going?" John K. stopped as a policeman waved to the high school band's drum major. The young man dressed in a crisp white uniform whistled to his followers, and the Marching Crossroads Coyotes executed a well-practiced maneuver to join the moving parade directly in front of John K.'s truck.

Faith looked behind her, where Alex and Kayla had stopped side by side. Gabby and Sam held their sparkly signs proudly, waiting to resume their marching. In the back of John K.'s truck, Carson and Chloe stopped their waving for a moment.

"We get to follow the band?" John K. tapped on his steering wheel.

"They didn't want to get behind the horses." Faith laughed. Tension seethed from the driver's seat.

"I just want this parade over with." He leaned out the driver's side window.

"Is it so bad to let everyone give you some kudos?" How could she help him get through this?

They were both silent until the band was far enough ahead, and the policeman motioned him back into traffic.

"There were friends of mine who didn't come home. Some of those who did are minus an arm or a leg." He sighed. "Those are the heroes."

Faith bit back her response. Nothing in her own life gave her the right to judge how he felt.

The band finished the school's fight song. The drum major tweeted his whistle and the drums played a new cadence. Brass instruments boomed out the opening of Stars and Stripes Forever, and the school's band picked up their pace. The crowd standing on either side clapped and cheered.

"Look!" Faith pointed. In front of the nursing and rehab home, John K.'s grandpa stood tall, saluting as they passed. Next to him, his legs covered with a beige blanket, Cody waved from his wheelchair.

"Can you drive a stick shift?" John K. rushed the words.

"Sure. I've driven every truck and piece of equipment on our ranch." What a strange question.

"Okay, then. Take over." John K. stopped the truck, opened the driver's side door, and jumped to the ground. He ran to the left side of the street, passing the last few rows of band members before dodging into the crowd.

"Oh for the love of ..." Faith slid behind the steering wheel, pressing down on the clutch to shift into first gear.

"Miss Faith?" Chloe had a desperate tone in her voice.

"Everything's fine. You and Carson just keep waving." She looked to the left side of the road. Had John K. decided to stand with his grandpa and his brother? There was no sign of him in the crowd or in front of the home. Nothing to do now but keep driving. Just wait until this crazy man was within earshot again.

24

"Carson, isn't that your Boy Scout Troop?" Faith pointed toward the five young men in uniform standing in a group next to Hope's truck.

"Yes, Ma'am. But I was supposed to give this sign to Mr. Billings." Carson handed the patriotic poster board to her.

"We'll just put it in his truck. Thanks for your hard work today." She tucked the poster under one arm and shook his hand with the other one.

"Here's yours." Chloe offered the 'Miss Crossroads Rodeo' sign to Faith.

"That is so beautiful." Faith held it at arm's length. "But I'll be going away to school soon, and I won't have a place for this. Would you like to keep it?"

Chloe smiled. "Yes, ma'am. Thank you." She skipped over to wait for Alex and Kayla to dismount.

"Miss Alex, could I have your autograph? You too, Miss Kayla."

Faith laughed. She didn't remember always having a

sharpie in her back pocket when she was Chloe's age. That girl did come prepared.

She scanned the crowd milling around the parade's breaking up point. Where had John K. gone? What would she do with his truck?

"Thanks again for allowing me to get to know Champ." Alex led the horse to stand next to Faith. "He's a real gem."

"Yeah. He's a pretty great guy." Faith patted the bay's neck. "Ready to unsaddle and load up, fella?"

"I'll take care of Belle for you." Aunt Tina began removing Belle's saddle.

A breeze ruffled the horse's tails as they stood, waiting for direction from Faith. Appetizing smells drifted in from the food trucks parked near the route. No time for food, though. She'd have to get the horses into their trailer and then decide where to leave John K's truck keys.

What had gotten into him today? She'd always thought of him as reliable. Why was driving in a parade so much harder for him than changing a tire on the freeway in the pouring rain? Would he really abandon Old Greenie after waiting so long to drive it?

"Hey," Kayla strolled up with Sissy. "What's going on? Why did John K. bail on you?"

"The question of the day." Faith removed her fancy black hat and placed it behind the seat of her truck. "I fully intend to ask him when I see him next. For now, I just need to get these horses home."

"Thanks again for bringing Champ." Alex stood next to Faith. "I hope I see you sometimes when I have an appearance around here."

"You're going to be a great queen. That part about me standing ready to fill in doesn't worry me at all." No, Alex wasn't like another person she knew who enjoyed skipping out on responsibilities.

"Yeah." Kayla grabbed her horse's halter. "Let's go get ready, Sissy."

"Should be a great year. Good luck in nursing school. See ya!" Alex ran toward a waiting pickup truck.

Faith stowed Champ's saddle and brushed him gently before wrapping his legs.

"Hey!" Hope ran up behind her. "I can take over for you. And Dad's here too."

"I'm okay." Faith turned toward John K.'s truck again. Why was everyone showing up right now except the one person she wanted to talk to? "You know, I could use some help. I need to find John K."

"Kayla told me he left in the middle of the parade?" Hope crouched to wrap Belle's legs.

"Lovely, right?" Faith tossed his truck keys up and caught them. "Should I just give these to O.D.?"

"Why don't you drive the parade route again and see if you can find him." Hope opened the back door of the horse trailer.

"Okay. I'll be back in just a minute to drive these guys home." Faith walked toward the vintage truck waiting patiently nearby.

"Don't forget, lunch at our house. We haven't had a proper open house since we moved in. O.D.'s mom and his Aunt Candace have been cooking all morning." Hope patted Champ, prompting him to enter the trailer.

"I promise I won't be gone more than two minutes. If I don't find him, I'll just lock his truck and give the keys to the nearest Billings Boy I find." Faith jogged over and opened the door. Even after all of the remodeling, it greeted her with a distinctive squeak. She could see why John K. was so attached to this old gem.

John K. stood next to the pharmacy at the end of Main Street. There was still a lot of activity at the end of the parade route. How could he explain to anyone what had just happened when he didn't understand it himself?

If only the band hadn't played that Sousa March. He and his mom shared the handicap of getting emotional during that song. Even without knowing the words, it always stirred his heart and brought memories of waving flags and men wearing uniforms.

Then, when Grandpa Dee saluted, and Cody waved with the same look of pride he'd sported since they were little kids, it was just too much. He didn't deserve any of that.

That was no excuse. No matter how emotional he felt, he shouldn't have left Faith to drive his truck through the rest of the parade. She must think he was some kind of maniac.

He owed her an explanation. But he wanted to provide it without going through several other unconcerned people on the way. He slid into the alley behind the movie theater and trudged toward the gravel lot near the railroad tracks.

Wait. Was that Old Greenie's motor he heard? Was Faith driving off without him? Well, he certainly deserved that after everything.

She drove by him on the opposite side of the street, then turned left. She must have seen him. Okay, time to face the music. He stopped where he was and waited for her to glide into a parallel parking spot.

"You looking for your truck?" She turned off the engine and walked around the front of the vehicle with his keys in her hand.

"You're doing a fine job driving it." John K. opened the passenger door and slid in.

"What makes you think I will give you a ride?" She stood outside the window, holding the keys in his direction.

"Because you have much better manners than I do." He hadn't pulled out this silly sheepish grin since way before he graduated high school.

"Okay. I need to go get *my* truck anyway." She returned to the driver's seat and started the truck's engine.

"I am sorry. I'm a total heel." The less he said the better.

"I won't argue much." She kept her eyes straight ahead. "But I'm sure there is more to it than that."

"So much more. If you have some time, I'd like to fill you in." He wouldn't blame her if she never talked or listened to him again.

"How about you come up to Hope and O.D.'s for lunch? Just Billings and Caldwells, not a lot of extra folks. I listen better after I get some nourishment." She glanced his way and smiled. That was a good sign.

"Mom invited me to do that too." So many people. Either he would have a lot of questions to answer, or he would be surrounded by uncomfortable silence. "You know, I think I'll just grab something at a taco truck and then go check in with Grandpa Dee and Cody."

"Okay. No problem." Faith stopped the truck next to her horse trailer. Champ and Belle were already loaded, and Champ had assumed his role as lookout from the small window on the passenger side of the rig.

"I'll call you later. Okay?" John K. opened the passenger door and walked around the truck.

"Sure. Tell your grandpa he looked extra sharp today."

How did she still smell like roses after driving his non-airconditioned truck all morning? He looked into her shining blue eyes for a second longer than he should have. Did he see a glimmer of understanding there? Could he find the words to explain his totally erratic behavior today?

"I will. See ya later." He opened the driver's side door and sat behind the new leather steering wheel. Processing everything that had happened today would not be easy.

Faith walked to her truck, stopping to peek inside the horse trailer before opening the driver's side door to get in. Hope waved at him from her pickup parked nearby.

What a day. Maybe Grandpa Dee could help him put it all in perspective.

"I love the way you can see our side of the valley from your kitchen window." Faith rinsed Hope's plate before placing it in the dishwasher.

"We had to add that window. I don't think O.D.'s Grandma was as obsessed with having a view over the kitchen sink as I am."

"Maybe his grandpa did the dishes." Faith laughed. "But, seriously, sister. This house is perfect. I know y'all have worked hard on it.

"Mostly O.D." Hope wiped the granite countertop with a wet rag. "It probably won't be our forever home. There are only two bedrooms, and we'd like to have kids someday."

"You'll figure it out." Faith walked to the side of the house that faced the concrete patio. "I need to go find Felicia and Candace to thank them for all of this great food. I should have just eaten a salad today, but the ribs and trimmings were terrific."

"Dad smoked the ribs down at our house. I think Candace did some of the cooking down there today too." Hope smiled.

"I think it is so cool they are spending time together." Faith poured herself another glass of tea.

"Me too. He's been so different since Mom died. Then, when the rodeo ended, I wasn't sure what he would do." Hope stood next to her at the window.

"We've all had adjustments to make. It's not easy for any of us to figure out what comes next." Except Hope. Apparently getting together with O.D. had been great for her. Faith kept that thought to herself. No way to bring it up without sounding jealous of her sister's happiness.

"Speaking of adjusting, did you ever find out what was up with John K. today?" Hope asked.

"I guess that would be for him to explain. I couldn't begin to guess." Faith peered back out toward the valley. She had thought of nothing else all afternoon. Hopefully, he would have some sort of answer for all of them soon.

"Hope, have you seen the aluminum containers I brought the baked beans in?" The screened door in the kitchen bounced closed with a *thwack* as O.D. and John K.'s mom came inside with an armload of trash.

"They're over here." Hope retrieved the two pans resting on towels near her sink. "I washed them."

"I'm so glad God finally sent me a daughter." Felicia hugged Hope.

"I don't think she enjoyed cleaning up this much when we were kids." Faith turned away from the window.

"Well, this sister of yours is a keeper for sure." Felicia picked up the pans and found the plastic lids next to the refrigerator.

"Here's the rest of the ribs." Candace brought a plate in and set it down.

"I thought I'd fix up a plate for Cody. Faith, I guess it's okay to take food into Pleasant Oaks, right?"

"People do it all the time. Are you going down there now?" Maybe John K. was still there.

"What about Dad?" Candace started another to-go plate.

"I'm not sure his teeth will handle the ribs. Better go heavy on the baked beans and potato salad for him."

Faith walked outside to stand under the new pergola O.D. had built on the wooden platform at the edge of the yard. She took a long deep breath, absorbing the peace of the valley below them. Was John K. feeling better, or did the episode at the parade still have him on edge?

"Hey!" Kayla jogged up to give her a hug. "Hasn't this been the best day ever?"

"Better than when you won Miss Teen Rodeo?" Faith laughed.

"I don't know. It might be. Riding down main street with that tiara attached to my hat. Pretty cool. Even though Mom was riding right behind us." Kayla shook her head.

"Hey, your mom is so proud of you. Be grateful she gets to share in the excitement." Faith reached for Kayla's hand.

"I know, Lainie. I'm sorry. Your mom would have been right in the big middle of the parade today too." Kayla hugged her, then raised her finger in the air. "Did you notice the television cameras at the review stand? I think they may have televised it live. I saw that Ty Porter and some other guy from the radio station too. We were big news."

Faith realized she hadn't thought about Ty once today.

"I guess it doesn't take much to be big news in a small town." She must have been so upset with John K.'s actions she didn't notice anything else. Just as well.

"So are you and John K. Billings an item now?" Kayla teased.

"I don't know. I think he just needs a friend." He certainly needed to talk to someone.

"He couldn't find a better friend than my cousin." Kayla winked at her. "I've gotta go. There's a fireworks show tonight, don't forget."

"Yeah. Have fun, Gracie." She managed to peck Kayla's cheek before her cousin ran toward her mom's Cadillac.

"Hey, Junior." She waved at her brother, who was admiring the newly refurbished barn. "Tell Dad I'm going back to town. See you later."

She jogged out to the baby blue truck and jumped in. Maybe she needed to check in at work to see how the residents liked the parade. Besides, she might find out how John K. was faring.

———

"So, you are okay with staying at this place for a while?" John K. settled on a loveseat next to Cody's wheelchair.

"It's just temporary. Hasn't been so bad since they moved my new roommate in." Cody used the remote to switch the TV channel to a baseball game.

"Mom said it's been good for Grandpa Dee too." Their grandpa snored softly on the bed across the room. "Won't we wake him up?"

"Nah. He'll be out for a bit. The parade wore him out." Cody adjusted the blanket around his legs. "I'll kind of miss seeing him every day when I go home."

"Any idea when that will be?" His little brother was handling these changes much more easily than he had figured.

"Now that Dad has the adaptations ready at home, I can leave as soon as I can handle stuff like moving from this chair to the bed, and take care of bathroom stuff on my own." Cody's voice dropped. "Maybe by the end of next week."

"Hey, terrific. But what about physical therapy?" John K.

stretched his sore ankle. For some reason, walking around after the parade had aggravated it today. Even more than the run up the hill yesterday.

"Well, there is that. Hey, let's go down to the room they do it in. I'll show you." Cody waved John K. off and propelled the manual chair with his own hands. "This is something else I've got to get better at."

"Okay. Lead on." John K. trailed behind Cody as they passed rooms with cheerful wreaths and signs on the doors. Antiseptic smells barely covered the unpleasantness wafting out of a few of the rooms.

"Where you headed, young man?" A nurse in bright pink scrubs stood in front of Cody.

"Cheyenne. I hear they have some kind of rodeo or something."

"Can't you control your little brother?" She stood aside and smiled at John K.

"No, ma'am. Stopped trying years ago."

Cody performed a sweeping left turn and continued down the next hallway.

"Here we are." Cody moved to the right as John K. entered the long room with a set of double bars dominating the center. A series of padded examining tables lined one wall, and a bank of devices with pull-down bars of several types stood on the other one.

"Hey. This looks pretty good." John K. walked to the bars. "Is this where they help you walk?"

"I just make a good attempt every day. Some of the girl therapists are kind of cute, and I hate to disappoint them. I spend most of my time over here, though." Cody navigated to the bars and reached down for a medicine ball. "This builds upper body strength." He held the ball over his head, then moved it down to the right, twisting his body to face John K.

Then he raised it over his head again, and back down on the other side.

"Hey. Great. That's how you're getting so fast with the chair." John K. picked up a resistance band. "I used these on my ankle before I came back home."

"How come you're not still doing PT?" Cody set the medicine ball down on the bench beside him.

"I guess I could." But that would require telling someone the whole story about his injury.

"There you are." The nurse dressed in pink appeared in the doorway. "Cody, you have more company in the dining room."

"Ha, ha! Mom texted me. She's bringing ribs!" Cody blazed past and headed down the hallway again. The nurse smiled at John K. as they followed.

"Hey Mom." John K. hugged her. "You brought some leftovers?"

"Yeah. Might as well share with your brother. There's plenty for you and Grandpa Dee too." She reached around his waist, turning to watch Cody position himself at the table.

"No, I'm good." John K. needed to get out into the fresh air. Short visits inside this place were plenty for him.

"Hey, buddy. Enjoy." He patted Cody's shoulder. "I'll see you again. Try not to give the staff too much grief, okay?"

"Who me?" Cody wiped his chin with a cloth napkin. "See you, bro."

John K. entered the four-digit code of the day into the keypad near the door and walked out to the covered porch. The musky smell of the blossoms in the hanging basket tickled his nose. He pulled his truck keys out of his pocket.

"Hey." Faith stepped down from her truck parked next to his in the parking lot. "How's your grandpa?"

"Asleep. I guess they'll wake him for supper." He had promised to call her. Was he ready to talk about today?

"I was hoping to run into you." Faith stepped closer.

"Are you coming to work?"

"Not until 11:00 tonight. I need to go home and take a nap myself." She looked down at her hands.

"I guess I need to get up to the cabin to see how much work they've gotten done today. Brad and his crew have been at it six days a week. He didn't have the words to explain yet. "Are you still up for our road trip on Wednesday?"

"Yeah. I guess." She backed up against the side of her truck.

"Okay. I'll pick you up at your house about 7:30 Wednesday. See you then, okay?" He reached out to touch her hand. He wouldn't blame her if she changed her mind between now and then. Would his feeble excuses be worth the wait?

You're working, right?

Faith read the text that popped up on her phone. She must have forgotten to turn the phone off today. Who texted at 2:00 a.m.? John K. Billings, that's who.

Yes.

How are my family members?

Your brother is sound asleep, but your grandpa napped too late this afternoon. Wide awake.

Do you allow visitors 24/7?

We don't publicize it, but yeah.

Was he really wanting to come into town to visit?

It will take about 30 minutes.

I will watch for you. Turning my phone off now.

She walked out to the front lobby. John K's Grandpa Dee sat in front of the television, flipping from one home shopping network to another, with the volume on the lowest setting. He wasn't bothering anyone out here. Even the birdcage in the lobby was covered so the feathered occupants could rest. Would he be interested in talking with his crazy grandson at this time of night?

Somehow, she had a feeling it might be exactly what they both needed.

25

"Faith, would you stick your head in at Mrs. Hale's room —I can see her light from here." The charge nurse pointed down the east hallway as Faith came out of the west one.

"Sure. No problem." She caught a glimpse of John K. sitting near his grandpa on the couch in the lobby. Not a lot of talking going on right now, but they both seemed comfortable.

"You okay, Mrs. Hale?" She stepped inside the room, speaking just above a whisper.

"Yes, sweetie. Just came back from the bathroom. Thought I might read a little so I can go back to sleep." The large lady scooted across the tile floor in her slippers and perched on the side of the bed.

"No problem. Since you don't have a roommate right now, you won't bother anyone. Can you reach that lamp from your bed?" Faith pulled the lamp closer. Mrs. Hale's daughter had told her this lamp had been on her mother's nightstand as far back as she could remember. Comforts of home made such a difference.

"Of course, that's better than the overhead light." Mrs. Hale struggled to cover her legs.

"Goodnight." Faith tucked the blankets around her and switched off the overhead light as she returned to the hallway.

"Everything okay?" The charge nurse stood when Faith returned.

"She's fine."

Faith walked over to a chair in front of John K.

"Should we take him back to his room?" He sat up straighter, settling the sleeping Grandpa Dee on his shoulder.

"I don't know. He'll wake up, and probably disturb Cody in the process. Here, I will help lean him the other way." Faith found a bed pillow that had been left in the lobby and propped the slightly built man away from John K.

"He seemed happy for a visit, but I'm not sure he knows who I am." John K. patted his grandpa's shoulder.

"You know, you will have to get used to that." Faith said. "It will be enough to keep him secure and comfortable."

"Makes me feel better being here too." His eyes met her in the dimness. "Got a minute to talk?"

"Looks that way." Faith pulled a chair closer.

"There was no excuse for me leaving you in the lurch during the parade today." He smoothed his blue jeans with his hand.

"It was a little unexpected. I don't think you were too excited about participating to begin with." She needed to let him do the talking.

"Nope. I keep telling people I'm not a hero, but they won't listen."

"Listening." She reminded him.

Headlights flashed through the front window as a car turned around in the parking lot.

"It was just too much. The patriotic music, the flags. This

guy saluting as we passed." John K. stopped for a moment, turning his head toward his grandpa.

"That day when I was injured. There was nothing heroic about what happened. The truck in front of the one I drove hit an IED. The explosion threw me and my buddy out of our truck too. I must have hit my head. When I came to, there were screams, and more explosions. I guess we were being fired on. I should have used my weapon, I should have ..."

Faith's hand covered her mouth. She held herself still, afraid to make any noise.

"All I did was run. My left leg hurt so bad. Like nothing I'd ever felt. But I ran. I just kept going and going. Somehow, I got behind whoever was firing, and they didn't see me. I found an old shack and hid there."

Faith reached out to touch his knee. "I'm glad you survived."

"Yeah, yeah. But don't you see? They classified me as missing in action until they found me. But I wasn't MIA. I was a deserter! I ran!"

He stood and walked toward the door. Faith followed, placing her hand on his shoulder. When he turned to face her, the porch lights reflected the tears in his eyes.

"So that's what I still do when things get tough. I run."

"Running makes me feel better too." Grandpa Dee's voice echoed from the couch.

Faith stumbled backwards, bumping into a nearby armchair.

John K. turned to walk back to the couch and helped his grandpa to his feet.

"Yeah. I remember that. Sometimes, you'd run down from your house to ours for breakfast." John K.'s voice shook.

"After your grandma had already fed me. Can't have too

many breakfasts." Grandpa Dee's steps were only slightly unsteady as he headed down the hallway to his room.

"I'll help him get back in bed." John K. followed, a step or two behind.

Faith sank into the couch. What a night this had been. She was more certain than ever that she had no right to judge John K.'s behavior, or any other veteran's for that matter. She had seen the long faces some of her patients wore, the sadness that often lived in their eyes. Their experiences while serving could scar them for the rest of their lives.

She closed her eyes for a moment. *Lord, thank You for putting me in this spot tonight. I hope I can continue to help John K. and his grandpa as they deal with their memories.*

"Everything all right out here?" The charge nurse walked out from the desk. "Where are Mr. Tollett and his visitor?"

"Mr. Tollett went back to bed. I think his grandson will be leaving in just a minute. Thanks for allowing them to visit, even though it's such an odd time." Faith watched John K. trail his grandpa into the room.

"We have to be a little flexible. I've talked to the director, and she agrees. These are adults we are serving. Making them adhere to our schedule is not always necessary."

Faith nodded. "Yes, ma'am. That's why I love working here. The patients are treated with respect. I guess I need to take another walk down the hallways." Faith smiled as she passed the spot where John K. and his grandpa had been sitting. Respect. Those two certainly displayed respect for each other. She turned to another hallway with a warm sensation growing in her stomach.

"Thanks again for letting me visit tonight." John K. stood at the front desk talking to the charge nurse when Faith returned.

"You're welcome. We love the families who care so much about our residents." The nurse nodded at him.

Faith walked over to the front door and punched in the new code for today.

"We still on for Wednesday?" John K. touched her hand as she pushed the door open.

"Of course. See you bright and early." Faith stood aside so he could exit. "Be safe."

"You do the same. Good night." The corners of his mouth lifted in a slight smile before he turned to walk out to his old truck.

John K. rolled over to watch the light growing brighter outside the camper window. He should be running, but maybe his ankle needed the rest today. The few hours after he returned from Pleasant Oaks had been some of the best sleep he'd had in a long time.

He kept thinking about Faith's response or the lack of response to his revelation last night. No empty platitudes about how he had done his duty or how he was still a hero. Her silence had been laced with understanding and respect. How much had Grandpa Dee heard? Somehow, that didn't matter. He was the first person John K. wanted to share his story with anyway.

He rolled over and planted his feet on the floor, remembering not to stand up completely. No use banging his head on the low ceiling in this trailer. He'd need to check out the cabin today. Mac and Betty would probably want to take the grandkids out in this trailer again soon.

Still coming to church with us?

He'd been happy to accept Betty's invitation to join them

today. Sharing his story with Faith had given him confidence to reconcile things with God too.

Sure. I'll follow y'all. Almost ready.

He pulled on his best blue jeans and rescued his cowboy boots from the teeny closet. Good news, there was a long-sleeved semi-dressy shirt in there too.

He stepped in front of the bathroom mirror. No time for a shave. Maybe Mac's church was okay with the stubbly cowboy look.

It took a minute to reach the cabin with his gimpy leg. Steps to the porch were done, roof was complete. Yes, he should be able to move in. The contractors would just have to work around him for a bit.

God, thanks for sending sunshine to warm my heart, and good friends to walk with me. You are good all the time, but this morning, life looks a little better.

26

Faith sat on Mom's favorite swing, rocking gently. Songbirds drowned out the crowing rooster behind the barn. Fleecy clouds strolled past. The sky changed from a rosy pink to blue. Getting up early wasn't so bad. A whiff of the rose bush Dad had planted near the porch brought a flood of memories of mornings with her mom.

There hadn't been many peaceful times like this. Mom was usually busy getting them all off to school or summertime activities, but there had been a few. Someday, maybe her shifts at Pleasant Oaks would allow more time to enjoy quiet mornings.

She scanned email on her phone. Nothing from the university where she would finish her degree this fall. At this point, maybe no news was good news.

She pulled up her camera and turned it around for a quick survey of her early morning face. Sort of strange to try to impress the oldest son of the family who had lived just over the hill from them for so long. If John K. had asked her for a date in high school, she would have melted into a nervous puddle on the spot. Today, a more calm, peaceful feeling filled her heart. He trusted her enough to share a huge burden last weekend. The least she could do was go along with whatever he had planned.

"Where you going today?" Junior walked out the front door with a banana skin draped over his hand.

"I don't know. John K. said he wanted to show me I could have big city experiences without leaving Arkansas." Faith had researched possibilities for days, but none of them would have to start at 7:30 in the morning.

"Remember, he's just a Billings Boy after all. Don't expect too much." Junior jumped off the porch and headed toward the barn.

"Whatever. You just mind Junior's business, okay?" She shouted after him. Her stomach squirmed a little. Maybe she should have eaten eggs and bacon with Dad.

Rumbling gravel and a low, steady engine noise brought her attention to the end of their road. John K's freshly painted army green truck came into view. Sunlight glinted off the back of the side mirrors. She smiled and stood up, opening the front door.

"We're leaving, Dad. It may be close to supper time when we get back," she said.

"Be careful, princess. Tell John K. I said 'Hey.'" Dad walked through the living room, wiping his hands on a kitchen towel.

John K. executed a sweeping turn in the driveway and waved at her dad as he pointed the truck back toward the main road. He jumped out of the driver's side and ran around to open Faith's door.

"Thanks!" Faith stepped up and settled herself in the passenger seat.

"You ready for an adventure?" John K. started the truck and proceeded up the long gravel driveway.

"Sure." Faith turned to look out the window.

"We have quite a drive, and we're not taking the freeway. So, get settled. I hope you're not starving because the place I'm headed for doesn't open till 10:00." He turned out onto the main highway.

"I'm fine. I've got a protein bar in my bag if I need it. I do most of the cooking at our house but Junior is the real eater."

Faith was grateful for the sunshine today. This long trip of John K.'s would not be much fun if the rain returned.

"So, you said something about big city experiences, but we're not taking the freeway?" She'd grown up driving all over these hills but she didn't know what to expect today. If only he'd give her a clue.

"I guess that was a little misleading." John K. laughed. "What I meant was, you can get the best of both worlds here in your home state. Why would you ever want to leave?"

This coming from a guy who had seen more of the world than she would ever dream of.

"Why did you join the Army then?"

"Well, that's a fair question. I guess you could say I didn't join the military to travel. I just wanted to make a difference. I'd be happy doing that right here if there was a need."

The truck bounced and twisted on a blacktopped highway headed north. Traffic behind them had no choice but to twist and turn at Old Greenie's pace since there was no safe place to pass.

"So, why aren't you in the Army Reserve? They do a lot of disaster relief and that sort of thing." Faith's hair blew in the breeze. Did his truck have air conditioning?

John K. was quiet for a long moment. Had she opened a wound with her question?

"Well. It sort of relates to the conversation we had at

Pleasant Oaks last weekend. To join up again, I'd have to explain the circumstances of my leaving the army."

"You were wounded. Doesn't that count?" This whole situation had her confused.

"Sure it does. There's just a lot to sort through." John K. accelerated to pass a slow-moving tractor on a rare straight stretch. "But you didn't answer my question. You talk about going to a big city for school. Why do you want to do that?"

"I want the best education. I think that only happens far from here. Besides, you've had your adventure. I haven't had mine." What business was it of his where she went to school anyway?

"Enter the reason for today's road trip. There is more to your home state than you realize."

"So you've said. I just hope this old truck gets us there soon." Faith jabbed him with her elbow.

"Hey, Old Greenie is every bit as dependable as the monsters you and the rest of the community drive. Just who had to be rescued on the side of a busy freeway in a rainstorm?" He poked her arm.

"Touché." She giggled.

They talked and laughed as the truck glided around curves and up hills on the way to whatever destination John K. had in mind. Her stomach growled. She might settle for the next truck stop that served sausage biscuits soon.

"I'm about to break the freeway rule. This one has some of the best views this side of heaven." John K. accelerated onto the entrance ramp to Interstate 49 and headed toward Fayetteville.

"Agreed." The wide road wound its way up and over long, sweeping bridges. Below them, valleys full of green treetops stretched as far as she could see. The blue sky provided the perfect backdrop. Even the puffy clouds played a part in the perfect scene. “God is really showing off today.”

“Yes, ma’am. Freeways are not always bad.” John K. slowed as they reached a tunnel through the mountains. “This is a big deal for our small state. Mr. Hopper should be proud to have his name on this feat of engineering.”

Faith’s eyes adjusted to the dimness of the overhead lights just as they pushed into the sunshine at the other end. She had been here before, on the way to football games, but hadn’t considered how amazing it was.

John K. stayed in the right lane, and soon exited to the older, narrower highway.

“We’ll be there just in time. Might even be the first customers.”

“So, where exactly are we headed? I’m not a total stranger to Northwest Arkansas.” She couldn’t wait any longer. Might as well just ask.

“I’ll give you a clue. If this little town was good enough for one of the smartest entrepreneurs in the world, it’s good enough for us.”

“Bentonville!” Faith laughed. Not exactly a big city, but it had certainly grown in the last few years. “But where exactly?”

“Trust me.”

She caught a glimmer of that rare smile again. She sighed and leaned back against the leather seat. Trust was a reassuring feeling.

“Well, what do you think” John K. gestured at the food in front of Faith.

“You’re right. I never imagined eating crepes in Bentonville, Arkansas.” Faith leaned back in the iron chair on the patio of the quaint and trendy restaurant. "They're not what I pictured. I guess I thought they were just extra thin pancakes."

"I thought you'd enjoy this. You can get your fill of veggies, and I get some ham and cheese, all wrapped up and ready to eat." John K. took a supersized bite of the buckwheat crepe. He'd have to be sure to tell his buddy Sam that this place was a hit.

"Strawberries and cream?" A waitress brought the surprise he'd ordered to their table. It was the same size as the ham and cheese crepe he'd just consumed. Hopefully, Faith would want to share it.

"Thanks! Do you need more coffee, Faith?"

She waved off the waitress.

"I'm good, thanks." She shook her finger in his direction. "Dessert for breakfast?"

"Brunch." He moved the cone-shaped serving dish closer to her. "When in Paris, do as the Parisians do."

"But I've been to Paris. Right now, we should do as the Bentonvillians do." Her laughter filled the little courtyard.

"Eat up, mademoiselle. More adventure awaits."

Eyes as blue as the sky twinkled as she licked whipped cream off her fingertips.

Yes, totally worth the trip.

Faith hurried to catch up to John K. inside the Crystal Bridges Art Museum.

"We walked through that gallery a little too fast." Faith stopped to look at a modern sculpture.

"Sorry." John K. stepped back in her direction. "Take your time. I might like to see some of those oil paintings up ahead."

"Our family has talked about coming here for years." Faith stood next to a wall full of what looked like burned wood. "It takes a bit to absorb it all."

"Surprisingly, our bunch has come here more than once." John K. sat on a bench behind her. "I guess Dad learned to compromise with Mom since we spend so much time at Razorbacks games."

"Hey. I've got an idea." Maybe he was tired of lagging behind with her. "Hand me your phone."

"Huh?" He pulled it out of his pocket.

"Trust me." It felt good to turn his advice back on him. She checked the apps on his cell and made sure that he would be able to receive a locator pin from her.

"Now." She handed the phone back to him. "You can see where I am, and I can see where you are at all times. If you want to go to the snack bar or even outside, I will be fine. We'll catch up again in a few minutes."

"O-kay."

Was he reluctant to share with her? Maybe this wasn't a good idea.

"You can always turn it off if you need privacy."

This might be a big change for someone in the habit of running away.

"No. That's fine." He put the phone back in his pocket and squeezed her hand. "Enjoy yourself. I may check out the new trail they built out by the parking area."

Faith wandered quietly for a while longer. John K.'s point about big city culture in a small town was certainly true. She had never imagined that a place as amazing as Crystal Bridges existed here in Arkansas. Besides, who knew a very masculine military type would appreciate the finer things in life? There was a lot more to this oldest Billings boy than met the eye. Not that what met the eye was that bad, either.

She smiled as she stood in front of her favorite painting one more time. For some reason, this portrait of an American Indian man tenderly reaching to touch a water lily pushed all the right buttons for Faith. He carried a large bird he had hunted on his back. Maybe a swan? He crouched and extended his hand toward the beautiful blossom. He seemed to recognize that even with the harshness of surviving in this world, there were precious moments to spend just appreciating God's creation. Just the reminder she needed that God was always here.

She sent John K. a text.

Ready to meet up and head out?

Sure.

His reply came quickly.

Don't say another word, let's just use these tracker things to find each other.

After leaving the elevator, she walked out to the front of the museum and spotted John K. standing under the giant silver tree that had become the trademark of this place. He lifted his hand to wave in her direction.

"Thanks for bringing me here." She stood in front of him, reaching for his hand.

"My pleasure." He pulled her closer, his arm fitting perfectly around her shoulders. "I guess we'd better head back home. It's a little warmer now than it was this morning. Greenie does have air conditioning, but you might not appreciate it."

"I'll be fine." Her face flushed. "Why won't I like it?"

"Grandpa Dee always called it 'two-fifty' air. Two windows down, fifty miles an hour. And on those curvy roads we can't always go fifty." He strode to the truck and stopped to open her side before walking around to drive. "We'll stop for gas so you can snag something cold to drink on the way home."

The miles passed quickly as they drove back to Crossroads. Faith mentioned several of her favorite exhibits at the museum and found they matched John K's fairly closely.

Blue skies gave way to dark clouds, and she rolled her window up to combat the cool breeze playing havoc with her hair.

"I knew the clear weather couldn't last all day." She peered through her side of the windshield.

"Long about August, we'll be wishing for some rainy days." John K. slowed to navigate a tight curve.

A flash of lightning was followed by a long slow rumble of thunder.

"Do you want to find a place to stop for lunch?" He asked as they neared a small town. "There is a first-class winery up here with a restaurant. Even if we don't 'indulge' they might let us sniff the cork or something."

"Sounds amazing. But maybe another time. Don't you think we'd better get closer to home before the storm hits?" Faith examined the dark sky as it roiled above them.

"Good plan. We can just drop in at Amy Lou's when we get back home. She's always got something cooking."

"I get your point about big city benefits near home. Arkansas is a great place." Faith smiled.

"And there's always Little Rock." John K. grimaced as he tightened his grip on the steering wheel.

The truck bounced and pulled hard to the right side. Faith held onto her seatbelt as the clouds released their burden of rain and John K. stopped on the side of the road.

"I don't believe this." He stared at her.

"Flat tire?"

"Ponchos are stored behind the seat. Give me a minute to get the spare out of the back."

She didn't try to contain her laughter as she reached for the door handle. She couldn't think of a better way to cap off this trip.

27

John K. stopped his truck in a space directly in front of Amy Lou's diner.

"I didn't think. You might have wanted to go home and clean up before we got here." Even though her hair had lost the majority of its bounce, he was impressed by how great she looked after their drenching on the side of the road.

"You know what?" Faith laughed. "We're among friends. If you're okay with the drowned rat look, so am I."

"You look nothing like a rat, and I don't think anyone will notice me anyway." He jumped down on the driver's side and ran around to open her door. It might help their case if it was at least raining on the Main Street of Crossroads. No such luck. The shower that had accompanied their flat tire seemed to have stayed north.

"I'm starved. I promise not to post pictures on social media." She crossed her heart before he caught her hand as she stepped off his running board.

The jangling bell on Amy Lou's door announced their arrival, but only a few heads turned to watch as they selected a booth. The lunch rush was long over, and dinner was still an hour or so away for most everyone.

"Hey. It's my favorite oldest nephew." Aunt Candace followed them to the booth. "Along with Caldwell royalty!"

"Thanks. I don't feel like a princess right now, though. I probably have mascara running all over my face." Faith sat down and checked the back of a spoon. Did she think she could see her reflection? He restrained a very unmanly giggle threatening to pop out.

"Nope. You must use the non-smear stuff. You look 'mahvelous.'" Making people feel at ease was his aunt's superpower.

"How long would it take to get a burger ready?" John K. leaned back in the wooden booth.

"I'll put a rush on it." Aunt Candace smiled. "Let's see, you like yours with a double patty, mustard and onions, no cheese, right?"

"You're good. I don't think I've ordered one since I moved up to the deer camp."

"I only memorize my favorite customers. How about you, Faith? Your usual Caesar salad? Our chicken salad sandwich is good today too." She tapped her pencil on her order pad.

"Your chicken salad is always good. On toasted wheat bread. And I'm extra hungry. John K., would you help me eat an order of cheese fries?" She returned the menu to its holder on the table.

"Always willing to help a lady in distress." He had a feeling she might eat the whole order herself, but he would never tell.

"Coming right up. Coke and sweet tea?" They both nodded.

Candace stopped at the table next to them, grabbing an empty glass for refilling.

"I had a great time today." Faith picked up a napkin to catch a leftover raindrop as it ran off the end of her nose. "But I think we are both trying to keep the local tire stores in business."

"Yeah, what's up with that? Maybe we should apply to work in a pit crew somewhere." He glanced past her as a familiar man walked in the front door. "Hey, Mac!"

"Well, looky here." Mac stood next to their booth with his wife. "I thought you were out of town today."

"We just got back." John K. stood up to shake Mac's hand. "Faith, these are my friends Mac and Betty MacDonald. They are my closest neighbors up at camp."

"Honored to meet you, young lady." Mac shook Faith's hand and motioned to John K. to sit down.

"It's very good to meet both of you." Faith responded.

"He missed you today." Betty nodded at Faith and turned to talk to John K. "He couldn't get enough volunteers to wash the trucks. He doesn't like the way I do it."

"You're my favorite helper. It's just delicate equipment is all." Mac patted Betty's shoulder. "Anyway, we got it done. Now I need a piece of pie to recover from sticker shock at the grocery store."

"Nice to meet you, Faith. We'll see you later, Mr. Billings." Betty walked past and found a table near the back of the diner.

"Get yourself a gem like that one." Mac winked as he followed his wife.

"You help him wash trucks?" Faith leaned forward to talk a little more softly.

"He drafted me for the volunteer fire department. I'm on standby during the week when most everybody else works in town somewhere."

"Yeah, I can see that. Military, fireman, you'd be great as any kind of first responder." Her sweet smile was the perfect partner for those blue eyes.

"I've got a lot to learn. Luckily, they don't have a lot of

dangerous fire calls. Mostly helping the sheriff with car accidents and putting out brush fires." He tried not to stare. He'd known this girl for years. Did her eyes shine even more with her makeup washed off?

"That's important. Right now it's the rainy season, but brush fires can get dangerous in the summertime." Faith moved to the edge of the booth. "I think I'll go check out the ladies' room before they bring our food."

He stood as she passed, then settled back on the hard bench. What a day. She had been a good sport on this big adventure. Not every day could a guy take a beautiful rodeo princess out for crepes at a French bistro and then count on her help to change his flat tire.

Faith waited in the freshly painted hallway outside the ladies' room. Amy and her family kept this little place looking nice.

"Your turn." Betty stepped out of the paneled restroom door, squeezing past her in the narrow space. "We sure do like that handsome guy of yours. It's been good to have someone besides me for Mac to talk to since he retired from the road department."

"He's not really ..." Faith stopped. No use trying to explain their relationship. Just what would she say? "Yeah, he's always been a good guy." There, that was truthful.

"Mac is trying to talk him into going to the fire academy. Our volunteer department needs a full-time trained employee, and Mac doesn't want to be the one." Betty stopped before turning the corner into the main part of the restaurant. "Yep. That boy's a good one to have around, all right." She leaned close to Faith's ear. "And easy on the eyes too." Betty laughed and hurried away, shaking her head.

The fire academy. Yes. A logical career move for John K. As long as no one called him a hero.

She caught a glimpse of herself in the mirror on the bathroom wall. Oh no. Probably would have been better if she hadn't looked. One of these days, maybe she'd have a date with John K. that didn't involve getting soaked on the side of a road.

When she returned to their booth, John K.'s aunt had placed their food on the table. Candace stood next to him, rubbing his back between his shoulders.

"This boy gets so tense." Candace laughed before bustling away.

"Only after changing a tire in a downpour." John K. smiled at Faith.

There was that smile again. So good to see. She sat down and picked up half of her chicken salad sandwich.

"So, we were discussing you being a firefighter." She bit into the sandwich, her taste buds appreciating the fine balance between roasted chicken and creamy mayo. A chunk of walnut provided crunch. The next bite brought sweetness from a whole grape.

"That's all in the talking stages." John K. used his fork to grab one of her cheese fries. "What about you? Won't you be headed back to college soon?"

"Yes. But I'm not sure where. That's not cool, since it's June, and classes start in August." She checked her phone to see if she had any more messages from colleges.

"Aren't you going to the community college?" John K. washed the fries down with a drink of his coke.

"I've learned all I can there. The associate degree gets me started, but I need to move up to RN soon, and then get accepted to a graduate program. It's a long road." It wasn't easy to explain this. Most people thought being a nurse was a clear, easy career path. It was a lot more complicated.

"From what I've seen at the nursing home, you are a natural. I know my Grandpa Dee thinks you hung the moon."

Heat rose to her cheeks.

"He is a sweetheart. I am glad you and your family come around so much. There are folks who never have visitors. It's so sad."

"I think I'm a lot like him. We both talk a good game about being independent and not needing anyone. But when it comes down to it, family is important. I missed that old guy as much as anybody when I was in the army." He pushed his plate away and looked down at his hands.

Faith finished her food quietly. She had worked at Pleasant Oaks long enough to recognize the signs. It wouldn't be much longer until John K.'s grandpa followed the path so many other residents traveled. No matter how many visitors came by, so many ended up retreating into their own world, transitioning from content to unhappy. From secure to frightened and even angry. Just bringing some brightness into their lives had become her chief goal at work.

"Cody thinks he'll go home soon." John K. reached into his back pocket for his billfold.

"Our rehab patients don't usually stay long. We're sort of a halfway house between the medical treatment at the hospital and their new situation at home. If your parents are ready for him, he probably won't stay much longer."

"I think they're ready. It won't be easy, but my mom will love having him there to fuss over. She may just drive him nuts." John K. picked up the ticket Candace had left.

"Well, my brother may be over there so much, the two of them will make *her* crazy." Faith laughed.

"Thank God for Junior." John K. reached across the table to touch her hand. "Your whole family has been a real blessing to us."

"That's what neighbors do." Neighbors. Was that how he looked at her? With her heading away to school again soon, wasn't that all she wanted? Why did that thought create such a queasy feeling in her stomach?

"Well, you ready to go home? I think I'd better go see what's up at my cabin before it gets totally dark." John K. stood up and guided her by touching her elbow as they walked toward the cash register.

That gentle touch was new. Maybe there was something brewing in his mind after all.

"I think I got spoiled by the air conditioner in the loaner truck." He broke the long silence of the ride home as he pulled up to the side of Faith's house. "I wonder if they could put one in Greenie without taking forever."

"Probably." Faith was in no hurry to leave the truck.

"Hey." His voice was quiet. He reached across the seat and held her hand. "Thanks for going on this crazy adventure today." He moved closer, his hand creeping up toward her elbow.

"I enjoyed it." Leaning in, she felt his breath on her forehead. When she looked up at him, his other hand slid behind her head, caressing her neck. With her eyes closed, the softness of his lips caressed hers. He moved back a little, and her eyes opened, meeting his with a wordless smile. "Thanks for a great day." Somebody had to say something. "Be careful driving home."

"Yeah." He paused, touching her hand again. "At least I don't think it's going to rain anymore. You take care too."

She stepped out of the passenger side, closing the door firmly. The fancy patriotic tailgate hurried away down the dirt driveway. What a day. What a day, for real.

John K. whistled as he stepped out of his truck. Mac had still not come to pull the camper away. Inside, he made a quick inspection tour. Didn't look like he'd left anything behind.

Climbing the short stairway to the porch, the ramp to his right looked like it belonged. Brad did a great job making things accessible for Cody.

Opening the front door, he walked into the still mostly bare room. If he were going to stay here, he would need to find some furniture soon. Was he going to stay? If only he could answer that question. What was his next move in life?

Dad had suggested using their account at the home improvement store to get a proper stove. He still didn't see the need. Maybe that decision should be up to Mom since she did the cooking for the family when they spent more than a night or two here.

In the mud room, the gleaming new hot water heater stood near the empty space where a washer and dryer would fit. Those should probably be the next purchases.

Outside the back door, the path that headed up to the old shack drew him. Maybe he should take a quick run. His ankle protested with a twinge, reminding him he needed to see a doctor.

Maybe sitting on the porch and watching the sunset would be better than running up the hill. Too bad there was no fridge, so no cold drink to take with him. A big sigh emerged as he settled on the steps for the nightly spectacle. The cleared driveway provided a glimpse of the nearby mountain as the sun spotlighted them before sinking behind. None of the paintings at Crystal Bridges could compete with this view.

Thanks for the peace that passes understanding, Lord. This has been a great day. The cool breeze brought in a woodsy, floral scent from somewhere nearby. Being alone out here was okay but having another special person sitting next to him on this porch would make everything perfect. Maybe someday. Maybe soon.

"Now, was that so hard?" Faith dried a plate and replaced it in the kitchen cabinet.

"Nothing tastes as good as when you cook it," Junior grumbled.

"But you ate it. No one was poisoned, and we all got full." She hung the dish towel on the rack attached to the kitchen island. "Chili dogs are easy. Open a couple of can of chili, boil some hot dogs, add pre-shredded onions and cheese. Dad worked long hard hours today, and this was a good stick-to-your-ribs meal."

"Yeah, yeah. I don't think he will be happy if you go away to school, though. We will probably keep the pizza delivery guys in town busy." Junior poured himself another glass of soda.

"Whatever works. I just won't always be here for every meal anymore. You might as well get used to it." Someday, this kid would have to grow up.

"How was your date, princess?" Dad was stationed in his favorite spot, feet propped up in his recliner.

"Great. I can't believe as much time as we've spent in Northwest Arkansas, we have never been to the Crystal Bridges Museum." Faith curled up in the corner of the couch. Dad turned the volume down on the local news channel.

"We could all use a little more culture. Just hard to work in more than a football game when we're up there. I'm glad John K. made the effort. Dave and Felicia raised some good boys." He sat back, reaching for the glass of tea that was always nearby.

"The Big River County fire department has some big news today." Tara Williams appeared on the screen.

"Hey, turn that up. I met this guy at Amy Lou's today." Faith recognized John K.'s friend Mac.

"Yes. We want to thank the voters for approving the increase in the county sales tax." Mac said. "Along with the grant we got from the state Rural Services department, our fire department will enjoy a real boost."

"You're hiring a firefighter, right?" Tara held the microphone for Mac.

"Yes, we will have two paid employees who will rotate so that we always have enough help during the week when most of our volunteers are away at work. Once we find the right people, we will send them to the fire academy to be properly trained. Makes us feel like a big-time department here in little old Big River County." Mac smiled. "The main qualification is commitment to helping our residents feel safe living in this beautiful part of Arkansas."

"Right. You heard it, folks. Firefighting is not an easy occupation, but if you have an interest, and you're willing to commit to the eight-week training course, you could have a very important job very soon. Check the KRVA website for more details on getting your application turned in. Now, back to the studio for a weather forecast."

"Well. Good for them. That's a big improvement for the folks who live out that way. I think the Billings family has a deer camp there." Dad leaned back and closed his eyes.

"Hope and I went out to there to make sure John K. was okay after his water heater exploded. It's a beautiful place."

Betty had said the fire department hoped John K. would be one of their trained employees. He'd be perfect. But it would require commitment. There wouldn't be many opportunities for road trips. Dates like the one they had today would be few and far between. That is, if he even wanted another date.

She closed her eyes, remembering how sweet John K. had acted when he'd brought her home. So different from the way Ty treated her. Ty had been aggressive and demanding, where John K. was tender and even timid.

Both Ty and John K. had lived exciting lives. Maybe John K.'s point about taking things slower made more sense. But did she want to get tied down to someone content to find a local job and stay put?

If she wanted to go away for her education, and he wanted to stay here, would that be their first and last kiss?

28

John K. leaned against what was left of the doorpost at the old shack. He stretched his left ankle out and propped it on a concrete block. The run this morning had been painful. Maybe using this "clutch foot" more lately was aggravating something. Time to put aside his stubbornness and check with the VA doctors.

Brush rattled nearby. He sat upright and his hand went instinctively to his right pocket. The cell phone wouldn't defend very well against whatever creature currently plowed through the woods.

"Oh, hey." The intruder's curly mop of blond hair poked out above the boulders. "I didn't know anyone was here."

"No problem. Just part of my morning run." John K. stood and extended his hand. Wasn't this the kid he'd met at his first brush fire? "John K. Billings."

"Thomas Jefferson Southerland. Call me T.J. Being named after a president can be weird." He hoisted his pack over his shoulder.

"Tell me about it." John K. failed to maintain his tough guy face. "My middle initial stands for Kennedy."

"No kiddin'!" His laugh rang through the pines. "Well, I'd better head on down the hill. I decided to camp up here last night after it stopped raining. You can see forever up here."

"Yep. Oh, be careful with those trash fires." Might as well get in a little dig before the kid walked away.

"I knew I remembered you." He stopped at the edge of the woods to John K.'s left. "Hey, I saw something on TV. Is the fire department looking to hire someone?"

"Yeah. Just drop by the station when you see a truck there. The chief would be happy to talk to you."

"Okay, see ya." The kid's long legs cut through the brush. He disappeared into the glare of the rising sun.

The offending ankle didn't improve on the way back down the hill. John K. walked straight through the new mudroom to the newly delivered refrigerator/freezer to grab a bag of frozen peas. Maybe fifteen minutes with this foot propped up would loosen it. Breakfast could wait since no one else was expecting it.

He had totally forgotten to check his cell phone while on top of the hill. What was Faith up to today? He pulled the phone out of his pocket and found the app she had installed at Crystal Bridges. Maybe he wouldn't know what she was doing without talking to her, but he'd always be able to locate her phone. What a crazy world.

Faith rocked the swing with her stocking feet, allowing the steam from her coffee to tickle the end of her nose. She should be sleeping, since her shift at Pleasant Oaks didn't start until 3:00 today. Staring at the ceiling as daylight crept into her bedroom did not appeal to her any more than it had when she was just a kid. Sitting here in Mom's favorite place warmed her heart, but the spot to her left seemed empty.

If Mom were here, what would she think of her road trip date with John K.?

"How did you stand riding for so many hours in that old truck of his?" That would have been the first topic of discussion. Her mom was not a patient person. These porch swing sessions were never more than fifteen or twenty minutes long.

"I don't know. I think I just enjoy how much he enjoys driving it." Faith would have explained. *"He revealed a part of himself to me that no one else sees."*

A mockingbird landed on the porch railing, practicing its latest repertoire with no regard to Faith's presence.

"Yeah, very good." She complimented the performance, startling the bird. Talking to a bird was no stranger than having a conversation in her head with her mom in heaven. Maybe she should study psychiatry in college. She'd need to figure out her own brain before analyzing anyone else.

Time to come back to the real world. She scrolled through her emails, deleting junk and special offers. She stopped on one that looked official from the University of Arkansas.

"Congratulations, you have met all requirements for admission to the J. William Fulbright College of Arts and Sciences for the fall semester."

"Whoop!" She jumped off the swing. The mockingbird that had settled in a gardenia bush flew off with a squawk, and coffee sloshed out onto her hand.

The acceptance letter was not a huge surprise. She had already completed basic nursing courses to get her associate degree and CNA license. It felt good to have an option to consider. Fayetteville was not very far away. It was familiar. After all the noise she had been making about having an adventure, would getting her undergrad so close to home seem like settling? Not really. This was an excellent program.

She sat back down and continued to look at emails. More junk. Then, what? Another one looked unusual.

"Louisiana State University is proud to extend an invitation to you to join us in beautiful Baton Rouge for the continuation of your college career this fall."

LSU and U of A in the same day? Wow! She looked out into the corral, hoping to see either Junior or Dad tending horses. Evidently, they were both dealing with cattle somewhere out of sight.

She dialed Hope's number. No answer.

CALL ME! I HAVE EXCITING NEWS.

She tapped on her phone after leaving the message. Why was no one around when she had something to share?

She glanced down at her phone and saw John K's location on the app she had installed. Why not?

"Hey!" She hardly waited for him to answer. "Are you busy?"

"Not at the moment. I'm thinking of checking the flight schedules for Dubai later on." He deadpanned.

"Dubai? Well, at least you wouldn't have to worry about getting a flat tire." Of all times for him to try his hand at comedy. "I just got some news, and I'm trying to find someone to share it with." Her phone buzzed in her hand. Hope was calling back.

"Tell me quick. I'm surprised I have a cell signal. You won the Powerball?" He laughed.

"No, I got accepted to both U of A at Fayetteville, and LSU. I got the notices this morning in my email!"

"Hey! Congratulations. They would both be crazy not to accept you. Now you have a decision to make."

"I have no idea how to decide."

"Well, I don't know if Baton Rouge has any French bistros that serve crepes. But, it's not far from beignets in New Orleans."

"Yeah. This decision will totally be based on what kind of food is available." Faith laughed. "Well, anyway, thanks for taking my call. I just needed to share with someone."

"I'm always up for hearing good news."

"And I'm not very good at keeping it to myself." But was it good news? Accepted by two colleges. Her decision had to be final soon since she had to be somewhere by the middle of August.

"Hey, sis! What's up?" Junior bounced up onto the porch. "Oh, sorry. You're on the phone." He made a point to tiptoe past her into the house.

"Sounds like you need to share your news with someone else." John K. said.

"Yeah. I guess. What about Dubai?" Had he been serious about that?

"Nah. I don't think their crepes are any good. Hey, congrats on some of your pieces starting to fall into place."

Silence. His connection must have failed. She immediately received a text message.

> Phone service comes and goes up here. Texts sometimes work better. Talk to you soon.

He was easy to talk to. After that whole "no need to leave home" speech he made yesterday, she thought he would advise her on which college to choose. But he didn't. This was her life, after all. Now, if she could just figure out what to do with it.

"I thought you'd sleep all day!" Junior slammed the door to the refrigerator as she walked inside. "Can you fry up some bacon? I can manage to do some toaster waffles, but I think I need some protein."

"Didn't you and Dad eat this morning before you went out?" When would he learn to fend for himself?

"No. He just made some coffee and put it in his thermos. Coffee. When it's already in the eighties and getting hotter." Junior poured a huge glass of orange juice.

Faith pulled out a skillet and peeled off a few slices of bacon. One thing was for certain. Whichever college she chose, she would not be living here. This family was suffering from a severe case of being spoiled. At this point, she didn't even want to share anything with Junior. He was too consumed in his toaster waffles.

When she had filled a plate with bacon, she decided to head out to the barn. Maybe Belle could use a ride this morning. She'd need to get her head cleared before the heat outside grew unbearable.

Stay with me, Lord. My brain is a mess today.

Her phone rang as she sat on the bench in the mudroom to pull her boots on.

"Did you call me?" Hope asked.

"Yes. Are you at work?" Maybe she'd drive into town instead of riding.

"Yeah. We've got a truckload of supplies to unload."

"I go to work at 3:00. Could I meet you when you break for lunch?"

"Chicken spaghetti day at Amy Lou's." Hope reminded her.

Food. Always food.

"Twelve o'clock?" Faith finished putting her boots on. She could get this ride in before lunch.

"See you then!" Hope disconnected.

Hope was happy with her job at Cedar Ridge ranch. They helped so many kids get through all kinds of issues. Her sister was super good at keeping a business rolling. They were fortunate to have her on the team.

If only Faith could snap her fingers and have all the knowledge she needed to be a nurse practitioner. She knew what her dad would say when she finally talked to him. "*Enjoy the journey, Princess. Treasure each day.*" She could treasure it better if she knew where she was headed.

The entry bell clanged as Faith opened the glass door at Amy Lou's. Hope waved from a booth about halfway back on the right.

"I ordered your tea." Hope turned off her phone and tucked it into her pocket. "Now, what's up?"

"How do you know something's up?" Faith laughed.

"It's all about what you didn't say. Not, 'hey, I need to talk.' Just 'are you at work?' Duh. It's a weekday, where would I be?" Hope put her napkin in her lap as the waitress stood nearby.

"I'll have a Caesar salad with chicken." Faith replaced the menu in its holder on the table.

"Your special, please." Hope smiled at the server. "Thanks so much."

"Spill it." Hope wasn't normally this fidgety.

"I have been accepted at Fayetteville."

"Oh, Lainie! That's great." Hope reached across the table to take her hand.

"And at LSU!" Faith sat back, watching Hope's expression drop.

"What? I didn't know you applied there."

"You know how much I like Louisiana. Ever since we went on the mission trip with the youth group. And then, I found out I would already have a friend. Alex is from there."

"But two acceptance letters. Oh my goodness. What are you going to do?"

"I don't know. When Dad finally came in from the fields a little bit ago, we talked for a minute. I don't remember him being this practical. Usually, he just says we'll pray about it." Faith pulled out a paper napkin from the silver dispenser, and promptly started shredding it.

"I think he picked up a little of that from Mom." Hope smiled. "So, practical, how?"

"He said to make a list of pros and cons for each place. Finances, specific courses I want, distance of housing from the school. All that stuff. I start work today at 3:00. When do I have time to make a list?"

"Dad, make a list? What has happened to him?" Hope moved her tea over to make room for the massive plate of spaghetti the waitress placed in front of her.

"I know, right? Hopie, I just don't know. I think I want to move away and have an adventure, and then I think, how can I? We haven't ever lived anywhere but here."

"I guess either way it will be an adventure. Just one place, you can be home in a couple of hours, and the other it would take all day."

"John K. said it was a choice between crepes in Bentonville and beignets in New Orleans." Faith used her knife to cut a piece of grilled chicken in her salad.

"You already talked to John K.?" Hope stopped in mid-bite and stared at Faith.

"He's easy to talk to." Faith could feel the blush on her cheeks. "Honestly, that's kind of making this harder too."

"You've only had one real date." Hope wiped her mouth with a napkin.

"And I don't know if I want him to ask me out again. He may be going to the fire academy to be a full-time employee at the fire department near their deer lease. Do I want to try to keep a relationship going long distance, or should we just stop it before it starts?" Faith's stomach already felt full, after only a few bites of her salad.

"Wow. I think we should pray about it." Hope reached for her hands again. "Lord," she whispered. "Please bring peace to Faith's heart. She has her whole future in front of her, and she needs to be sure You are there for every step. Your plan is perfect. Amen, and Amen."

"I can't believe Dad is making lists, and you are doing the praying." Faith patted Hope's hands. "The world is topsy-turvy."

29

Scree, scree, scree. John K. reached into his pocket to silence his phone.

"That's a great notification. Mine just dings." Brad threw his toolbox into the back of his truck.

"I guess we'd better go see what's up." John K. laid down the board they'd been cutting for the railing on his porch steps.

"Give Old Greenie a rest. We'll take my truck."

"Oh no." John K. read his text messages as Brad attached a flashing light to his dashboard and started the truck's engine. "Housefire. Possible entrapment."

"Uh-oh." Brad accelerated, and gravel flew as he turned out onto the road leading to the main highway.

"I've got the directions to the house in my GPS." John K. was grateful once again he'd caught onto this technology. When he'd joined the army, he dragged his feet, avoiding change as much as possible. They'd taught him to be flexible, to use available resources. *Lord, take care of these people until we can get there, and help us help them. Amen.* Prayer was another resource he was grateful for.

Mac was already in full protective gear when they arrived at the station. Two more local firefighters rode on the department's pumper truck.

"Do we need Dumbo?" John K. asked as he ran inside the concrete building to find a protective suit.

"Not this time. One of you grab an oxygen tank and make sure it has the face mask attached."

Mac jumped into the pumper truck and started it.

John K. retrieved the turn-out pants and jacket from the locker Mac had assigned him. He put his helmet on, just to free up his hands. He picked up his air pack and mask, hoping he wouldn't need it.

He walked to the back of the locker room and found an oxygen tank, complete with hoses and masks for possible victims. *Please, God, let them be okay.*

"Got the O-Two." He shouted on his way out to the truck.

"Right behind you." Brad clomped through the building, slamming the metal door on his way to the driver's side of his truck.

"It's the Margrave place. You know where that is?" John K. pulled up the app with directions on his phone.

"Pretty sure. Just try to tell me about the next turn before I get there."

John K. wished he had offered to drive. The passenger seat on these bumpy, curvy roads was not his favorite location.

Mac's siren preceded them, and they glided up into the driveway of a log house with a metal roof and a porch that stretched across the front. Smoke rose from the building's back.

Brad and John K. jumped out and ran in the direction of the shouting behind the house, the oxygen tank bumping against John K.'s right leg.

"Anyone else inside?" Mac shouted. "Pets?"

"No. It's just me and him." A gray-haired lady coughed after speaking.

Mac's pumper truck was positioned near a shed, and the two other men unfolded the hoses, training water on what must have been the kitchen.

The lady mopped her face with a dishtowel as she held an older man's arm. John K. ran to them, helping the man settle in a metal chair behind Mac's truck.

"Oh, bless you. I got him out, but couldn't tote his oxygen too." She reached for the mask, and John K. turned the valve to begin the flow of oxygen.

"There's a tank inside?" John K. moved away from her. "Where?"

"In our bedroom, at the front of the house." Her eyes widened.

"Mac!" He ran to where the chief helped aim a hose at the back of the house. "There's an oxygen tank inside. The room is not involved yet, but shouldn't we get it out?"

"If you can grab it quickly, go ahead. But hurry, I need you back here with a hose."

He ran. *Please Lord, please Lord, please Lord.*

He cleared the front steps in two bounds and turned the knob on the door, grateful it was not locked. Which way? He headed left and grabbed the green tank from its spot next to an unmade bed. *Thank you.*

Smoke crept in from the right, but he didn't feel any extra heat. He turned and ran back through the front door and down the steps. Sirens from the highway announced the arrival of a truck full of paramedics from the closest town.

"You got it?" Mac met him outside.

"Sorry. Not a fan of explosions." John K. took a huge curving path around the house toward the people sitting behind the pumper truck.

"Man, we need to get you trained. I got enough to worry about out here without trying to run herd over my firefighters." Mac pushed his helmet back on his head. "You all right?"

"Right as rain, Mac. Thanks for checking." He had better spend the rest of this day following directions. No use causing his friend more stress. At least, this tank had not turned itself into a missile, like his water heater. That was a bit of good news, for sure.

"We lucked out today, guys." Mac gathered the firefighters for a short meeting after the gear was once again stowed at the station. "The Margraves aren't hoarders like a lot of our neighbors out here. Minimal flammable stuff made it easier to contain that fire. We are also fortunate to have responsive medical personnel nearby. Those folks got all the attention they needed in a short time. Good job all around."

John K. and Brad exchanged fist bumps.

"Don't forget, the board is accepting applications for two paid positions. I don't know what your current jobs pay, but this would be at least as good as a lot of part-time gigs in town. Give it some thought."

"Chief MacDonald?" T. J. stood just inside the still-raised overhead door. "Could I talk to you for a minute, sir?"

John K. patted the kid's shoulder, then turned to walk outside with Brad. "Can you give me a lift back to the cabin?"

"Sure." Brad walked to the driver's side of his truck. "I'm not sure how I left my saws anyway. Hopefully, no one took a liking to them while we were gone."

"I guess we'll see." John K. settled into the passenger seat. Yeah. He'd better not hear anyone talk about his boring life out here in the woods.

"I'm so glad y'all came to visit." Faith led Kayla down the hall toward Cody's room.

"We haven't seen him since he's been here," Kayla spoke just above a whisper. "It was a little hard to convince anyone to come with me. Not their favorite kind of place." Another teen-aged girl and two boys followed in a shoulder-to-shoulder group.

"Yeah. I get that. Hospitals are a little less intimidating." Faith reached for her hand. "But Cody will be tickled."

"We're his friends. We'd want the same thing if it was us." Kayla smiled.

Faith knocked on Cody's door.

"Y'all decent?" She pushed past the patriotic wreath Cody's mom had brought for their room.

"We can be!" Cody's grandpa was in fine form.

"Cody, you have some visitors." Faith led the way, and the teens crowded in behind her.

"Hey! It's the Coyote crew!" Cody navigated his wheelchair closer to Grandpa Dee's bed.

"What's up, Cody?" One of the boys stepped up to shake his hand.

"Hey, Faith, can we go out in the courtyard for a bit? Want to come, Grandpa Dee?" Cody grabbed a baseball cap from the table next to the television.

"No. You kids have fun. The People's Court is coming on." Grandpa Dee turned up the television's volume.

"Great idea. Come on, guys." Faith walked through the back gathering room of the home and entered a code into the pad by the courtyard door. "Y'all stay as long as you like."

Cody led the way, and his friends walked out into the sunshine, bumping each other playfully.

Faith's phone buzzed in her pocket. She couldn't check the messages until she took a break.. After checking on two more patients, she grabbed a bottle of water from a vending machine and sat at the breakroom table.

When's your next night off?

John K.'s message appeared.

I work 3-11 every night until Monday night. Off until Thursday morning.

Ooh. Tough schedule. You may need to rest those two days.

Not the whole time. What are you thinking?

Not sure yet. would like to see you.

Sounds good. What have you been up to?

Went on an actual fire run today. Ended well.

Firefighting seemed to be his niche. He would no doubt be headed for the academy soon.

Glad you stayed safe. Talk to you soon.

She couldn't stand waiting too long to talk to him again. How would this work when she was at school? Even if she chose Fayetteville, he'd be gone for eight weeks in the Southern part of the state.

I know you need to go to work. we'll figure something out. Take care.

Good way to end a text conversation. Nice to know he cared.

In the hallway, she stopped to take a good deep breath. Time to start waking folks and getting them ready for supper.

"Hey Faith," Kayla called to her from the door of Cody's room. "We're leaving. I know you get off late tonight, but do you want to go for a ride or something?"

"Yeah. That sounds good. I'll just come by your house instead of going home. I'll need to unwind for a bit anyway."

"Mom and Dad are out of town at a cattlemen's convention. That house gets lonesome." Kayla smiled.

"You should just stay with us." Faith said.

"No, they'll be home tomorrow. See you tonight." She stepped inside Cody's room, then followed the other three to the front door of the home.

"Don't forget the code." Faith waved as they went by.

"Thanks, Ms. Faith." One of the boys shook her hand.

Ms. Faith? She was only a few years older. At least he was being respectful.

Faith used a cloth napkin to wipe the chin of the lady she was assisting with her supper. Grandpa Dee nodded in his chair nearby. She'd need to take him to join Cody, who always ate in his room. She'd actually be sorry to see John K.'s baby brother go home in a few days. It did the residents so much good to have younger folks around.

A text notification buzzed in her pocket.

"Here you go, Mrs. Wallace." She moved a covered glass of tea with a lid and a straw closer to the lady on her left. I'll be back in minute. I need to get Mr. Tolliver back to his room.

"No sleeping at the table." Mrs. Wallace admonished Grandpa Dee.

Faith smiled. No one else had this much fun at suppertime.

"Thanks, sweetie." He talked less these days, but he was always pleasant and respectful. Must run in the family.

"No problem." She navigated the hallways, reaching their room near the back. "Brought your grandpa home, Cody."

"Hey, thanks. And thanks for bringing your cousin and the others a while ago."

Faith collected the paper from his tray and placed it in a nearby wastebasket. "I think that was all Kayla's idea. Hard for me to believe she graduated and will be headed to college this fall."

"I'll be doing that next year at this time." Cody moved to the other side of the room as Faith got Grandpa Dee settled in bed.

"Yeah. You've done well keeping up with things."

"Can't quit." Cody sat back in his chair, closing his eyes for a moment.

Would he ever tell anyone if he was in pain? Recovering from a spinal injury was complicated, even for a young person.

"Okay. See y'all later. Behave yourselves."

"Aww man. Did you hear that, Grandpa Dee?" Cody spoke louder as she left to go check her messages. "They never let us have any fun."

Faith sat at the break table with a cup of yogurt and fruit.

Call me on your next break if you don't mind.

How strange. This message was from Tara Williams.

"What's up?" Might as well find out now. Whose truck was she wanting to remodel this time?

"Hey! Thanks for calling. I thought you might be interested in an event happening next week." Tara spoke quickly.

"What kind of event?"

"Hope might have told you our station is holding a benefit

gala for some local charities. Cedar Ridge Ranch is one of them." Tara explained.

"I think she did mention that. So it's happening next week?"

"Yes, Tuesday night. It's kind of odd that it's not on a weekend. But it was hard for them to coordinate with the entertainer's schedule, and we want to have a live spot or two, so we had to work with our station management as well."

"How can I help?" Her mind was working overtime.

"Well, you know how our station has been working closely with the local radio station? I will attend with one of our anchors, but we need a date for the radio guy. We'd use a station car, and it would be a double date."

"I don't know." Surely, it wouldn't be Ty. Weren't there other deejays at that station?

"I'm not sure who the radio station is sending. Could I pencil you in as a *maybe*? That would help me out a bunch. Since Cedar Ridge is one of the charities, it kind of makes sense to have a rodeo queen there anyway."

Faith took a deep breath. She hadn't made any plans yet with John K. It might be fun to dress up and go to a community event.

"I'll be glad to go." She hadn't even used Tara's 'pencil me in' line. "Can you give me some ideas on what to wear?"

"From what I've heard, it will be formal, but not black-tie. The theme is western, so one of your rodeo queen outfits would be perfect." Tara sounded excited.

"Okay. I'll probably have to persuade Hope. She's not big on dressy occasions." She was doing it for Hope. It was a double date with Tara. Everything would be fine.

"Tara," Faith swallowed hard before speaking again. "I looked up some background info about Ty. I would not want to end up being his date for this. So, please let me know if that seems to be what the radio station has in mind." She took a breath. It felt good to say that.

"I think it will be the new general manager they hired. I'll make sure to let you know if it sounds like they are sending Ty. I don't blame you for trying to stay away from him." Tara agreed. "I think this will be a fun evening. See you Tuesday."

"Okay. See you then." Faith disconnected. She hoped that she wouldn't be this nervous every time someone mentioned Ty. Putting him behind her for good would be a big positive.

30

Faith stopped in Kayla's driveway and killed the engine of her truck. It was strange arriving so late at night at her uncle and aunt's house. Kayla stood on the front steps, the porch light casting a dark shadow.

"Hey." Kayla walked out to meet her. "Let's just go around to the back. We can sit on the deck and talk. There's even a TV if we want to watch movies or something."

At the locked gate protecting their swimming pool, Kayla entered the security code and they stepped inside. Crickets and tree frogs provided soft background music as the muted lights in the pool lit the area. They'd had lots of pool parties over the years. The recently-added deck made a big difference.

"This is so nice." Faith ran her hand over the smooth faux wood banister as she made her way to a comfy deck chair.

"Dad let me help design it and pick out the materials." Kayla curled up in an oversized chair. "I come out here a lot when I need to think."

"So, what's up? We probably both need our beauty sleep." Faith settled into the soft cushions.

"I don't sleep much these days." Kayla stood up to retrieve two bottles of water from the small fridge near the grill. "There's just so much to think about. My reign as Miss Arkansas Rodeo Teen doesn't officially start until January, but Alex is calling me all the time to tell me about some event or clinic she thinks I should attend. And I start school at Fayetteville in August."

"I know it's a lot. But your mom and dad are a big help, right?" Faith remembered those weeks right after high school graduation. Overwhelming even without the added Rodeo Queen title.

"Yeah, sure. But now and then I need someone to talk to who understands. You and Hope are more like sisters than cousins. Now that she's married, I just hoped I could talk to you when I'm feeling stressed." She placed her feet on the ground and leaned toward Faith.

"Of course, you can. Funny you should mention college." Faith rolled the bottle of water between her fingers. "I got some news today too. I've been accepted to both U of A at Fayetteville and LSU. Not sure what I'm going to do."

"Wow. So how does that fit with your plans to be an oncology nurse?" Kayla asked.

"I don't have to be too picky until my post graduate degree. I can take my pre-med and get my RN just about anywhere. Fellowships at M.D. Anderson for oncology NP are really competitive. So having a good undergrad program helps." It felt good to talk this through with someone.

"So you're thinking about Houston. Didn't your mom ..." Kayla swallowed.

"No. She refused to go there to get treatment." Faith cleared her throat. "I'm still trying to accept that. I know it would have meant a lot of travel. I didn't have any business telling her what to do. I still wonder if things would have been different if someone had been more aggressive with treating her cancer." She closed her eyes. Her mom's decision had changed everything between them. Mom relied more on Hope since her younger sister wouldn't try to convince her to change her plans. Dad and Junior had stayed completely out of the discussion, just trying to comfort and support Mom through the whole journey. Probably what she should have been doing as well.

"I know you could help a lot of people if you go there for your training." Kayla crossed her feet under her and stared toward the pool.

The crickets and frogs increased their volume. Faith slapped at a mosquito.

"Well, I know you need to get home." Kayla tented her fingers and rested them on her chin. "I guess I just want to know you'll be around to talk to. Leaving home this fall will be a big deal for me. That's not even mentioning the whole Miss Arkansas Rodeo Teen stuff and trying to keep my college grades up after the first of the year. Thanks for listening, Lainie."

Faith stepped over to wrap her cousin in a hug. "You know I'm here for you, sweetie. Call or text me anytime. I'll always get back to you."

"You're the best." Kayla wrapped her arms around Faith's back and hugged her tightly.

"Sleep tight." Faith walked off the deck toward the pool gate.

"Don't let the bedbugs bite." Kayla laughed.

Faith strolled the moonlit path outside the gate toward her truck. She could totally understand Kayla's fluttering emotions. Even as frustrated as she was with her home situation at times, stepping out on her own would be a big change for her as well. *Stay with us, Lord.*

"So, what do you think?"

John K. read the subject line of the latest email from his army buddy in Northwest Arkansas. Jason had attached an advertisement looking for workers on a traveling combine crew. He took a minute to look at the details again before answering.

"Still mulling."

The idea checked a lot of boxes for him. Driving big equipment, traveling all over Western Kansas and Eastern Colorado, substantial pay. No long-term contract. Right up his alley. But how would this affect Mac's idea about going to the fire academy?

He rechecked the dates for the next course for rookie firefighters. Even if the board selected him as one of the new paid firefighters, he could do this traveling harvesting thing for a few weeks before committing to firefighter training. This sounded more like a solid maybe.

What would Faith say? Funny how she crossed his mind when he had a decision to make these days. She had her own decisions to make, her own career to consider. He had no intention of slowing that down. After all, even his most definite plans were very indefinite right now.

Maybe he'd go into town and take her for pizza on her next day off. Just talking it through might help settle his wandering brain.

Want to go get some supper Tuesday night?

What time did she say she got off work last night? Eleven? It was almost noon now. Should be fine. He hit send.

Dots indicated she was reading his message and formulating a response.

Actually, I have something to do on Tuesday.

Okay.

Maybe Wednesday? Do you do church?

She did have a life. He had no right to expect her to be sitting around waiting on him.

Yeah. But we could get coffee or something afterward.

Sounds good. Take care.

Wednesday. The traveling farm crew idea could wait until then.

———

"What about that one, way in the back?" Hope leaned into Faith's closet, pulling aside a rhinestone-studded jacket.

"Yeah. That might be perfect." Faith pulled out the emerald tea-length dress, measuring it against Hope.

"Your legs are longer than mine, so if I borrow a full-length one, it would have to be altered." Hope held up the dress, admiring herself in Faith's full-length mirror.

"There's no time for that, for sure. This one would hit you a little below the knees, but the color would look great with your hair and your hazel eyes, when they look more green. Faith pulled Hope's hair up off her neck. "With an up-do, the neckline would look great too."

"I am glad KRVA wants to include Cedar Ridge in their fundraiser this year, but you know formal events are not my cup of tea." Hope sat down on Faith's bed, settling the dress beside her. "O.D.'s dad bought all of the guys new suits for our wedding instead of renting tuxedoes. I think he's set."

"You know the guys could show up in blue jeans anyway. It's a western themed thing." Faith moved hangers in her closet, trying to pick out an outfit for herself.

"Oh no. If I have to dress up, so does he." Hope laughed. "Do you know who your date is?"

"Nope. Tara said she'd text me with details. Someone from the radio station." She couldn't risk a look in Hope's direction. Her face was flushed, just thinking about the possibility of a date with Ty.

"Did I tell you Dad bought a ticket to this thing?" Hope found a garment bag in Faith's closet and zipped the green dress into it. "He's taking O.D.'s Aunt Candace."

"Really?" Faith turned face her sister. "Well, good for him. She's a sweetheart. I think they can both use a night out."

Faith's phone dinged as a text came in from Tara.

Here's the 411 for Tuesday night.

We will pick you up in the KRVA SUV Tuesday about 6:30.

Faith waited for moment to see if there was a third text message.

Who's We?

Me, Bill Carson and the radio station manager, Evan Lewis

Can't wait to see you. our fav rodeo queen.
YOU will be the star of the show

Tara's message was punctuated with crowns and horse emojis.

Send me your physical address for my GPS.
We will pick you up in the TV station vehicle.

Will do.

A double date, and Ty would not be involved. Might be fun after all.

"Well, I guess I'd better get back to work. They'll be looking for me at Cedar Ridge." Hope carried the garment bag into the hallway. "Thanks for loaning me this dress." She stepped closer, hugging Faith's shoulder with her free hand.

"Bye, sis."

John K. adjusted the plastic bag full of ice that rested on his foot and leaned back in the kitchen chair he'd brought to the front porch. From this vantage point, he could see so many things that needed doing. Sitting still for a sore ankle was certainly not what he had planned for today.

He checked the business hours for the Veteran's Administration in Fort Smith. Tomorrow's trip would be shorter if he went to the branch office in Crossroads but facing his dad's friend Steve and talking about his last days in the army would not be pleasant. Better to sit and wait his turn where he could talk to someone he'd never met and would never see again. Beads of sweat popped out on his forehead. Even thinking about seeking treatment freaked him out.

He changed the screen to display the application for the fire department's paid position.

"The ideal person for this position will be physically fit, energetic, and above all, dedicated to the community of Big River County. We are looking for someone who is readily available and committed to our community for the long term. Firefighting skills can be taught. Helping our neighbors should be second nature."

Commitment. That word stood out. He certainly loved to help others. But at this point, was he ready to commit to staying around? He'd been home from the army for months. Firefighting seemed to be a good fit for him. But staying in this location long term? Was he ready for that?

Maybe he could be more settled if he had one big adventure first. The combine crew sounded perfect. He'd be making good money, providing a needed service, working outside. Why not make it happen?

"Okay, Jason. Send me some wheres and whens." He started an email to his buddy. "I think I'm in."

Now, to see if the VA doctors agreed that he was ready.

"How does my hair look?" Junior bumped Faith as he ran down the hallway past Grandma's antique mirror.

"What in the world?" Faith laughed.

"There's a TV truck outside. Gotta look my best for my audience."

"Oh, you goof." Faith stopped at the same mirror. The rodeo queen image did still fit, even if she was a runner-up. She moved the last problem strand of hair into place. No one else would notice.

"You look gorgeous, princess." Dad stood behind her.

"You clean up pretty good too." She poked him in the arm. "Looking forward to your date tonight?"

"I wouldn't call it a date." His ruddy cheeks showed a tiny blush.

"Well, Candace would." Faith pecked his cheek. "And I think it's wonderful. Let's go meet mine on the front porch."

"Junior, are you gone?" Dad hollered after her brother, who was halfway to Faith's pickup.

"Yep. Cody came home. I gave them a while to get settled, but we're going to hang out tonight."

"Be careful with my truck." Faith yelled. She was confident he would, but it did make her feel a little funny not to be driving it herself. Time to step out of her comfort zone just a bit.

Three doors slammed at the news station's SUV, which sat in their driveway.

"Hi, Mr. Caldwell." Tara approached from the passenger side. "This is my boss, Bill Carson. Bill, Smiley Caldwell."

"Great to meet you. Got to admit I miss hearing you at the rodeo." Bill extended his hand toward Dad.

"That was a lot of fun, for sure." Dad shook his hand firmly. "Time to move on, though. Good to meet the behind-the-scenes man from our favorite TV station."

"And this is his daughter, Faith." Tara continued.

"Miss Rodeo Crossroads." Bill smiled. "It's a pleasure."

"Faith, Smiley, this is Evan Lewis, the new general manager over at the radio station." Tara waved at a young man who looked a little uncomfortable in his bolo tie.

"Hi." Evan moved forward to greet them. "Thanks for agreeing to go with me tonight, Faith. I haven't met many people since I got here from Chicago."

"Chicago?" Dad spoke up. "Faith has talked about going to medical school there. Y'all will have something to talk about."

Another guy from a big city. After Ty, Faith was beginning to rethink that whole plan.

"Y'all have a great time, princess." Dad squeezed her hand as Evan opened the back passenger door for her. "See you soon."

Faith tucked her long skirt around her boots in the back of the SUV. Dressing up for a date was fun now and then. She closed her eyes for a moment as Evan walked around to get in the other side. If only she could be going with a certain handsome ex-soldier tonight.

31

"Thanks to all of you for being here tonight." Mac sat in an armchair at one end of the open fire department garage. "It takes all of us doing what we can to keep this thing going. We all have different talents and abilities. Hopefully, we won't ever have to face a real catastrophe out here. In the future, I want to spend more time on education. If we teach folks how to keep their places mowed, it will be easier to keep their houses safe. Along with that, we can keep them informed about burn bans. But that can't happen if we're all just volunteers. Having a couple of paid employees will enable us to spend more time educating the community."

John K. nodded at Brad and his wife Christy who sat nearby. Christy held Brad's hand and listened intently. On the other side, T.J. and his grandad whispered to each other.

"As you know, we have some highly trained firefighters among our ranks. We will still rely on them for their expertise. For these full-time positions, we are willing to train someone new. The fire department has received a grant that will pay for the basic firefighting course at the State Fire Academy in

Camden. This includes lodging and two meals per day. All you have to do is get yourself down there and take along some bread and peanut butter for your lunches." The crowd chuckled.

"The most important qualification is love for your neighbors here in Big River County. We all enjoy living out here away from the hustle and bustle. Those who have to leave to work in the city want to know their homes are safe while they are gone. Between these two new employees, the station would be covered at all times. That doesn't let you volunteers off the hook, though. We still need you every bit as much."

"We ought to just pay you, Chief." A gray-haired man spoke up.

"No. I don't need that responsibility." Mac smiled at Betty. "If the wife decides she wants to pull up stakes and head to the lake for a week or so, I would like to go with her. As the Bible says, we have learned to prefer one another. And I prefer sitting around the campfire with her to watching after this place. No offense to y'all."

Laughter again. John K. smiled. These were good people. They deserved to feel safe and protected.

"Okay. Anyone who wants to apply, please stay and talk to me afterward. The rest of you, don't forget our ice cream supper next Saturday night. Invite your friends, and anyone who has an electric ice cream freezer, please bring it. If you have the crank type, you'll be the one in charge of cranking. I served my time doing that when I was a kid. Good night, and may God watch over all of you." Mac stood up as the crowd headed toward the open overhead doors.

T.J. handed Mac a manilla envelope. "Here's my application, Mr. Mac."

"Thank you, young man. How old did you say you are?" Mac opened the envelope but didn't remove anything.

"Nineteen, sir."

"He's out of school and he told me he couldn't think of anything he wanted to study in college. He'd probably make a decent mechanic, but if he wants to be a firefighter, he'd have to learn." T.J.'s grandfather stood behind him.

"Okay. I'll give this to the board, and we'll let you know." Mac said.

Brad and Christy stood on the other side of Mac.

"I've got my application too. I'm around here most of the time, building and fixing things for folks. It would be good to have something steadier that my family could count on." Brad held his paperwork out to Mac.

"Great. Thanks for applying, Brad." Mac nodded at Christy. "I guess you'd better get home to those sweet young'uns."

"Yes sir. Their grandma's liable to be filling them with sugar before bedtime." Christy laughed. We'll see you Saturday night."

"Thanks Brad. We'll let you know something soon."

Mac turned to the desk behind him and picked up a packet of papers held together by a paper clip.

"Here. You need to fill this out." He handed the papers to John K., moving closer to talk softly. "Our main problem is going to be choosing between those other two. Brad is a good guy, and he's helped here for years. This T.J. is just a kid. In some ways, it might be better to train up a young man like that. He might stay around longer. I wish we had three positions open."

John K. looked over the papers. They wouldn't be hard to complete. Did he want to commit to a paying position here? Firefighting seemed to be right up his alley. Why was he so unsure of this?

"I'll take these home and bring them back tomorrow." He

shook Mac's hand. "See you later, buddy. You and Ms. Betty have a restful evening."

John K.'s headlights illuminated the dirt road on the way back to his cabin. He remembered the words of the man at the Veteran's Services office yesterday. "Your whole life is still ahead of you. Let us help you continue to serve in whatever way you want."

What did he want? Would he feel like he was making a contribution at the Big River County fire department, or should he think about going elsewhere? What if he decided to join the Army Reserves? Would the fire department be happy when he had to go on training missions? Or maybe he would want to leave the area altogether and move somewhere else. He'd love to be a trained firefighter, but getting the training paid by the Big River department implied a commitment to staying here for a while. Was he ready for that?

Faith turned toward Evan as she caught Ty smiling from across the banquet room. She had wished for a night without being reminded of him. At least since he'd shown up with another young lady, they'd managed to avoid each other. Evan had been the perfect gentleman, and she'd appreciated being able to enjoy the actual awards being presented.

Still. That sly smile in the midst of that red beard haunted her each time she looked in Ty's direction.

"Now, a special award, presented for the first time tonight." The young anchor from Tara's station stood at the microphone. "The Better Together Award. This is presented to a pair of business partners or a couple who have made outstanding contributions to the Crossroads and River Valley communities over the past year."

Dad and Candace leaned on elbows at the table next to Faith's. Hope, seated at the same table, looked down at her clasped hands.

"This year, we present the award to the new general manager at one of our favorite truck dealerships. His youthful leadership has helped to strengthen the local economy in an industry that has been in recovery mode for a few years now. Along the way, the Billings Boys have continued their support of local causes, sponsoring sports teams, holding pep rallies, and becoming synonymous with community spirit in our area. His wife has become an integral part of promoting healing and physical activity in her new role as the voice and face of Cedar Ridge Ranch. From their new location in the old Caldwell Rodeo arena, they are doing amazing work for all sorts of folks who need an extra boost after an injury or disability. Tonight's recipients of the first-ever Better Together Award—Hope and O.D. Billings."

Faith popped to her feet, and others in the audience joined her as O.D. followed Hope to the stage. Restraining the impulse to use her fingers to form a whistle, she applauded enthusiastically.

Tara smiled and winked in Faith's direction.

"My sister and brother-in-law." She whispered to Evan as she sat down.

"I gathered you knew them." He laughed.

Faith beamed with pride as Hope uttered a brief thank you, and O.D. stepped forward. She turned her head to the right and didn't see Ty at his table. A relieved sigh escaped her lips.

"I'd like to thank KRVA and the local radio station for their support. Without local media, businesses couldn't get their message out at all. Hope and I are invested in this community, and plan to stick around. I hope you never need the services provided by Cedar Ridge, but feel free to come by Billings Boys for a cup of coffee. You might just leave with a great new ride!"

The audience applauded again as Hope and O.D. left the stage.

"Come with me to the restroom," Hope whispered in her ear as she passed.

Chuckling, Faith informed Evan she would return, and followed her sister's retreating figure. Usually the picture of composure, she knew Hope probably needed to unwind for a minute before she could sit still for the rest of the banquet.

"Just as I thought." A rough voice reached her ear just before she was pinned to the wall next to the ladies' room. "You're too good for a lowly deejay, had to go for the upper management at the station." Ty's nose was inches from hers as he pushed against her.

"Leave me alone." Faith managed a growl and balled her hand into a fist.

"Ready, Ty?" The tall, dark-haired girl she'd seen with Ty exited the restroom. He stepped back before Faith had a chance to knee him.

"Yeah. No reason to hang out where we're not wanted." He grabbed the girl's elbow and hurried away.

Faith stepped inside the restroom, her cheeks ablaze.

"What happened?" Hope asked from just inside the door.

"Nothing." Faith moved past her to check her face in the mirror. No use letting that creep ruin both of their evenings.

"I am so proud of you!" She pasted on a smile and hugged Hope.

"I'm exhausted. They called me the face and the voice of Cedar Ridge, but I don't want to go to many more of these things." Hope reached up to check a bobby pin in her hair.

"You are beautiful. Give me a minute and we'll go back and

let you get some more recognition." Faith closed the restroom door behind her. Yes. She definitely needed a minute.

John K. stopped flipping channels on the remote to watch the end of the local news.

"Tonight, a gala celebrates the contributions of outstanding members of the River Valley community." The anchor switched to a video. As the camera panned the crowd, a familiar face showed up near Tara Williams. Everyone on his screen was dressed to the hilt, but one particular blonde rodeo queen outshone them all.

So, Faith's Tuesday obligation was a date with this guy in the totally fake western style suit. Why did that make the back of his neck prickle? They certainly didn't have any kind of agreement about dating other people. No denying this, though. Seeing her with someone else was not a pleasant experience.

He continued to watch a report on the presentation of an award to O.D. and Hope and remembered his mom mentioning this last week. Fancy dress balls weren't the Billings family's cup of tea by any means. It was perfectly fine for his brother to represent the dealership and the family at this event. He'd just need to convince Faith that he could be her escort the next time something like this came up.

The display on his phone showed the app she had added at Crystal Bridges. No harm in checking it, right? Looked like she was headed home now. Should he call her to get her opinion on his firefighting decision? What if she was still with Mr. Drugstore cowboy?

Wow. He certainly didn't need to talk to her when he was

feeling so defensive, and even possessive. They did have a date planned for tomorrow night. *Take a chill pill, John K.*

"Thanks so much for bringing me home." Faith reached to Tara, who was in the front passenger seat of the station's vehicle.

"I'll walk you to the door." Evan stood beside her in the gravel lot next to the Caldwell house.

"Thanks, but I'm fine. Looks like Dad left every outside light on. I'll probably just sit out here on that swing for a bit." Faith nodded at him. "I had a lovely evening."

"Me too. I feel like this is a very welcoming community." He started back around the SUV. "I'm sure we'll run into each other again."

Faith sat on Mom's swing, listening to the chorus of crickets and tree frogs, with an occasional moo from one of Dad's cows. All of the lights out here were overkill. They had plenty of motion detectors that would have come on as soon as the car stopped in the driveway. As always, she appreciated his caring heart.

Maybe she'd go inside and change out of this fancy skirt and boots. Dad and Candace may have gone out for coffee, but surely Junior would be home soon, and they could get a movie started.

The wooden seat of the swing slapped the back of her legs as she stood up. She took a step to the right and a hand covered her mouth as a strong arm pushed her left elbow into her stomach.

"Mmmphh." She struggled, trying to swat at her attacker with her right arm.

"Yeah. That won't do a lot of good. I don't think anyone is

close enough to hear your scream out here, but I can't take the chance." Ty spoke loudly into her left ear. "I told my date I had to go to work. Little white lie, but I'd rather be here with you."

She opened her mouth enough to bite his hand.

"Okay. Is that the way it's gonna be?" He spun her around and slapped her sharply across the face. "You don't think I'm good enough for you, but I am stronger."

Faith doubled over, tears washing her stinging cheek. She had to get away. She tried to straighten up, but he stood over her, smacking the other side of her face.

"You really do live out in the boondocks, don't you. Didn't take much asking around, though. Everybody knows where the Caldwells live." Ty stretched a piece of duct tape across her mouth and pulled her behind him as he ran toward the barn.

She tripped over her skirt and jerked her arm away as she fell to the gravel.

Ty kicked her in the side.

"Just stop. You ARE coming with me." He pulled her up by both arms and drug her to his Mustang, parked just behind the barn. Motion detector lights illuminated the pasture and the back of the structure.

Lord, please help me. Faith struggled to stand, staring at Ty with her eyes open wide. She couldn't scream, but she would make sure he didn't forget her eyes and the hatred she was transmitting to him.

"We might have to drive a ways to get to a good place for this little talk I want to have with you. Get in." He opened the passenger side door, but Faith managed to back away.

If only she could turn enough to get her knee ready for a perfect strike.

"Okay, then. You don't want to sit by me?" Ty drug her to the back of the car. "Then ride in here." He held her with one arm and opened the trunk with the other. He pulled her hands roughly in front of her and wrapped more duct tape around both of her wrists. Shoving her down he lifted her legs to push her inside before slamming the lid.

Faith's heart pounded inside her chest. Her cheek still burned on the left, and blood trickled down from somewhere near her scalp on the right. The rough floor of the trunk pressed against her eyes and her forehead.

The car sped out of their driveway, shifting her body into the side of the cramped space she rode in. She rotated her hands. If he drove far enough, she might be able to free her hands before he stopped again. Her phone buzzed in the pocket of her skirt. Somehow, she needed to access it to call 9-1-1. Moving around slowly, she used her legs to help her flip over until she faced up, toward the lid of the trunk. She wiggled her thumbs, moving the duct tape and loosening it slightly.

Music blared from speakers over her head, and her body shifted as Ty drove much too quickly around the curvy roads. They were undoubtedly leaving town, maybe headed for the river.

Ty cursed from the front of the car. The car stopped abruptly. Where were they? Would there be anyone around to help her?

Something glowed in the dark. The emergency trunk release. She strained and stretched to reach up with both hands. At the back of the car, she got a whiff of gasoline fumes.

Ty must be near a gas pump. If she pulled this lever and climbed out, would he see her? Of course he would.

More cursing. He mumbled something about the pump not working. His footsteps stomped away. Now was her chance.

Reaching higher, her fingers locked around the hatch release. She pulled and the trunk opened. She had to get out and get it closed before Ty came back. She moved her left foot up and over the edge of the trunk and reached up with her bound hands to boost the rest of her body over. Her hip, ribs and shoulder slammed against the concrete as she hit the ground, but she ignored the pain.

From a kneeling position, she turned her head to look in the direction of the gas attendant. Ty stood inside the glass door. She struggled to her feet, reached up to slam the trunk, then stumbled away from the car into the shadows next to the gas station.

Her heart pounded as he returned to the vehicle to pump gasoline. If only he would leave without opening the back to check on her.

Tears rolled freely down her stinging cheek as she leaned against the dumpster at the side of the building. Ty inserted the nozzle into the side of the car, shifting from one foot to the other. After pumping for a bit, he slammed the nozzle back into its slot and ran around to the driver's side.

Thank You, Jesus.

32

Faith waited, her pulse pounding so hard her upper body rocked with each heartbeat. A strange creaking noise caught her attention, and she slowly turned to look behind her. The sign from Mrs. Gino's Italian restaurant swung back and forth in the next parking lot. The red Mustang spun out onto the highway, throwing gravel behind it. Her hands squirmed against the tape. The wiggling caused it to cut into her wrists. She reached up with both hands and used her fingertips to lift one end of the tape that covered her mouth. She peeled it off, little by little, taking a big cleansing breath when her lips were free.

Easing out from behind the dumpster, she made her way across the parking lot. The toes of her boots caught in the hem of the burdensome skirt. With each slow step, stitches ripped in the skirt, until she finally reached the glass door of the gas station and pushed it open with her shoulder.

"What the ...?" The dark-eyed man behind the counter took a step backward as she walked toward him. "Where did you come from?" He peered out to the parking lot. "Did that guy leave you here?"

"Sort of." Faith held her arms toward him. "Could you call 9-1-1 for me? I can't reach my phone."

"Wow." The man came around the corner with a box cutter. "Hold still, lady. I don't want to cut you." He placed the blade in a gap between her hands and sawed the tough gray tape.

"Okay. Now, let me call the cops, okay? We'll talk more in a minute." He ran behind the counter again.

"Yeah. George out at the Toot and Moo. There's this lady who needs help." He stared at Faith, his eyes growing wider. "Well, I'm not sure what happened. I don't know about an ambulance ... She's conscious and everything."

"Is it okay if I talk?" Faith reached for the phone.

"Sure." He handed his cell phone to her.

"This is Faith Caldwell. I was kidnapped by Ty Porter. He is driving a red Mustang. Sorry, I don't have the license number." She licked her lips, hoping to soothe the pain.

The operator on the other end maintained a calm voice.

"Do you know which way the subject is headed?"

"He left the gas station next to Mrs. Gino's Italian Restaurant headed north a minute or two ago." She needed to sit down.

"Can you give us a physical description of this man?"

"About six feet tall, red hair and beard. Dressed in a dark suit, maybe a tuxedo." She had tried not to notice him at the banquet, couldn't care less what he was wearing at the time.

"Do you think he is armed?"

Faith swallowed hard. What if he had a gun?

"I don't know. I don't think so, but he will be very angry when he finds out I'm not in the trunk anymore."

"Okay, ma'am. We are sending officers after him and someone to talk to you. Do you need medical attention?"

Faith shook her head, and then stopped herself. Might as well be honest.

"I might. Thank you. I will be here." She handed the phone back to the attendant and sank to the floor in front of the counter.

"Wow." George wiped off his phone and then his counter with a disinfectant wipe. "Okay. I hate to ask, but could you move to that bench outside the door? I mean, if it's not too much trouble? If a customer comes in, they won't be able to get up here to pay."

"Oh, sure." Faith reached into the pocket of her skirt. Her phone was there, but no billfold, no identification, no money. Outside, she found a bench to the left of the door. Seated with her back against the glass window, she closed her eyes, her head pounding. What if Ty came back before the police arrived? She could be back inside in two quick steps. Best to keep a close watch on the road anyway.

Her hands trembled as she pulled out her cell phone, selecting her dad's number. His voice mail answered immediately.

"Daddy. I am okay now, but I need a ride. Please call me back." Her parents had provided a safety net since she was old enough to date. A message like this was sure to prompt a response from him with no judgements. At least not until she was safely at home.

A real live conversation would be much better than a voice mail.

She found the group text with Hope, O.D., and John K.

> Somebody call me. I will need a ride after I talk to the police.

Hope and O.D. probably had their phones silenced like her dad. It might be a long time before she heard from anyone.

A mini-van pulled up to the pump, and a man jogged toward the door. He stared for a moment as he opened the door and walked inside. She reached up to take off the rest of the duct tape from her face in one quick motion. *Owww*

I'm closest again

John K.'s text was followed immediately by her phone ringing.

"Where are you? Never mind. I can track you with my phone. Are you okay? What happened? I'll be right there. The police? What in the world?"

Tears streamed down her face as she listened to him ramble. She could visualize him struggling into his shoes, grabbing his truck keys, and heading out his front door. It was such a relief to just hear his craziness.

"I'm okay. Do you know where Mrs. Gino's restaurant is, near the river? I'm at a gas station next door. I can't wait to see you." She leaned back against the glass. What little she had eaten at the awards dinner churned in her stomach.

"Thank God. For real. Thank God you are okay. I don't care what happened. But I am dying to know. I'll be there as fast as Old Greenie will drive."

"Hey, send Dad my location. Okay?" Her chest rose and fell with a deep breath.

"You got it. Love you."

Did he really say that? A smile tried to creep onto her sore face.

Blue lights flashed as a patrol car turned into the driveway.

"The police are here. I'll see you soon." She disconnected and closed her eyes again.

Thank You, Lord. As John K. said: For real. Thank You.

Faith rose as one of the officers entered the gas station, and the other, a female officer approached her.

"Hi. Can you tell me your name, please?" The officer stood a few feet away with a small note pad.

"Faith Caldwell." What must she look like in a torn-up dress, by herself, at a gas station in the middle of nowhere?

"Where do you live, Ms. Caldwell?"

"Just outside Crossroads." Faith's phone jangled in her pocket. "Officer, do you mind if I take this? It will be my dad."

"Go ahead, but please tell him you will call him right back." She stepped away, making eye contact with her partner through the glass.

"Dad." Faith managed to keep her voice from trembling.

"Faith, what happened? Are you okay?"

"Yes. I am fine. The police are here. I promise I will call right back."

"John K. called and told me where you are. I am on the way. I love you, little girl."

"Love you, too, Daddy." She disconnected and focused on the police officer again.

"Do you have some form of Identification?" The officer moved a little closer again.

"No, ma'am. I don't know if my wallet is in that car or at home." She couldn't help thinking what a blessing it was that her phone was in her pocket. This night could have ended so differently, in so many ways. She took a deep breath and tried to organize her thoughts.

"So, tell me what happened. Where had you been, and how did you end up here?"

"I was at my house. Ty Porter came up from behind me and grabbed me."

"Did you see him? How do you know who it was?" The officer prompted.

"I know him, know his voice. It was him." She shuddered, remembering the moment he had grabbed her. Why didn't any of the self-defense moves she had learned help her tonight?

The officer's eyes had softened while she listened. She stopped writing and touched Faith on the shoulder. "There is a medical crew on the way. Are you injured? Were you assaulted?"

"Oh no. I mean. I may have some bruises. He slapped me, and I fell out of the car after I opened the hatch. But, no. He didn't ..." She couldn't utter those thoughts out loud.

A vintage green pickup rolled into the parking lot nearby. It barely stopped before John K. jumped out and ran toward them.

"Excuse me, sir. Did you witness what happened here?" The officer turned quickly to face him.

"No, ma'am." John K. stopped a few feet away, holding his hands out in front of him.

"Then please stand back until I finish talking to this lady." The officer pulled her radio out of her pocket, and her partner turned away from the clerk to come outside.

"Ma'am. Is the man who left you here?" The officer whispered.

"No. This is a friend I texted before you arrived." Faith sat down on the bench. Her knees were sore, and she wasn't sure they would hold her up much longer.

"Okay. I think that is all we need for now. Please wait until the medical crew looks you over before you leave. Their exam might be important if this episode ends up in court." She nodded at her partner, and they walked back to the patrol car.

John K. waited in front of the bench. She struggled to stand, then stepped off the curb into his arms. His heart pounded almost as hard as hers as he pulled her against him. She closed her eyes, inhaling the fresh cottony scent of his T-shirt. He hadn't pelted her with questions, even though he must have a million forming in his head. For now, his strong, steady presence was exactly what she needed.

She leaned back and looked up to meet his deep blue eyes. The stubble of his fledgling beard rubbed her forehead. She couldn't believe he still hadn't spoken.

"Thank you for being here." Had she spoken loud enough for him to hear?

"My pleasure." His eyes locked with hers and he pushed her back to arm's length. "I'll be here as long as you need me."

A siren blared as a rescue truck pulled into the station. She turned as the paramedics jumped out but made sure to keep hold of one of his hands.

"Would you like to come over and let us take a look at you?" A stocky young man held his hand out toward her.

Faith turned to look at John K. once more before she released his hand. She slowly moved toward the open back door of the ambulance and sat on the bumper.

"Will you be taking her home?" The police officer asked John K.

"I would be glad to." John K. nodded, watching as the medic shone a light in Faith's eyes.

A white four-door pickup pulled in, parking next to the rescue truck.

"But I think this might be her ride." He walked over to greet Faith's dad as he stepped out of his truck.

"Is she okay?" Smiley stood a short distance away as the medics examined Faith's bruised knees.

"She says she is." John K. stood with his hands in his back

pockets. Okay was an understatement. Whatever had happened before he arrived, Faith had handled it with tremendous strength and courage. Her attitude was matter-of-fact, unshaken. What core was she tapping into to maintain her composure?

This man standing next to him had not taken his eyes off Faith since he arrived in this parking lot. The expression on Smiley's face was worried but calm. Puzzled but proud. Maybe he had a clue now about Faith's behavior in a crisis. The firm foundation was on full display here tonight. John K. had never felt it was important to be inside a church building every time the doors were open. Maybe there was something to be said for making attendance a habit. Regular reinforcement might be a good thing.

John K. stepped back as the paramedic took off his gloves and helped Faith rise to her feet. Her dad closed the gap between them with two firm strides.

"Oh, Daddy." She dissolved into Smiley's embrace.

"I'll call you in the morning." John K. made sure she could read his lips as he walked toward his truck. He blinked back tears. He'd been glad to be the first responder for her again. This time was much different than a flat tire in a rainstorm. Even though she was a grown woman, he knew only a father could provide the comfort she needed tonight.

33

On the porch swing with her coffee, Faith read her text messages from Hope and Kayla. Settling here had a been a little difficult today, with memories of Ty coming up behind her in this spot. No way would she allow him to steal the peace she always felt here. The presence and strength of her mom lingered here. Nothing and no one would ever erase that from her life.

After the police called just after sunrise to report that Ty had been apprehended, she'd be fielding questions all day. Nothing had sounded appetizing for breakfast, but she needed to eat. Maybe she'd go inside for a bowl of cereal soon.

With her eyes closed, she recalled a sermon her dad had preached shortly after her mom passed away. He had talked about the origin of the word "*Selah*" as it was used in the Old Testament. A musical term, it was a signal to pause, to listen. She was a fairly good listener but pausing long enough to do that was sometimes an issue.

Without opening her eyes, she heard birds in the nearby oak trees, the leaves rustling with the passing breeze, the far distant sound of a train. She inhaled deeply through her nose, puffing air out through her lips. *Selah.* Pause and listen.

Her phone jangled. She opened her eyes slowly. John K. had promised to call. So, of course, he did.

"Good morning." Her voice still sounded raspy to her ears. Had she tried to scream through the duct tape? So many details were blurry in her mind.

"How are you?" His deep voice comforted her.

"I'm good." Pause. Listen. "Really, I am."

"When you told me you would be busy Tuesday night, you mentioned you were also off work today. I'd like to see you, but it's totally your call."

"Sure. Dad is taking me to the police station in a bit to pick up my wallet, and they may want to talk to me again." Her skinned knees throbbed. She might have to take some more pain reliever soon.

"So, maybe supper?" He prompted.

"Yeah." She smiled. "I just won't want to be around a lot of people. Not even going to church. How about a picnic?" She had a sudden inspiration. Mount Nebo, at sunset. There was nowhere more calming on earth. Well, at least around here. "If you don't mind, I'll drive. I'm a little nervous about being a passenger right now. You can leave your truck here."

"You're okay driving with your injuries?"

"Modern truck, automatic transmission." She grinned.

"Touché." He laughed.

"About seven?"

"We're not going back to Bentonville, right?"

"Oh no. It will be a bit of a drive, but not too far from here." She hesitated. Thankfully, the road to the top of the mountain was not extremely long.

"Okay then, see you about seven. Bye."

"Bye."

She closed her eyes again after disconnecting. Could she somehow fast forward this day to get to seven o'clock?

John K. leaned a kitchen chair on its back legs and propped his feet up on the cabin's new front porch railing. Banging and even mild curses reached his ears from the tiny bathroom where the workers installed a new handicap-accessible shower. There was certainly no room for him to help them, and he wouldn't know what to do anyway.

With all the changes happening here, this little place didn't feel like home anymore. Mom thought she could improve that situation by decorating. She did have a talent for such things, but he still doubted he would ever feel completely comfortable here again. In some ways, he missed the homey little travel trailer he had borrowed from Mac.

He stood up, pulling his phone out of his pocket. Maybe he should go back up the hill to give Faith another call. He couldn't get the expression on her face out of his mind. How could someone look so wounded and vulnerable and still be so full of strength and resolve? Last night had revealed parts of her personality he should have expected but surprised him anyway.

His ankle didn't feel up to that walk again so soon today. Would Faith's picnic involve a hike? No matter. He could do that for her, for sure.

He scrolled through his emails and found one from the Veteran's Affairs representative he had talked to yesterday. She had been very helpful, with no judgment when he explained why he didn't qualify for hero's benefits.

"That's the most common thing I hear when I talk to a wounded warrior," she explained. "But the sacrifice you made just by volunteering to serve makes you worthy of all the benefits your country has available."

As promised, her email gave him contact information for medical resources. It also mentioned several veteran's groups full of people who would understand where he came from. Talking about this was still new, but he began to see how necessary it was.

"Hey, what have you decided about the combine crew?" Jason's email got right down to the question of the day.

"I'm planning to let a doctor clear me. I may need more PT on this ankle, but maybe he can give me some exercises to do until then. I'll have a definite answer tomorrow." He wanted to run this by Faith, but Jason didn't need to know that. How could he accept a job two or three states away from her? Last night had proved to him that his comfort zone was much nearer to wherever she was.

The application for paid firefighter stared up at him next. That decision was becoming much clearer. Firefighting sounded like a perfect direction for him. But now was not the time. Mac needed two people committed to this community, to staying right here. It wouldn't be fair to use the grant money set aside for his training if he ended up moving away. Brad and T.J. were much better choices.

Just where was he headed? Each time he asked himself this question, one blonde-haired, blue-eyed beauty popped into his head. Would she see him as a stalker if he followed her wherever she decided to attend college? He probably needed to talk to her about that tonight too.

Lord, why are You making this so hard? Finding someone I want to spend all my time with should be a good thing. But there are so many obstacles. Could You see what You can do about that, please?

"Hey dude." Brad stopped his truck at the foot of his front steps, stepping out onto the gravel driveway.

"What's up?" John K. greeted him.

"Just wondering if they're going to be ready for me to do some trim work in the bathroom tomorrow." Brad pushed back his baseball cap. "Are you going to be here for a bit?"

"Yeah. I guess I'll go into town to check on Grandpa Dee and Cody, but that will be a while yet. I'll need an operational bathroom soon to get cleaned up. Let's go see how they're doing."

John K. opened the front screen door. Anything to make time pass by. He'd much prefer to just go see Faith right now.

"Prince Charming is here." Junior burst through the back door, making his announcement as he opened the refrigerator door.

"Be careful what you dive into." Faith walked out to intercept the hungry teen. "Some of that is for my picnic with John K."

"My picnic with John K.," Junior mocked. "Are you planning to take this apple? Too late." He chomped into the piece of fruit he held.

"I guess not. Just chill a minute while I go tell him to come inside. I need to get things ready." She found the small ice chest dad stored under the kitchen island.

"I'll tell him." Junior headed back out the door.

Faith wrapped a bowl of freshly baked beans in a towel to keep them warm. She filled the chest with canned sodas, then covered them with ice. A plastic bag of loose-leaf lettuce and a bowl of homemade chicken salad nestled on top. In a reusable shopping bag, she placed a loaf of bread, a roll of paper towels, and a bag of chips. She opened the pantry door and stretched to the top shelf for a box of plastic utensils.

For so many picnics, the whole family had loaded into

whatever Dad was driving and headed to the nearest water. John K. had grown up the same way, so simple food would be fine with him. Tonight, the view was more important than the menu. She was counting on the peace of that unforgettable sunset to erase the memories of last night. Most of all, she needed John K. sitting next to her to view it.

"So, let me get this straight, you'd be driving a piece of equipment taller than this house across a huge field?" Junior opened the back door for John K.

"Possibly. There would be all kinds of vehicles there, from ordinary farm trucks to bigger ones with dump beds and the humongous combines." He waved at Faith as he reached the kitchen and leaned against a counter behind her.

"What are you talking about?" This didn't sound like firefighting.

"John K. is going on a traveling combine crew all over Oklahoma, Kansas, and Colorado." Junior popped the top on a soda and took a long swig. "He's going to make so much money. I think I need to go too."

"What? I thought you planned to drive customers around the Billings Boys lot in a golf cart this summer." Faith added a box of utensils to her bag.

"Golf cart or combine?" Junior held his hands up in a balancing fashion. "Help me talk to Dad. I think I should go with John K."

"Did John K. actually invite you?" Faith laughed. "You'd better cool your heels just a little bit. But okay, we can talk about it later. Dad is in town this afternoon, so he said he'd bring y'all a pizza for supper. See ya soon."

John K. picked up the ice chest and she led the way outside to her truck.

"Little brothers, right?" She laughed.

"Hey, Cody would be right in the middle of this too, if he

could." John K. placed the ice chest in the bed of the truck. "It does sound pretty exciting. I haven't decided if I'm doing it yet." He stood beside her as she opened the driver's side door. "The important question right now is, how are *you* doing?"

"I'm okay." She looked up into his face. How many times had she said those two words in the past several hours? For the first time, she might mean them. Just having him next to her made all the difference.

34

"Great choice for a picnic spot." John K. leaned against the passenger door of Faith's truck as they started up the last curvy access to Mount Nebo.

"What is it they say? 'You can take the girl out of the country, but you can't take the country out of the girl'?" Faith flashed a smile in his direction.

"Hey, you will see your share of big cities in your lifetime, I'm sure. But nothing beats the view from up here." While he served overseas, he'd been back on one of these mountains in every dream.

She was silent as she fell into the rhythm of slowing slightly before each curve, accelerating through it, and preparing for the next one. Probably much like the way she won her barrel racing competitions. Graceful, effortless, fearless. The same way she'd survived whatever had happened last night.

"I am such a fool." She turned the steering wheel a little harder than normal on the next curve.

Had he sent her telepathic messages? Would she be ready

to talk about it soon?

"No more than the rest of us." He could state that without a doubt. The biggest fool was not the driver today.

"I am trained in self-defense. How could I let Ty get the better of me last night?"

She was quiet for the next few turns as they met some traffic coming back down the mountain.

John K. waited. There was no use interrupting. She would finish her story when she was ready.

"I thought we'd head for sunrise point first and then come back this way." She turned on her left turn signal at the stop sign. "Don't you love these old cabins? I try to picture what it was like to build them way back in the day."

"Yeah. Imagine hauling lumber up here. Or did they just cut it and mill it all onsite?" Okay. He would allow the abrupt change of subject. But he did want to know more about this Ty character. His cheeks flushed, imagining what he would do if he ever met the guy.

She parked in a lot just before the road circled at the east end of the mountain.

"I told him I wanted nothing to do with him more than once. I guess that made him mad. When I went to the awards banquet with his boss instead of him, that must have sent him over the edge." Her eyes were clouded with tears as she cut off the ignition and turned toward him. "Was this my fault for going out with him in the first place? Did I lead him on?"

"First and most important. This was not your fault." He reached for both of her hands and looked her square in the eye. "No one deserves aggressive treatment like that, no matter what. As for leading him on, I can't answer that. Why did you go out with him the first time?" This was clearly none of his business. Would she end this conversation here and now?

He waited again as she took a deep breath.

"Ever since he helped us get entries for the truck giveaway at the Black Friday event, he seemed exciting and charming." She closed her eyes. "I'd had guys compliment me before, but he just made me feel noticed. Like I was special."

"Well, you are." His strategy to be silent wasn't working well.

"Thank you." She smiled, squeezing his hands. "The first time we went out, it was like he couldn't keep his eyes off me. Unfortunately, he had the same trouble with his hands." Her cheeks brightened, and she glanced away, releasing his hands.

The heat rose in John K's neck. Guys who couldn't keep their hands to themselves pushed all his buttons. It wasn't an easy thing to do, but girls deserved more respect than that.

"I knew he wasn't the type of guy my family would approve of, so at first, I didn't tell anyone we were seeing each other. I know that was wrong ..."

"You're an adult. Who you date is nobody's business." He wouldn't let her feel guilty about this. That was exactly what creeps like this Ty character wanted.

He squeezed both of her hands inside his again, urging her to continue.

"He was there at the pageant, and he kept trying to get me alone. He got more and more aggressive. I told him then I didn't want to see him again."

"But he still didn't get it?" He released her, turning to look straight ahead, hoping to hide the anger building.

"Yeah. I thought he did. He honked and waved when I was sitting on the side of the road in the rain." She chuckled.

"What? Of all the ..." He leaned back against the truck door. If he ever got his hands on this scumbag ...

"It's okay. A great guy came to my rescue that day." She reached across the seat to pat his leg. "Let's get out and walk. We can talk more later."

At the front of the truck, he draped his arm over her shoulder. The sun warmed his face and a soft breeze touched his cheeks. Incredible. Green treetops stretched before them, just past the rough boulders that lined the paved driveway.

A group bustled around to their left, standing back as a young man wearing a black helmet strapped himself into a harness attached to a bright red canvas kite.

"Hang-gliders!" Faith pulled him nearer to the jumping-off place.

The young man walked between two boulders close to the edge of the mountain, then took a few running steps before leaping into the air. The small crowd watching applauded and cheered.

John K. pulled Faith against his side as she pointed with her left hand.

"What a view he has from there!" She turned to peer up at him.

"Amazing." He gazed into her eyes before she turned to watch the hang glider again. That guy's view couldn't compare with this one right here.

"How far do you think he'll go before he lands?" She took a few steps forward.

"He has a spot picked out. He'll start steering that way soon." John K. caught a glimpse of a crew waiting in a flat area below them to the north.

"Have you ever done that?" She reached around his waist, still following the glider into the valley.

"No. I haven't worried too much about trying to fly. Might be fun, but I feel safer on the ground." Did he? Then why did he make a habit of running when things got scary?

"Are you ready to go find a picnic spot?" Faith turned back toward the truck. "It may get crowded on Sunset Point in a little bit."

"Sure." He still didn't know what happened before she ended up in the trunk of Ty's Mustang. At this point, it might be better if he didn't know. He followed her to the truck and stepped into the passenger side.

"So. This double date last night was Tara's idea. The new general manager at the radio station needed an escort for the awards dinner."

Once again, she read his mind. Maybe if he said nothing, she would finish her story this time.

"Ty was at the same dinner, but he had another date. I was enjoying the evening, until he cornered me outside the ladies' room." She looked straight ahead, juggling her truck keys in her hand. "He was angry that I was there with his boss. But then, his date came out of the restroom, and they left. I thought that was the end of it."

"And after the banquet?" At this point, prompting her to continue might be helpful.

"Tara and her boss and Evan—the radio guy—took me home. Dad and Junior were still gone, and it was a nice evening. I decided to sit outside."

That was the limit. She slumped forward, and tears ran down her cheek.

"I don't know where he was hiding. All the lights were on outside. Why didn't I see him? What if I didn't have my cell phone in my skirt pocket? What if he didn't stop to buy gas? What if the pump worked and he didn't go inside? What if he checked the trunk when he came back out?" She took a gasping breath.

"Hey." He pushed a lock of hair off her forehead. "No more *what ifs*. You were strong and brave and wouldn't put up with being a victim." He took her shoulders in his hands and pulled her up to look into her eyes. "God still has plans for you, Faith Caldwell."

He pulled her closer and pressed his lips to hers. She straightened and smiled at him.

After allowing him to wipe a few more tears off her cheeks, she started the truck and drove toward the other end of the mountain.

Faith pulled up to the stop sign that marked the only intersection on the mountain and smiled at John K. again. There was no embarrassment about breaking down while telling him what happened with Ty. It felt good to share with him. All she felt like doing now was smiling.

He could have told her how foolish she was to go out with someone she didn't know. Some people would say she got exactly what she deserved. John K. had hardly talked at all. Then, that kiss. So tender, so undemanding. He seemed willing to let her reveal herself at her own pace. Exactly what she needed right now.

"Are we looking for a table?" John K. rolled his window down and rested his arm part of the way out.

"Oh, I don't know. If you think we can juggle things on our lap, we might just find a bench where we can watch the sunset. Those will be scarce on a nice night like this." Faith pulled into a parking space near the visitor's center.

"I'm game." John K. jumped out and grabbed the ice chest. "Lead on."

They walked past the crumbling foundation of an old hotel that had lodged early wealthy tourists and made their way to the rocky edge of the mountain. A glance behind her showed John K. moving a little hesitantly over the uneven ground. Maybe she shouldn't ask him to carry the ice chest much further.

A couple placed a small child in a stroller and walked back toward the parking lot. Faith headed for the bench they had vacated.

"How's this?" The view from this end of the mountain wasn't as spectacular. The Arkansas river was the definite highlight as it wound its way below them. She took a deep breath before settling on the wide cedar bench.

"Looks great. Unless you're serving a four-course meal, we should be fine without a table." He sat beside her, placing the ice chest in front of her feet.

"Will you give thanks?" She sat with her hands in her lap. Was she wrong to expect this from him?

"Of course." He didn't hesitate. "Heavenly Father, thank You. For your perfect creation that is on display everywhere we look. For the food that Faith has prepared for us. And," He cleared his throat. "For protecting us from harm even when we don't make the most intelligent choices. Amen."

Well. She smiled before opening her eyes. *Yes, Lord, most especially for that. Amen.*

"Nothing fancy." She reached into the shopping bag and found the paper plates. "Here, you can start with this. I made some chicken salad. I wrap mine in lettuce, but I brought you some bread." She opened the ice chest.

"No need for bread. We can do without the carbs."

Did he mean that, or was he being polite? Well, either way, it made things easier.

"The real star of the show will be Mom's baked bean recipe. It has shown up at every Caldwell picnic since I was little. I brought some Styrofoam cups to serve it in." She stuffed the chicken salad into the lettuce wraps and handed him one. "Don't worry, the beans are not too awfully healthy. They have bacon in them and just enough sweet from the brown sugar. We've also got some potato chips. Oh, and

Junior threw in his must-have. A box of Twinkies for dessert."

"Man, what a picnic! I would have been happy with PB and J." He smiled before taking a healthy bite of the lettuce wrap.

She sat against the hard back of the bench with her cup of baked beans. For her, this was comfort food. As long as she could find Mom's favorite brand of barbecue sauce, this recipe never disappointed.

He stood to get a soda from the ice chest, then walked around the bench for a minute. He evidently had more trouble sitting still than she did.

"So, what's this about a traveling combine crew?" She had shared her story. It was only fair he filled her in now.

"Yeah. A friend of mine turned me on to that. He said you can make good money. To be honest, now that the cabin is livable again, there are not enough projects to keep me busy. The walls are starting to close in." He tore off a piece of paper towel and wiped baked beans off his chin.

"I heard on the news that your friend Mac was looking for a paid firefighter. Aren't you interested in doing that?" She didn't tell him that Betty thought he was a shoo-in for the job.

"Firefighting sounds like a good fit for me. They only have two positions, and there are two other applicants. I'm just not sure I want to stay in this area very long. It wouldn't be fair to let them pay for my training and then bug out on them." He folded his napkin and Styrofoam cup inside his paper plate. "Want me to make a trash run?"

She handed him her trash and watched as he made his way to a can near the parking lot. He wouldn't be going to the fire academy? Because he didn't want to commit to staying around here? What would he do after this combine job? Harvesting wouldn't last long. Then what?

"Looks like the show's about to start." He pointed at the

pink clouds and purple horizon before nestling beside her and placing his arm around her shoulders.

She sank into his side and rested her head against him. Yes. This was the perfect spot, for real.

"I need to thank you." His voice was so soft, she thought she imagined him speaking.

"Why?" She sat up, looking into his face.

"After I talked to you about my last day in the Army, it was easier for me to talk to the Veteran's Services office. They are going to hook me up with medical benefits. I might need some more treatment for this bum leg of mine."

"Great. Not about needing more treatment, but about them helping. That's what they're there for, right?"

"Yeah. They also have group therapy for vets still dealing with tough situations."

"Excellent!" Better not act too enthusiastic. "No one understands like someone who has been through it." This was a huge step for him. She would pray that talking to others would help him.

"Thanks. You make me feel comfortable. I didn't know how important that was. It's more than comfort. I love you, Faith Caldwell."

She waited. His eyes searched hers. She felt his breath on her face, and he moved closer. The kiss he offered this time was firmer, more definite than the one in her truck. She pulled away for a moment, then sat up to kiss him back, reaching up to wrap her arms around his neck.

"Don't miss this." He turned toward the view, scooting her against him. The sky was blazing with every color imaginable. The river below sparkled in response.

"I love you, John Kennedy Billings." She leaned against his chest, facing the sunset. He was right. She never wanted to miss this. If only they could sit here forever.

Her breathing slowed. Her body stilled against him. Was she falling asleep? Why was he not insulted by that?

"Hey." He stroked her shoulder with his fingertips. "I need to take the ice chest back to the truck before it gets too much darker." Walking over those rocks with his bum ankle wouldn't get easier with only the park vapor lights to show him the way.

"Sure." She sat up but didn't move very far away. "I didn't think about the long drive home in the dark."

"I would be happy to take the wheel this time. Driving any kind of vehicle is my superpower." He locked his fingers into hers.

"Speaking of driving. Junior is probably already talking to my dad about this harvesting trip. I could use some extra money before I go back to school too. Do you think they could use a couple more hands?"

Perfect solution. Being so far from her was his only holdback for this idea.

"Of course. I don't think they're flooded with applicants."

He kissed her forehead as she rested against him. They did need to get back down this mountain. But he needed to clarify one more thing first.

"May I make one more suggestion?" He sat up, brushing her hair away from her face. "If you ever find yourself needing an escort for some kind of fancy event, business or pleasure, would you keep me in mind? I actually clean up fairly well."

"You are now on my shortlist." She laughed out loud. Her eyes brightened, and he couldn't resist one more kiss. He pressed his lips to hers. She reached up to his neck, pulling his head closer to deepen the kiss.

He pulled away, touching her lips with his finger.

"That will be quite enough, young lady. Let's go." He

handed her the shopping bag, then hoisted the ice chest onto his right hip. Yes, time to come down from this mountaintop before there was no turning back.

35

"I can't believe John K. is actually on a combine today." Junior pushed his cowboy hat down firmly on top of his head as he drove Faith's truck down a two-lane highway.

"He's driven the tractors pulling trailers, and then he sat beside one of the combine drivers yesterday. I guess he's ready." Faith's window was rolled up, but the breeze the big equipment generated through the driver's side window kept her hair flying. She was glad her little brother enjoyed this summertime job. Hopefully, she had been a little bit of a calming influence. Her dad's instructions had been simple. *"Help your brother remember who he is. We don't want him getting into any more trouble than he would if he stayed home."*

"I can't believe I totally missed out today, even on the tractors. That was the coolest thing, being in the right spot to catch all that grain as it came out of the feeder." Junior took his hat off and laid it in the seat between them. "It takes finesse to be in the right place at the right time."

"Yes, you are the king of finesse." She'd insist he roll his window up and use the air conditioning soon. No use getting super grimy too early today.

"But today, all we're hauling is lunch. I didn't hire on to be a caterer." Junior slowed down a bit to stay behind the tractor's flashing lights.

"Believe me, they will be happy to see us when the time is right." Faith looked behind her to make sure the big water jugs and ice chests were riding well in her truck bed.

"Thanks for talking Dad into this, Lainie." Junior turned to look at her.

"No problem." She couldn't have imagined sending Junior off without her. She was glad the director of her nursing home had allowed her some time off. Truthfully, it wasn't about her little brother at all. At this point, she just wanted to be as close as possible to the oldest Billings Boy.

"Here we go. Field number two of the day," Junior announced.

They bumped off the pavement into a field. Trucks towing the harvesting headers pulled into place, and the three combines positioned themselves to attach the wide contraptions to the front of their machines.

It hadn't taken long to get caught up in the rhythm of this process. The more experienced workers made the work look effortless.

With headers attached, the combines staggered themselves in the field and began the process of cutting and threshing the wheat. Faith didn't know what she had expected, but this was much more fascinating than she had imagined. The sun reflected off the back of the vehicles before them, and Junior moved into the end of the line.

"Where will we stop for lunch?" Junior rolled up his window and moved ahead slowly.

"Jason will radio us." Faith held up her two-way. Maybe

tomorrow she could arrange to ride with John K. They hadn't talked much since they joined the crew earlier in the week.

Long, hot days had been followed by grabbing a quick supper and falling into bed. She smiled. It looked like there would be plenty of time for them to talk later. Even better, she looked forward to those moments when no words were needed.

"Time for a break." Jason's voice came through her radio. "Faith, you and Junior watch for me on your right. If you'll follow my truck, we'll find a spot to get these guys some water and food."

"There he goes." Junior pulled off the well-harvested path and bounced through the stubble behind Jason's black pickup. They passed the tractors and combines and glided to a stop.

One by one, all the other vehicles slowed and stopped.

"Who's driving that last combine? It's coming in kind of fast." Junior leaned out the driver's side window.

"Run!" Faith pushed him out of the truck and scooted over to the passenger door.

"What …?" John K. stepped on the brakes again. He hadn't needed to stop much since they reached this field. The tractor with its trailer had been in just the right spot, and he had moved forward smoothly, allowing this huge machine to do its job.

"Is that Faith's truck? Why did she stop? I'm getting too close." He geared down, slowing the huge rig just enough. He wouldn't hit anyone before he stopped.

What was that smell? Hot, rubbery.

"Get out!" He bailed out of the left side of the combine, landing on his sore foot.

A huge explosion knocked him to his knees. He stood up, fighting off the pain as he ran, and ran, and ran.

"Faith, are you okay?" Junior helped her get to her feet behind Jason's truck.

"The tire blew!" Jason sped past them toward the combine John K. had been driving. "I've never seen anything like that. Is he okay?"

Faith pushed Junior away and ran past her pickup.

"Wow! Look at this!" Junior pointed at her baby blue truck. The driver's side door was completely caved in, and the whole pickup rested at a crazy angle. "Good thing we weren't in there!"

Faith stopped, her hand against her mouth. What in the world had happened? Where was John K.?

She turned to look at the combine and saw him stumbling, falling, getting back up, running, running, running.

She took off, her cowgirl boots bouncing over the stubble. She ran past the other combines and trucks, pushing off hands that tried to slow her down.

"John K. Stop! Wait!" Even with his sore ankle slowing him, she didn't think she could catch him. "Stop! I'm coming with you!"

He fell to his knees, and she ran around him, leaning over to hold his face in her hands.

"Stop running. I'm here."

His cheeks were wet with tears. He looked up with a blank stare. His hands reached for her, pulling her down next to him.

"I'm here." She rocked gently as he collapsed into her embrace.

"I thought you were dead. Your truck. Your brother. The explosion."

"We're okay. The tire on the combine blew up. Everyone is okay."

"No." His voice was clear and firm. "I'm not okay. Don't leave me, Faith."

"I'm not going anywhere." She couldn't hold back her own tears she held him even tighter. "Not without you."

Jason's black pickup bounced over the rough stubble and stopped less than fifty feet away.

Junior hopped out of the driver's side. "Whoa, man! That was awesome!"

Faith and John K. stood, their arms linked.

"Awesome? Well, maybe." John K. reached out to shake her brother's hand.

"It was a first for me. One of the other combine operators said it was pyrolysis. All I know is it was the biggest bang I've ever heard." Jason stood behind Junior. "The paramedics will be here shortly. They'll want to have a quick look at you, John K."

"I'm fine."

Faith squeezed John K.'s hand.

"But, sure. It won't hurt to visit with 'em for a minute." He squeezed hers.

"Your truck is toast!" Jason walked nearer to Faith.

"Just a truck." Faith tried to look past him. Would it be fixable?

Jason opened the passenger's door. "Ready to head back?"

Faith was so happy that John K.'s friend didn't question how they ended up so far away from the scene of the explosion.

"Junior, why don't you ride with Jason?" John K. hobbled

over to open the tailgate. "It might be easier for me to crawl up in the back. Me and the nurse will ride back here."

"Really?" She stood back as he struggled to hoist himself up onto the tailgate. "Wouldn't the cab have worked better?"

"Nope." He grabbed her hand and pulled her up next to him.

"All right, but let's scoot back. This wouldn't be a good time for either of us to bounce off."

"Why did you come after me?"

Good question. "You need to stop running. Someone needs to help you see that." The truck bounced over a rut and she fell against him. His arms reached around her, stabilizing them both for the next bump.

"My heart knows you're right. My gut and the rest of my body just needs to catch up." His blue eyes locked into hers. "It may take a while."

"I'm not going anywhere. Not without you."

Neither of them spoke again until the pickup jolted to a stop. Faith's stomach went cold as she fully took in her truck's destroyed driver's side

"That big tire did all of that!" Junior ran around from the passenger side of Jason's truck.

The other crew members were still gathered nearby. Someone handed her a bottle of water. She passed it to John K.

"I'll need to update my dad, I guess." She pulled out her cell phone, taking a shaky step away from John K. "I'm still on his insurance."

"Yeah, you call your dad, and I'll call mine." He squeezed her hand. "I'm sure he has connections up here who can start the repair process."

Junior walked around the truck, shaking his head between bites of a thick ham sandwich.

"Dad. We're okay." She said when he answered.

"I always feel I should sit down when a call starts that way," Dad responded.

"This time, it's just the truck. Junior and I are fine." Faith was breathing a little easier now. John K. paced a short distance away, holding his phone away from his face now and then to look at another screen.

"I'll send you pictures. The bottom line is, you need to contact the insurance company and let them know where we are and what's going on." She spoke to her dad, but her attention wandered to the tall sandy-haired guy talking on his own phone.

John K. was noticeably limping. Had he reinjured his leg during the combine accident, or maybe during the crazy hundred-yard dash afterward?

"We'll get right on it, princess. I am just praising God that you kids are okay."

"Oh, and Dad." She turned and took a few steps away from the crowd. "John K. is dealing with some serious issues right now. It's his story to tell, but ... Well, I just feel like I need to be here for him until we can get him some treatment. I don't know what that will look like, but I'm not coming home without him."

Dad's deep breath echoed through the phone. "I'll be praying. Just remember. This is his journey. You can be there to support, but you can't do it for him."

"You're right, as always. I love you, Daddy." She turned toward the agitated man stomping circles in the Kansas wheat field. This would not be an easy journey for either of them.

"Okay, Dad. Hold on, and I'll tell her." John K. held the phone away from his mouth and walked closer to Faith. "It's kind of crazy, but Dad was already working on a dealer trade with a dealership just up the road from here. If we have your truck towed there, the guy who planned to drive the new truck to Crossroads can take you and Junior home tomorrow." His eyebrows raised as he pulled the phone up to his mouth again.

"Sounds like a God thing. We'll just need to figure out how to get her home when she's fixed. If ... she's fixable." She frowned at the truck. Might be a big 'If.'

"Okay ... Yeah." He reached for her hand. "Dad, I think I might finish out the week with this crew, and then ..."

Faith dropped his hand and propped her hands on her hips, pinning him with a glare.

"I mean ... Wait. This is a two-seater truck, right? Can he fit all three of us and our luggage?" One side of his mouth curled up in a crooked grin as he spoke into the phone.

"Yeah. Okay. Sounds like a plan. Love you too. I'll see you late tomorrow night." He disconnected.

"What part of 'I'm not leaving without you' did you not understand?" This man.

"Okay, okay!" He showed her that rare smile again.

Now, if she could just convince him to go to counseling when they got back home.

Whew. What a day, Lord. Thanks for keeping all of us safe. Please stay with us the rest of the way home. Amen.

36

John K. sank onto the concrete slab and rubbed his ankle. The physical therapist had not limited his activities. She said the pain would tell them what to concentrate on the next time. He hadn't broken any speed records coming up here this morning. It just felt good to get back in a routine, and the climb up to this old shack both calmed and exhilarated him.

Echoes of his morning Bible study rolled around in his head. Paul's letters were such every day, practical advice. Today, in the second letter to the Corinthians, he had talked about forgiveness. John K. wanted to tell Faith about it. Something like "the punishment inflicted on him is sufficient. Instead, you ought to forgive and comfort him, so he will not be overwhelmed by sorrow." Ty didn't seem sorrowful about this. Was that what God wanted him to pick up from this? He needed to forgive Ty?

The wind stirred the tops of the majestic pines, causing them to sway and creak. He stood up to listen, to watch them move and recover, withstanding the pressure. The wind stopped completely, and then the slightest breeze moved across his cheek toward his ear.

"Okay. I'm listening." With his eyes closed, the pines rustled again. God was here, in the tiniest breeze, whispering. It wasn't about Ty. Faith would have to come to terms with the way he had treated her. No, this message about forgiveness was about him. He was the guy who needed comfort and needed to forgive himself. Even after he came to terms with God about that terrible day when he was overseas, he was still punishing himself, still running from God's whisper. Accepting God's forgiveness had to happen before he could accomplish anything else in his life.

"Amen." He opened his eyes and looked down toward the cabin. Time to move on.

The phone rang in his pocket.

"Hello."

Faith's voice was barely above a whisper. "Your Grandpa is giving us a concert today. I hope you can hear him. I don't want to move closer, or he might stop."

"I see the rainbow through the rain."

John K. sank back to the concrete. Grandpa Dee's favorite song. "Oh, Love that Will Not Let Me Go." Tears streamed down his face. How precious that Faith was sharing this moment with him.

"Did you hear?" She spoke again as mild applause erupted in the background.

"Yeah. Thanks so much." He wiped his face with his forearm.

"He's having such a good day today. I thought someone from your family might want to be here." Faith spoke a little louder.

"I was planning to drop by later, but I'll call Mom. It's hard to catch his good moods these days." He stood up again.

"I know. I'm working a short shift today. I've got a deposition at one to prepare for the trial."

"I'll be there when you get out. I need to run by the VA office to check on my treatment schedule, but I can do that anytime. Thanks again for calling. That was exactly what I needed to hear this morning."

"I expected to leave a message, your reception is usually so bad."

"Just like you love to say, 'It was a God thing.'"

"Well, I've got to go help someone. Looking forward to seeing you soon."

"Yep. See ya." He disconnected and stood still for another moment. What a God thing, for real. He had heard about God sending angels to help people. He never knew they looked like rodeo princesses. It was time to make sure this angel would be a part of his life from now on.

He walked a few steps away from the trail that led back down to the cabin. The view from the other side of the little shack was fantastic. The sky was so clear and bright this morning. The river valley spread below him in a patchwork of plowed fields, pine forests, and cleared homesites. Ribbons of asphalt led all the way to a couple of small communities. In his quick trips up here and back down, he had never stopped to take a good look. He might spend more time up here if there were a cleared spot and maybe even a wooden deck, like the one he had helped O.D. build on their hilltop.

He punched another number on his phone.

"Brad, are you busy?"

"Not too busy, buddy. What's up?" Brad replied.

"I have an idea for a little project. The issue will be getting materials to the site I have in mind." John K. smiled. Brad might balk when he saw the potential building site.

"Okay, I'd have to take a look." Brad sounded hesitant.

"Are you home so I could come talk to you about this?"

"Yeah, come on over."

"Well, I'd kind of like to have it done around the Fourth of July. Is that doable?"

"I won't know until I take a look, buddy."

"Sure, I get it. It's not big and involved. I'll be right over."

Not big. Just involved.

I hope You're okay with this crazy idea, God. If it works, I'll owe You big time.

"You okay?" Dad met Faith just outside the conference room in the courthouse.

"Yeah, I'm fine." She hugged him close.

"Thanks for coming in, Faith." The attorney walked past them with his briefcase. "I'll get that deposition filed. I hope we'll have a court date soon. Meanwhile, are you sure you don't want us to get a protection order?"

"Whatever you think is right. I don't want to underestimate what Ty might do." She linked arms with her dad and peered out the window toward the front of the courthouse. Hadn't John K. said he would be here?

"We're not letting her wander around alone very much these days." Dad squeezed her hand.

"Okay. See you soon." The attorney hurried down the stairway.

"There's a very worried young man outside with your cousin Kayla Grace." Dad called the elevator. "Did you do okay in there?"

"I did fine. Only a couple of questions bothered me." She stepped in beside him and punched the button for the first floor.

"Like what?" Dad's hands clenched and unclenched.

"Like, what condition was I in that night? Had I had any alcohol? Had Ty and I argued a lot during the evening?" Maybe it wasn't the questions, it was the way they were asked. "It's like they wanted to see if I had provoked him, maybe if I deserved what he did to me."

"Well. You know better. Those same things will be asked during the actual trial, so this prepares you, I guess." He held the door open as she stepped into the lobby.

"Hi!" John K. reached for her hand and smiled at her. "You okay?"

"Yeah. More than okay." She held his fingers. "Glad to get that over with."

"I'm glad too. That Ty is a real creep. I hope he ends up in prison." Kayla looked around nervously.

"I don't know what the judge will say about punishment," Faith said. "I just wanted to be sure folks know he's not what they think." She locked arms with John K. as they headed toward the parking lot.

"It's late for lunch, but can I buy y'all a piece of pie?" John K. stopped as he reached his truck.

"Sure. Let's head down to Amy Lou's." Dad said. "The trucks will be fine here for a little bit."

Kayla and Dad took the lead, stopping now and then to look in store windows.

"I won't be able to stay long." John K. said. "Turns out there's a group counseling session this afternoon, and then I want to go eat supper with Grandpa Dee tonight."

Faith looked up at him, placing her arm around his waist to keep him close as they walked.

"I'm so glad you're here."

"Me too." He leaned down to brush her lips with a quick kiss. Faith looked up to catch a smile from the store owner inside. Light reflected off a diamond ring in a velvet case in the window. Her cheeks flushed.

"I guess we should catch up." She tugged on John K.'s hand and jogged a few steps to stand behind her dad as he pressed the crossing button at the corner.

"Well, look at this crew." Candace greeted them as she placed napkins on the table. "What are we celebrating?"

Faith felt their eyes on her. Celebrating?

"It's always a party when the Caldwells invite a Billings along." John K. broke the ice skillfully.

"For a fact, nephew. You need menus?" Candace moved closer to Dad.

Faith noticed red creeping up Dad's neck. Maybe there was something more happening here than met the eye. She couldn't help smiling.

"No. If you'll just tell us what kind of pie Amy Lou has today, we'll make it quick."

Faith didn't listen to the recitation. Pie wasn't her thing, but if it meant spending a few more minutes next to her new best friend, she was all in.

"Apple. And sweet tea." She managed to speak at the right time, and Candace walked off, scratching on her order pad.

"So, Faith. Have you decided about college?" Kayla tapped her fork on the table.

"As a matter of fact, I have."

"First I've heard of this." Dad turned his gaze back from following Candace across the room.

"I think I will be pretty near you at Fayetteville." Faith reached for Kayla's hand.

"Ooh! I am so glad. We can room together!" Kayla stood up partway to reach across the table for a hug.

"I'll bet you will be required to be in the freshman dorm."

Faith winked at John K. "I'll probably find a little apartment somewhere close to campus."

"We'd better get cracking on that." Dad pulled out his phone. "It's almost July, and we're talking the middle of August, right?"

"So, no big city adventure right now?" John K. turned to look her way.

"Fayetteville is plenty big for the time being. I might set my sights somewhere else for grad school." Her mind filled with details. School hadn't been at the forefront of her mind, especially during the harvesting trip. Dad's assessment was an understatement. Time to get cracking for real.

Conversation dwindled as they enjoyed the sweet, filling treats Candace brought. John K. finished his pie quickly and reached for her left hand under the table, twining his fingers through hers.

"John K., thanks for inviting us, son. I'll go pay your Aunt Candace." Dad stood, picking up the ticket.

"I need the ladies' room." Kayla scooted out. She stopped at the edge of the table. "I'm so excited, Lainie!"

"Lainie?" John K. laughed.

"Oh, there are things you don't know about me, Mr. Billings." Faith elbowed him.

"Gives me hope and a future." His eyes sparkled.

She took a quick breath. A future. With him? Nothing sounded better right now.

"That reminds me." He pulled her a little closer on the bench. "What are your plans for the fourth?"

"Of July?" What a silly thing to say. Of course, the fourth of July.

"Yeah. I think our little fire department will be helping at some local displays, but I was hoping to tell them I couldn't be there. Is that terrible?" A cloud crossed his face.

"Not a bit. I totally get that." Her quiet tone matched his.

"Well, how about you and I spend the evening together? Maybe we can go for a drive. I'll be sure to check my tires first."

She laughed. "It's a date."

Kayla returned from the restroom, and Faith walked to the door with John K. The three of them smiled as they watched Dad linger over paying their bill.

John K. held the door for the group as they walked out of Amy Lou's. Faith exited last and caught his hand. The walk back to his truck was much too short.

"Well, I guess Old Greenie and I had better hit the road." John K. waved at the others as he patted his truck's hood.

Dad and Kayla waved and walked on.

"Thanks again for being here." She leaned closer.

"My pleasure." He kissed her forehead and then the top of her nose. "I may be trying to pick up some more odd jobs for the next week or so. With your work schedule, it may be hard to get together. Text me, or call. I will miss you."

"It's nice to be missed." She pulled away. Just a little over a week until the Fourth. Being together was becoming a wonderful habit.

"Yep. The view from up here makes all the hard work worth it." John K. shook Brad's hand. The new wood smell grew stronger as the July sun beamed down on them.

"If you use it much, you'll want a canopy over it." Brad moved his hat back and mopped his forehead with a bandana.

"Honestly, there won't be a lot of parties up here. It's too hard to lug stuff up here from the cabin." John K. faced the valley, trying to recognize landmarks.

"Tell me about it. I was glad Mac suggested you hire that

team of horses. I would guess that's the way the materials got up here for this house too." Brad leaned on the back wall of the shack.

"Funny, I hadn't thought much about the first folks who lived here. It's just been a run-down shack as long as I can remember. I'll bet they chose this site for the view and then regretted it. Nowhere to even plant a garden." He pulled his phone out of his pocket. "Hey, that's Mac. I need to meet him at the highway. He's bringing me a park bench."

"We did a good job. I'm happy to help you with your big Fourth of July plans." Brad picked up a hammer and placed it in his tool belt. "I hope it has the intended result."

"Me too." John K. half jogged and half slid down the path toward the cabin. "And thanks for the extra lanterns. This would be no fun to try to navigate after dark tomorrow night."

"You got it. See ya, buddy!" Brad yelled from the top of the hill.

John K. stopped to open the door of Mac's trailer, which was back in its old location in front of the cabin. There was no reason to bring Faith out here without suitable sleeping arrangements being made. This plan had all the trappings of a military operation. Grandpa Dee would be proud.

His Grandpa had not followed too much of the conversation when he'd run this crazy idea past him. His only response had been, "Going hunting this time of year?" Conversations with his mentor were becoming difficult.

"Will this do?" Mac unloaded a forest green bench from the back of his truck.

"Should be perfect." John K. helped him set it on the ground. "We'll have a quilt to sit on to watch the fireworks, but it will be good to have something to lean back on if we want it. I'll have to get Brad to help me take it up to the new platform."

Mac laughed. "I still think it's funny. You told her you wanted to avoid fireworks, and what are you planning to do?"

"I need to stop avoiding every kind of explosion. I think with my best friend Faith nearby, I can start to handle them better." John K. paused. It was getting easier to talk to others about his triggers. "Do you think we can see most of the displays in the area from up there?" John K. said.

"I reckon that will be the best view for sure. Oh, and Ms. Betty will have your picnic ready. We'll leave it in the little trailer for you."

"That's perfect. You'll find some cash on the table. And thanks again for the loan of the trailer again." John K. said. "It just wouldn't be right to have a lady out here so late at night with one place for both of us to sleep."

"I admire you for that, son." Mac shook his hand. "Just wish I could have convinced you to come to work for me."

"I appreciate the offer. But Brad and T.J. will be perfect. I'm still a little too flighty."

"Flighty? Not a word I would use for the fine, dependable young man I'm looking at." Mac opened the door of his truck. "I hope we'll see a lot more of you and your young lady around these parts."

"I hope so too." John K. waved as his friend backed up and turned around. God had sent him so many good friends over the past few months.

Faith reached for John K.'s hand as he stood on the concrete stoop of the old ramshackle building. She thought of the times when he'd called from here. Rugged, strikingly handsome, but a little lonely. A lot like John K. had always been. She'd been happy to notice lanterns hanging in the trees on the way up here. The sun had not quite gone down yet, but soon that pathway back to his cabin would be treacherous.

"You can see the little trailer from here." She pointed down the hill. "That's what you lived in while they fixed the cabin, right?"

"Yeah. I knew it might be too late to take you back home tonight, so we each needed a place to sleep."

"Attention to detail." She nodded. "Admirable."

"Come around the back of the shack. That's where the real view is. I didn't even know until just recently." He held her hand and guided her past the crumbling building.

"Wow." There was no other word for it. The vista of the valley and the river from here rivaled Mount Nebo. "Amazing. It's mostly farms and trees, but there are a couple of little towns too."

"My geography skills are terrible. I couldn't even tell you what towns those are. I'm counting on the folks down there to provide us some entertainment. See, it's not even dark, but it's already starting." He led her to stand in front of the bench, where a quilt was folded on top of an ice chest.

"I hope everything in there is still cold." He set down the picnic basket he had been carrying. "My neighbor, Ms. Betty, fixed our picnic. Want to see what's in it?"

She nodded. The effort he had put into this date was incredible.

"How long has this platform been here? It's the perfect place to look at the view."

"We finished it yesterday." He sat on the bench and opened the basket, handing her a rolled-up cloth napkin with silverware.

He held her hands in his. "Father, bless this food. We are so thankful for the hands that prepared it. Please use it to nourish us so we can spread Your love to others. Amen."

Faith's stomach trembled. This was truly a special occasion. If he had gone to this much trouble, she had a feeling she would remember this night for the rest of her life. Tears clouded her eyes, but she blinked them back. No need to get emotional before his whole plan played out.

They unwrapped one special treat after another. Spareribs, fried chicken, potato salad, lemon bars, and watermelon, along with sodas and sparkling water.

Below them, roman candles, fountains, and fireworks of every description prompted her to laugh and point in all directions.

"This is great. And I guess we're far enough away from the explosions that it's not bothering you much, right?" She leaned back, allowing him to take her empty dishes and stow them in a bag.

"That was the plan." He stood up and walked to the edge. "Right over there is the headquarters of the little fire department I work for. They'll be starting their extra special display in just ..." he checked his phone for the time, "a minute or so."

He spread the quilt on the platform in front of them and sat, beckoning her to join him.

Whistling, whizzing, and booming was a little closer now, but John K. seemed to take the noise in stride. He pulled her close, and she rested against his chest. They laughed as they oohed and aahed in unison to some of the colorful displays.

He turned his head and placed his finger under her chin, pulling her mouth into the perfect spot for a passion-filled kiss.

She closed her eyes, waiting for more.

Boom!

Her eyes snapped open. John K. sat upright but didn't move away.

"Faith." His husky voice was just above a whisper. "Could you sit on the bench for a minute?"

She stood up and sat on the park bench, watching as he pulled something out of his pocket and knelt in front of her.

His eyes met hers, and she held her breath.

"I've heard of angels rescuing people before, but I never knew I would need one. I knew God would always be with me. Lately, he has reminded me that we are not meant to go through this journey alone." He opened the box he held in his hand. "We both have goals and ambitions. Some of our plans will work out, and some won't. God has the best plan for both of us. The bottom line is, I love you. I want us to do this together. You and me. No matter where He leads us. For as long as we both shall live."

The tears wouldn't stay in place anymore. A tiny one drifted down her cheek.

"Faith Elaine Caldwell, will you share forever with me? Will you marry me?"

"Of course!" She held his face in her hands and kissed him, once, twice, a third time. "I'm not going anywhere without you!"

He slipped the diamond on her finger. Behind his head, every color imaginable framed his sandy blond hair, spotlighted his smile, made her gasp in amazement.

He sat beside her as the fire department's grand finale concluded.

"You know that when I get through with therapy, there's a chance I might re-enlist. While you're in school, I will try to find another fire department that will send me to the academy. So, I'll be gone for a while." His eyes locked on her face.

"Don't try to talk me out of it, now!" She laughed. "We'll have to work out the timetable for this. We're both pretty good at event planning."

"This platform reminds me of the one O.D. built for his and Hope's wedding. But, I'm not sure if ..."

"Oh, no. Not handicap accessible. Hardly even able-body accessible. I have a place in mind. I'll let you have some input, but believe me, every girl has her wedding pretty well planned out."

"I just have one song request. 'Oh Love That Will Not Let Me Go.' Can you fit that in somewhere?" His voice was so soft, she barely heard it.

"I can't think of anything more perfect. Because ..."

"I know." He pulled her close again. "You're not going anywhere without me."

The fireworks yielded to a sky full of stars as Faith's heart found its forever home.

EPILOGUE

John K. scanned the faces in the crowd. No graduation ceremony held a candle to this one. The past ten weeks of training had been the hardest and most satisfying in his life, bar none. He spotted his mom first and returned her happy wave. Dad sat to her left, O.D. on her right, then Hope, and then the face he'd missed the most. Faith blotted a tear running down her cheek. He wasn't surprised that she, above all the others, understood what a milestone today was.

"Thank you, again, gentlemen and ladies, for your hard work."

He shifted from one foot to the other as the speaker concluded his remarks.

"You will all be a credit to the departments you are joining, and your communities are fortunate you chose to serve."

The crowd applauded, and the graduates cheered, slapping each other on the back, hugging, and doing a ridiculous amount of hand-shaking. He smiled at the guys he'd come to know and trust with his life. *Thanks, Lord.* It was a wonderful thing to add so many good friends for the road ahead.

"See ya, Billings!" Jake Henry waved as he ran to find his family.

"Yeah, man. Take care." He waved, moving toward the center aisle between the folding chairs in the gymnasium.

They would both report to the Fayetteville fire department in a couple of weeks. Without the training he'd just finished, that would certainly have been a big change from the Big River volunteer department and their once-in-a-great-while grass fires. He was confident he could handle whatever came up now.

"Hey!" O.D. slapped his shoulder as he reached the audience. "Good job, bro. Football star, war hero, firefighter. Can't wait till you make astronaut."

"Won't happen. No interest in being weightless any time soon." John K. laughed and hugged his brother. "Y'all couldn't figure out how to bring Cody?" He lowered his voice.

"Nah. He knew it would take a lot of logistics. He said, maybe next time." O.D. looked away, pulling Hope closer to him.

"Congratulations, John K." Hope wrapped him in a hug. He spotted Faith over her sister's shoulder, wringing a tissue into bits.

"Thanks for being here." He stepped away from Hope and pulled Faith close to him, pressing her cheek into his chest.

"I am so. Proud. Of you," she whispered, before he silenced her with a kiss.

"You know your text messages after they put us through the Maze and the Gauntlet, along with some emergency talks with God, gave me the courage to get out of bed the next morning." He held her far enough away to see the light shining from her eyes.

"Congratulations, son." Dad shook his hand, and Mom sidled in for her own hug.

"Thanks, everybody. Now, let's continue this celebration over lunch." John K. handed his framed certificate to Mom. "Will you take care of this for me?"

"I think we can find a place for it." Mom smiled and winked at Faith.

"You realize the line for barbecue will be impossible," Dad said, leading the way to their trucks. "It's game day."

"Oh well. It will be worth the wait. We won't have to be in a rush since we don't have tickets today. I can catch up on all the family gossip while we are in line." John K. followed him, pulling Faith along. "I guess I'd better get filled in on the details of this wedding a certain someone is planning."

"I guess you'd better!" Faith laughed. "Come on, my truck is over here. I'll tell you all about it on the way over."

John K. reached the driver's side door a few steps ahead of her and held his hand out. "I'll drive." As she placed the keyring in his hand, he caught her arm, pulling her close. "I have missed you so much." He kissed her thoroughly, loving the feel of her body pressed against his.

She relaxed in his arms and placed her head against his chest. "Just one more week of separate apartments in Fayetteville." She whispered, leaning back to look into his eyes.

"Good thing we'll be good and busy until then." He held the driver's side door as she stepped up and then scooted over to her side. *Yes, Lord. A very good thing.*

"What's John K.'s truck doing here?" Faith closed the passenger door of Hope's truck as they arrived at Emma's Victorian house in Paris.

"Remember I told you he asked how strict you were with

the tradition about not seeing each other before the wedding?" Hope took a shoebox from Faith's hands.

"Yeah. We're supposed to have a 'reveal' of my wedding dress just before the ceremony. But that's not until 2:00. It's only nine in the morning." Faith stepped back. Everything was planned to the minute. Now was supposed to be the 'get ready' time for the girls in the beautiful house where she'd purchased her dress. The guys were supposed to be relaxing somewhere else. "What's going on, Hope?"

"Calm down. It's okay." Hope held Faith's hands. "Today is going to be so special. Just give your sweet man a few minutes for a surprise." She prodded Faith toward Emma's right-side garden gate.

Faith walked under the drooping willows and massive oaks in Emma's backyard. This really was a magical place. But what did John K. have in store for her? Her heart pounded. She took a deep breath and closed her eyes. *Yes, Lord. I hear you. Selah. Pause and listen.*

The cool breeze of the autumn morning tickled her face. She opened her eyes and followed a tinkling noise of wind chimes toward the back of the garden. Yellow and bronze leaves drifted onto the pathway at her feet.

Just before she reached another gate that led to an alleyway, a linen cloth covered a table near a hydrangea bush. Two china plates flanked a small candelabra, and the flames flickered in the breeze. Fluted glasses sparkled in the morning sunlight.

"Mademoiselle." John K. stood next to the table, dressed all in black with a white towel hanging over his arm. He pulled out a delicate iron chair and gestured for her to be seated.

"*Merci*." Faith held back a giggle and settled into the chair.

"Brunch for mi'lady." John K. opened the back gate and stepped out for a moment, returning with a bottle of sparkling white grape juice. He poured it into the glasses with a flourish and stepped through the gate again.

Faith resisted the urge to turn around to watch him. What a crazy, romantic man she had snagged. Two crepes, rolled up and wrapped in paper, appeared on the table.

"How did you get these?" She laughed as he sat across from her.

"You took care of most of the planning, but I had this one little trick up my sleeve. There was a little bit of down-time during the past ten weeks. My buddy in Bentonville came through for me." He picked up his glass. "A toast."

Faith raised her glass, the smile she had been holding back spread across her face.

"To the woman of my dreams, on the morning when our lives change forever. May God continue to bless us no matter where we roam." He leaned forward and clinked his glass against hers.

"This is amazing." Faith tasted her crepe. "How is it so hot, out here in the garden?"

"They actually brought a food truck. It's parked just outside Emma's back gate." John K. pointed. "The owner said she'd been wanting to come to Paris for a long time. Today's the day!"

"Yes, indeed it is." Faith reached across the table for his hand. The beautiful diamond on her finger sparkled as much as it had during the fireworks when he'd placed it there.

Today was a mountain-top celebration for them both. With God's help, they had put the past firmly behind them and were ready to conquer all future rocky obstacles together.

ABOUT JENNY CARLISLE

Jenny Carlisle has been writing stories since she learned to hold a pencil.

Raised in Southeast Kansas, with her younger sister by a divorced Mom, letters to her Daddy helped develop her writing voice. After her mom's remarriage added 4 new siblings and a move to Arkansas, she graduated from high school in her new home. She studied journalism in college but left her studies when she married her best friend and began a career with the state of Arkansas. Storytelling continued in spiral notebooks while she waited for their three kids at scout meetings and band practices.

Membership in Fiction Writers of Central Arkansas and later, the Arkansas Chapter of American Christian Fiction

Writers, provided her with a writing home. She held a variety of offices in both groups and attended numerous conferences and workshops. Besides honing her writing skills, the benefit of these associations was lifelong friendships.

She submitted articles for publication in *Gospel Tidings*, a nationally published magazine associated with the Churches of Christ. For over 10 years, she was a monthly general interest columnist for *Ouachita Life* magazine, based in Southwest Arkansas.

Her self-published projects, *Turn, Turn, Turn* in 2017, and *To Everything a Season* in 2021, encourage readers with a mix of nostalgia and hope for the future.

Her lifelong dream of publishing a fiction novel came true with the release by Scrivenings Press of *Hope Takes the Reins* in March of 2022.

She continues to inspire with blog posts and monthly newsletters while enjoying the process of writing and publishing the stories that fill her heart. She loves participating in book-signing and "author talk" events at local farmer's markets and public libraries. She is always on the search for opportunities to speak about her books, and her writing journey.

Jenny's goal is to use the talents God has given her to reach out with hope and a wistful smile to all who read her work.

ALSO BY JENNY CARLISLE

Hope Takes the Reins

Crossroads Series—Book One

O.D. Billings has lived in the shadow of his brothers all his life. Even his name brings him down, so he has used only initials for years. Now, his older brother has returned home from the army, rejecting the role his family expects him to assume in their pickup truck dealership, and the younger brother is intent on risking his life on the back of a bucking bull. O.D.'s fans at the rodeo love his confident swagger during tie-down roping competitions, but every trail he heads down on his own seems to wind up going nowhere.

Hope Caldwell's world is still reeling after her mom's recent death from cancer. She thrives on keeping the family's rodeo business going. Getting back to normal seems impossible when she overhears her uncle's plans to sell out. How can she continue without the only way of life she has known for all of her nineteen years? Can she rely on the help of a big-talking cowboy? Or does he have too many problems of his own?

MORE CONTEMPORARY ROMANCE FROM SCRIVENINGS PRESS

Roadtrip for ~~One~~ Two—Book Two

Recovering from heartbreak is hard when the ex-fiancé tags along ...

Dallas wasn't in the plans when Bree Henley set out to use the nonrefundable honeymoon tickets from her canceled wedding. Nor was running into ex-fiancé Nathan Hart. But their mutual friends and the weather have other ideas. A hurricane cancels their cruise and Bree decides to turn the disaster into a roadtrip for one, never imagining Nathan would object.

Nathan is furious when he uncovers the plot to get him back with Bree. But he can't just let her go roaming around the big city of Dallas alone. Though he knows calling off their wedding was the right thing to do, he still cares for Bree. And before he knows what hits him, he's volunteered to tag along. Suddenly, it's a trip for two.

Spending the week together might remind them of why they fell in love. But is it enough to overcome the obstacles standing in the way of "til death do us part"?

Get your copy here:

https://scrivenings.link/roadtripfortwo

Love Delivered

A novella collection

***Romance at Register Five* (by Amy R Anguish)**—Mack McDonald isn't happy about the Grocerease app coming to his grocery store.

But he's committed to the sixty-day trial period, and braces himself to lose money. Kaitlyn Daniels loves how the Grocerease app helps her make ends meet so she can assist her mom, the reason she moved to small Sassafras, AR. Mack and Kaitlyn struggle to overcome differing opinions on the perks of the app. But if they don't, it could keep them from something even better.

***Where Love is Planted* (by Sarah Anne Crouch)**—Ivy Aaronson is surrounded by family at their flower shop in West Texas—just the way she likes it. But she's given up hope on ever finding a man who understands her choices. When attorney Grant Keller orders flowers for his mother, Ivy wonders if maybe there are indeed some considerate men left in the world...until she finds out Grant's relationship with his parents is less than ideal. How can Ivy ever find love when every man she meets puts career over family?

***Sweet Delivery* (by Heather Greer)**—After winning Cake That, Will Forrester thinks his Pastry Perfect Baking Dreams have come true. The sweetness fades when a chain bakery moves to town, and Will must adjust his plans to keep his customers. Hiring Erica Gerard is one of those changes. As they work together, Erica challenges Will and offers new ideas to improve the bakery. Soon, Erica and Will start bringing out the best in each other. But Erica harbors a secret, and if it's discovered, Will might never be the same.

***The Mermaids, the Ex, and USSS* (by Rachel Herod)**—Braig Sanborn is the most loyal employee the United States Shipping Service has ever seen, which is why he agreed to transfer across the country with only a few weeks' notice. Bailey Bivens is so busy planning a friend's wedding, she didn't expect to fall for the carrier who delivers packages to her house. When they both find themselves in too deep, will they agree the relationship was doomed from the start?

Available February 14, 2023:

https://scrivenings.link/lovedelivered

Forever Home by Hope Toler Dougherty

Book Three in the Forever Series

With a fulfilling job and a home of her own, former foster child, Merritt Hastings, relishes her stable, respectable life. Dreaming for more is a sure way for heartache. When a contested will turns her world upside down, she must revaluate what's important to her, what's worth fighting for, and what's worth sacrificing.

Patience has never been Sam Daniels' strong suit with his history of acting quickly and asking questions later, and he's ready for changes in his life...now. Too bad the plans for acquiring a radio station didn't include a contract. Now he's out of a job, out of a radio station, and out of prospects.

While his life is in flux, at least he can help Merritt steady hers, or will he rush in and overstep ...again?

Will the sparks flying between these two opposites lead to a happily-ever-after or heartbreak for both?

Get your copy here:

https://scrivenings.link/foreverhome

---

www.ingramcontent.com/pod-product-compliance
Lightning Source LLC
Chambersburg PA
CBHW060623100726
47907CB00006B/1743
9781649172662